HELENA LANDLESS

DEANNA MADDEN

ISBN-10: 0692559159
ISBN-13: 978-0692559154

Cover design by SelfPubBookCovers.com/Daniela

Flying Dutchman Press

2015

AUTHOR'S NOTE

Charles Dickens left his last novel, *The Mystery of Edwin Drood*, unfinished when he died on June 9, 1870. What follows is a reimagining of the story from the point of view of one of the novel's characters, Helena Landless.

—Deanna Madden

For Doug and Gypsy

1

When I was six, I saw a man bitten by a cobra. It happened in the marketplace in Colombo, where my brother Neville and I had been taken by our ayah, a young Indian woman who was hired to watch us. The cobra belonged to a fakir who earned a few rupees by charming it out of a basket. That day a circle of people had gathered around him. The crowd seemed as mesmerized by the fakir's flute as the cobra that was slowly rising from the basket. It was as if time stood still. The only thing that moved was the cobra, and it rose so effortlessly that it hardly seemed real. It reminded me of a rope trick I had seen another fakir perform. Only this time in place of the harmless rope end was the flat hooded head of the cobra. I watched, entranced, until the music died away. We all held our breath, waiting for something to happen. Then the cobra lunged at a man in the crowd wearing a white turban. The man screamed as the cobra sunk its fangs into the arm he had raised to shield his face. The basket was knocked over, and people scattered in all directions. Our ayah hurried us away and afterward begged us not to tell what had happened. We never told, but for a long time both Neville and I were haunted by bad dreams. To this day it is one of my most dreadful memories of Ceylon.

Neville and I were born in Ceylon, he six minutes ahead of me. Our father was an officer in her Majesty's service who died so young we couldn't remember him. Our mother remarried because she had no way to take care of us, let alone herself. She died when we were six, leaving us orphans at the mercy of our stepfather, a tyrant who begrudged us food and sometimes beat us. When he died thirteen years later, we were sent back to England to be wards of Mr. Honeythunder, a philanthropist who took an interest in orphans of the empire. Mr. Honeythunder had no intention of taking us into his household. Even before we arrived in England, he had made arrangements for us. He had found a cleric in Cloisterham, a sleepy cathedral town some three hours distant from London, who would tutor Neville, and a seminary for young women located near the cleric where I could study as well. This was his plan for us until we would come of age, at which time he would wash his hands of us entirely.

So it was that Neville and I, accompanied by Mr. Honeythunder, who thought it his duty to hand us over personally to our next keepers, arrived in Cloisterham around dusk on a brisk November evening, having traveled first by train and then by omnibus. We were met by Mr. Crisparkle, the cleric at whose house Neville would lodge. Mr. Crisparkle was a boyish-faced, middle-aged man with a kind and generous nature, much to the relief of Neville and myself, for we had feared someone more along the lines of our benefactor. After we had disembarked from the omnibus, he escorted us back to his home in Minor Canon Corner, where dinner awaited us. Several guests had been invited to help welcome Neville and me, and for a few minutes we were engaged in a flurry of introductions.

Altogether there were nine of us at dinner that night. We barely fitted around the lace-covered table in the small parsonage dining room. Mr. Crisparkle sat at one end of the table beaming at us and old Mrs. Crisparkle, his mother, a tiny frail woman, sat quietly at the other. I found myself seated between John Jasper, the local choirmaster, and his nephew Edwin Drood, an amiable young man of about my own age. Across from me was Neville, who had contrived to place himself next to Rosa Bud, or Rosebud, as she was sometimes called, a pretty blue-eyed fair-skinned girl of sixteen. Neville had barely taken his eyes off her since he walked in the door. Of course she was quite unlike any of the young women he had encountered in Ceylon, but I thought he ought not to appear quite so obviously infatuated with her. He was all solicitous attention. Had she enough meat? Would she care for more potatoes? You would have thought he had personally prepared the dinner. On the other side of Neville was Miss Twinkleton, the head of the Seminary for Young Ladies at which Rosa was a pupil and at which I was soon to be. She was a woman of indeterminate age, who had a mass of corkscrew curls that quivered when she moved and was given to frequently fanning herself. Neville did not seem at all concerned whether she had food on her plate or not.

We sat uncomfortably scrunched together because an extra setting had been added for our guardian, Mr. Honeythunder. Although we had known Mr.

3

Honeythunder for only three days, Neville and I were only too eager to be free of him, and I daresay he felt the same about us. His interest in orphans was reserved for those at a distance, not close up. In the time we had been with him, he had barely asked us a word about ourselves, instead heaping all sorts of proclamations and platitudes on us when he paid any attention to us at all. Now he dominated the meal just as he had dominated all conversation since we had arrived in London. In a booming voice he lectured all of us on the plight of the poor and scarcely gave anyone else a chance to speak. It threw a frightful pall over the table. I felt sorry for Mr. Crisparkle, who tried so valiantly to change the topic to the benefits of exercise or the excellence of the mutton. Across the table Neville was showing far more interest in pretty Rosa Bud than seemed to me proper for a young woman who had been introduced as almost engaged to the young man on my right. I tried to catch Neville's eye, but he ignored me just as shamelessly as he did poor Miss Twinkleton, whom he heartlessly abandoned to Mr. Honeythunder. I was worried what Edwin Drood might think about my brother's attentions to his intended, but he seemed not to mind in the least. With the best good will in the world, he divided his attention between the mutton and me.

"I understand you're from Ceylon, Miss Landless," he said, not raising his voice enough to draw Mr. Honeythunder's attention. In fact, so loud was Mr. Honeythunder and so absorbed in pontificating on his favorite causes that he probably would not have noticed if we had all commenced to talk.

"Yes, we only arrived a few days ago," I said, keeping my voice low too. "Everything still seems quite strange."

"England strange?" he said. "Fancy that! And to me it's all so ordinary."

"I assure you it's very different from Ceylon," I said.

"And did you like it there?" he asked.

I hesitated. He had very blue eyes I noticed. Altogether he was a handsome young man and seemed sincerely interested in my opinion. I could of course have told him about the flowers that bloomed everywhere, the lush gardens, the heat, the rains, the bazaars. On the other hand, I couldn't very well tell him about my stepfather or how Ceylon had not been a happy place for me because of him. In the end I simply said:

"Not having lived anywhere else, I'm afraid I've very little to compare it to." It was a truthful answer, even if it wasn't the whole truth.

"You were born there?"

"Yes, Neville and I."

"Ah, your twin brother." He glanced across the table at Neville, who had just turned once more to share some pleasantry with Rosa and was regarding her as if she were the most exquisite creature he had ever seen. I would have kicked Neville if I could have been sure of getting his legs under the table and not someone else's. I wondered if I ought to apologize for the attention he was lavishing on my dinner partner's intended. I would definitely have to have a talk later with Neville about how to behave around other men's fiancées.

"I believe Septimus said you were orphans?" Edwin Drood remarked, gallantly overlooking my brother's behavior.

"Septimus?" I repeated.

"Mr. Crisparkle. He was named Septimus because he

5

was the seventh child born into his family, and in fact all the others before him died."

I glanced at Mr. Crisparkle, who seemed completely untouched by this family tragedy. "Yes, our parents died when we were young."

"Rosa and I are orphans too."

"I'm very sorry to hear it," I told him.

"Well, I have Jack, and he's wonderfully good to me."

Jack, I surmised, was Mr. Jasper, the dark brooding man with a mustache who sat on my left. Thus far he had rebuffed any small attempts on my part to strike up a conversation. I wondered if he was always so antisocial or just in a bad humor on this occasion.

"Are all the women in Ceylon like you?" Edwin said, reaching for his wineglass.

"What do you mean?" I asked.

"Oh, you know, do they have that sort of air of mystery about them that you have?"

He gave me such a charming smile that I couldn't help but smile in turn. I liked his breezy manner. He was so artless. He simply said whatever he thought. I had always heard that Englishmen were reserved, but Edwin wasn't like that.

"I don't think there's anything mysterious about me," I protested.

"Ah, but you're wrong," he said. "Take your name, for instance. Beautiful and mysterious."

"Landless?" I asked, surprised, for it had never seemed to me either beautiful or mysterious.

"No, I meant your given name—Helena."

He said my name so softly I think I blushed. I glanced across the table to see if Rosa Bud was listening, but apparently she was not. She was telling Neville something that they both seemed to find highly amusing.

"I guess I'll get to see the East for myself soon enough," Edwin said, sounding a little less sunny. "I go to Egypt to work in our foreign office as soon as I turn twenty-one." He sighed and reached for his wine. "I'm not happy about it, but I haven't much choice. It's all arranged. I must go."

He looked again across the table at Rosa Bud. "Pussy's not happy about it either."

I gathered Pussy was his nickname for Rosa but did not want to ask why he called her that. Maybe she reminded him of a kitten. She was such a pretty thing with her golden hair and fair skin. She had a glow of pink in her cheeks and a pink ribbon in her hair and was wearing a pink frock.

"Miss Bud goes with you then?" I asked.

"Yes, as my wife. It was all arranged for us years ago by our fathers." He heaved a deep sigh.

"You mean it was arranged that she would go with you to Egypt?" I asked. It seemed strange to me, but then so did many other things in this foreign land which was supposed to be my mother country.

"Oh, no, I meant our marriage," Edwin said. "We were just babes when our fathers decided we ought to marry. They were good friends and I suppose it seemed the thing to do. We've grown up all our lives knowing we would be married. There was never any question about it."

I wondered if that meant he didn't love her, but of course I couldn't ask him that. Besides, how could anyone not love a creature so pretty and sweet? I saw how close Neville's dark curly head was to hers as he whispered in her ear. I hoped nobody else noticed and glanced quickly at Miss Twinkleton, Rosa's chaperone. That good lady was so flustered by Mr. Honeythunder suddenly demanding how many young women of the lower classes she had in the course of her years as headmistress admitted as charity cases to her school, that she was quite speechless and apparently far too distracted to notice any impropriety regarding her charge.

"You're so fortunate not to have your future all mapped out," Edwin said, poking at his potatoes as if they were at fault. "It must be wonderful to have the freedom to choose what you will do with your life."

"My brother and I have little choice right now about our lives," I told him. "Mr. Honeythunder controls our money, and so we must do as he says and go where he sends us or we will find ourselves out on the street without a shilling. We had no choice about coming to England, nor had we any choice about where we were born."

"But the future—" Edwin said, "you *do* have a choice about the future."

At that moment Mr. Honeythunder struck his hand on the table so hard we all jumped. "Do any of you know how many widows of soldiers are in need of assistance?" We all looked at him guiltily. Miss Twinkleton dropped her fork as if she had been caught in an act of theft. "I thought not," he declared with an air of satisfaction, as if we had all confirmed his worst suspicions about us.

"It's the not having a choice that I find hard to bear," Edwin said so close to my ear that I felt his warm breath. "There's nothing wrong with Pussy. And going to Egypt could be a lark if I wanted to go there."

"Perhaps it won't be so bad as you think," I suggested.

"Sometimes places turn out very different from what we expect." I didn't add that in fact they sometimes turn out worse. England, for example. I had had no idea it would rain so much, that the sky would be so relentlessly gray, that the cold would chill me to the bone, or that the customs would be so baffling. After all, in Ceylon I had always thought of myself as English.

"That's what Jack says. He's been in the East too you know."

I turned to Mr. Jasper and made another attempt at conversation. "Mr. Drood said you were in the East. Where, Mr. Jasper?"

Edwin's uncle looked at me distractedly. His dark eyes blinked, as if trying to focus. "What?"

Was it possible he had drunk too much wine, I wondered. I had seen a similar look on my stepfather's face when he had drunk too much. I always knew that was the time to stay out of his way. However, this was not my stepfather. I knew I shouldn't be quick to judge. I repeated my question.

"It was a long time ago," he said coldly. Then he turned back toward Mr. Honeythunder as if I had rudely interrupted, and I felt I had once again blundered. No doubt I was remiss in not devoting my attention to Mr. Honeythunder, yet I had now heard him holding forth on widows, orphans, and the poor for three consecutive days and the topic was becoming quite tedious.

I must confess that I had no great inclination to have a conversation with Mr. Jasper, while Edwin, on the other hand, I could have talked to all evening without growing bored. I had led a very confined life in Ceylon, where I had had little opportunity to receive the attentions of young men. Perhaps for that reason I found the attentions of Edwin, who was overall so charming, to be sweet indeed. It was hard to understand the relationship between him and Mr. Jasper, who was his guardian and his uncle but could not have been yet thirty. The two were completely opposite in appearance and temperament. Edwin had blonde hair and blue eyes, and was friendly and good-natured. Jasper, on the other hand, was dark and morose with tormented eyes. I wondered if something had happened to him, if he had suffered some unhappiness that had left its mark upon him, or if he had come into the world with that air of melancholy. A few minutes later I noticed Jasper's hand start to tremble as he reached for his wineglass. He quickly drew it back and hid it in his lap. It occurred to me that he might be ill. I wondered if I should say something.

"I daresay you must think me awful," Edwin said, drawing my attention back to him again. "Here we've only just met and I'm baring my soul to you. Do you mind?"

"No, of course not," I said. "You are a most entertaining dinner partner."

"Am I?" He beamed as if I had paid him a wonderful compliment. "Pussy says I'm an awful bore. Whenever we're together, we end up quarreling."

It seemed a bit disloyal of him to tell me this. I glanced at Miss Bud and my brother and wondered what they were talking about with such animation. Certainly not widows and orphans.

"I do wish I could show you around Cloisterham," Edwin said. "There are ever so many quaint old nooks and crannies I'd like you to see."

"Can't you?" I asked, tempted by the prospect of

spending more time in his company and exploring our new world.

He laughed, and I saw my mistake at once. Of course he couldn't show me around. He was practically engaged to Rosa Bud. It wouldn't have been proper for him to be seen strolling around Cloisterham with another young woman.

"How I admire you," he said. "You aren't a bit like us. We must seem awfully stuffy to you. All this fuss about what is proper and what is not. It's such a lot of nonsense, isn't it?"

I tried to protest, but he interrupted me. "You're absolutely right. Why shouldn't I show you around? Pussy wouldn't mind. Why should it matter what the good people of Cloisterham think? They live in this little backwater and know nothing about progress. But the world is changing, Miss Landless. Twenty years from now you won't recognize it."

His enthusiasm was infectious. "I'm sure you're right."

"Of course I'm right. There will be more railroads, more people, bigger cities."

"And will people change?" I asked him.

"They'll have to. It stands to reason."

I felt caught up in the vision he had conjured up. He made me want to step into that future world and see what it was like. It would be better than ours. Of that I was certain. People would be happier.

"I wish—" he said.

But I never got to find out what he wished because at that moment Mr. Crisparkle said, "Good heavens. It's almost seven."

We all turned our heads toward the mantel clock.

"There's still plenty of time to catch the omnibus," Mr. Crisparkle told Mr. Honeythunder, "but perhaps it would be wise to start back now."

"Goodness, yes," Edwin said, pulling out a gold watch on a chain and scowling at it.

"It takes at least twenty-five minutes to walk back," Miss Twinkleton observed.

"More like five," Edwin whispered in my ear.

The rest of us chimed in with our concern that Mr. Honeythunder not miss his ride. We helped fetch his hat, gloves, and cane. Mr. Crisparkle and Neville volunteered to escort him, and soon they were off.

After the door had closed behind them, we were like children let out of school. Even old Mrs. Crisparkle and Miss Twinkleton looked relieved to be rid of Mr. Honeythunder. The atmosphere was suddenly lighter and more festive.

"Rosa, you must sing for us," Jasper announced, sitting down at the piano to accompany her.

"Oh, I couldn't," she said, looking alarmed.

"Nonsense, of course you can."

"Oh, go on, Pussy," Edwin said. "Show us what Jack has been teaching you."

She looked as if she wanted to refuse, then reluctantly went to stand beside the piano.

Edwin promptly sat down on a chair so close to me that my skirt brushed against his leg. "Do you sing, Miss Landless?" he asked, leaning closer.

"I'm afraid I don't," I told him.

"Ah, you just don't want us to ask you to sing for us, do you? I'll bet you have a voice like an angel."

Before I could protest, Rosa began to sing. She sang

with a sweet true voice that well matched the plaintive love song Mr. Jasper had chosen. He watched her lips intently while she sang, his fingers moving skillfully over the piano keys. Such scrutiny must be unnerving, I thought, as if he were waiting for her to make a mistake; but as she sang bravely on, her eyes avoiding his, I realized that was not it. He stared at her lips as if nothing else in the room mattered, as if he and Rosa were alone. Was this the way he conducted her music lessons I wondered? There was something disturbing about it. I looked quickly around the room—at Miss Twinkleton and old Mrs. Crisparkle, who were politely attentive, and at Edwin, who smiled back at me, as if he had been waiting for me to look his way, but no one else seemed to notice anything amiss.

I felt sorry for Rosa. She was pretty and charming but seemed so vulnerable. We were both orphans, but clearly she had not had to endure the kind of abuse I had at the hands of my stepfather. She had been coddled. Everyone loved her. Who would not love such a sweet child? And yet, there was something she lacked. The strength to stand up against the world when it has done its worst to you and defy it. My stepfather had beat me but he had not broken my spirit. The wrongs I had suffered had made me stronger. Rosa had never suffered like that, and I would not have wished it on her for the world, but I feared what might befall her. I knew the world could be cruel and it was a lesson she had yet to learn. My heart went out to her as a fellow orphan at the mercy of a hard world. Despite our differences, we were sisters.

Rosa was still singing when Neville and Mr. Crisparkle returned. It was yet another sad song about two lovers parting. Did she know no other kind? Her eyes shone with tears and her voice trembled. Mr. Crisparkle sat down beside his mother, and Neville came to lean against the piano and gaze adoringly at Rosa. He had hardly taken up this vantage point when her voice faltered and she burst into tears.

"I can't," she said. "I can't go on."

The room erupted in a murmur of concern. Rosa swayed slightly, as if she were about to swoon. In a flash I was at her side. I took her arm and half led, half carried her to a small divan.

"Lie down," I said. "You'll feel better in a minute."

Neville and Edwin were beside us now.

"I guess it was too much excitement," said Edwin.

Neville tucked a small embroidered pillow under her head.

"Oh, dear," said Miss Twinkleton. "I knew I should have brought my smelling salts."

"Perhaps a glass of wine?" suggested Mr. Crisparkle.

"I don't think it's necessary," I said.

I rubbed the backs of Rosa's hands while she lay there with her eyes closed looking deathly pale.

"Jack, you expect too much," Edwin admonished his uncle. "You're such a taskmaster."

I looked over my shoulder. Jasper still sat at the piano, his hands poised above the keys, as if a magic spell had been cast over him that froze him at that moment in time when Rosa's voice had broken. Then he did something strange. His eyes closed and his hands moved silently over the keys, as if he were continuing the piece in his mind. It was a strange pantomime, but with everyone's attention directed to Rosa, no one seemed to notice except me.

"You wouldn't let Jack bully you like that, would you, Miss Landless?" Edwin said.

"Indeed I would not," I said.

Neville and I exchanged quick looks. Perhaps because we were twins, we often experienced a kind of telepathic communication. That was true now. He knew exactly what I was thinking. We had both endured our stepfather's temper. I had vowed early on that he would not break me. After the first time he beat me, I had refused ever to let him see me cry again. If I could stand up against him, why then I could stand up against anyone.

"I think she's coming around now," Edwin said, and indeed she was.

The next time I looked toward the piano, Mr. Jasper was gone. He had quietly slipped away during the commotion over Rosa.

"I don't know what came over me," Rosa said, sitting up. "What happened?"

"You fainted," Edwin said.

"Well, I told you I didn't want to sing."

"I bet you fainted on purpose," Edwin said.

"I did not," said Rosa. "That's a mean thing to say."

"Then I apologize," said Edwin. "I didn't mean to be mean."

Now that Rosa had recovered, Miss Twinkleton declared that it was time to leave. I would go with her and Rosa and begin a new chapter of my life as a student at the seminary. I had dreaded this moment of parting from Neville, who had been my closest companion, but I could comfort myself that he would be close at hand and I could see him often. I worried about how he would fare without me, for he had a hot and rebellious nature, and it was often only through my influence that he held himself in check. The moment of parting, however, was to be postponed a bit longer. Neville and Edwin would walk us to the seminary.

The night was crisp and cold. There was a full moon in the sky and many stars. Edwin gallantly offered Miss Twinkleton his arm. Neville followed with me on one arm and Rosa on the other. I watched Edwin as he walked ahead of us. At the corner he glanced back and smiled at me. Rosa was telling Neville about a play they had done at school, and he was completely absorbed in her story.

"Is Pussy boring you?" Edwin asked.

"Pussy?" Neville said. I could feel his arm stiffen. "If you mean Miss Bud, no, she's not boring me in the least. As a matter of fact, I find her conversation quite fascinating."

"There, Eddy," Rosa said with a small pout. "If you don't appreciate me, there are others that do."

"Not appreciate you?" Edwin said, stopping in the middle of the street we were crossing. "Of course I appreciate you. Aren't we engaged to be married? Aren't you my future wife?"

Rosa sighed. I watched Edwin walk on, hopelessly out of my reach.

A few minutes later Rosa, who had been glancing back over her shoulder, let out a small cry.

"What's the matter?" Neville asked, also looking back.

"I thought I saw something move."

Behind us the deserted street stretched away in the moonlight and the houses loomed darkly with lit windows. The trees threw long shadows. Somewhere a dog barked.

"I don't see anything," Edwin said. "You're just imagining things again."

"Perhaps it was a cat," said Miss Twinkleton. "There are a lot of cats about lately."

"Yes," said Rosa, "you're right. It was probably just a cat."

We walked on, but Rosa talked less now, and from time to time glanced anxiously over her shoulder. Soon we reached the wrought-iron gate of the Nuns' House, an old brick building which housed the seminary. A brass plate mounted on the gate announced 'Seminary for Young Ladies, Miss Twinkleton.' We all said goodnight and then Rosa and I accompanied Miss Twinkleton to the door. I took one last look at Neville and Edwin Drood standing at the gate. I wished that I could go with them instead of entering this crumbling old building where I knew no one, except of course Miss Twinkleton herself and Rosa. I imagined how Neville and Edwin would walk back through the streets, talking about the things that young men talk about and getting to know each other. I hoped they would become friends, but I wished that I could be part of that friendship too. It seemed unfair that I had to be excluded. Well, I would have to get used to it, I supposed. I would have to satisfy myself with seeing Neville occasionally, and I would never have the opportunity of walking alone with Edwin through the dark and deserted streets of Cloisterham. Sighing for all that could not be, I waved a last good-bye.

Miss Twinkleton immediately sent us off to bed. I was relieved to discover that I would be sleeping in a small room adjoining Rosa's. The other young women had all retired for the night so I was spared having to meet them until the following day. For this I was grateful. I felt a little overwhelmed by all the new people I had already met that day.

"I'm glad that Miss Twinkleton arranged for me to be near you," I told Rosa after we had put on our nightgowns. "This way I won't feel so alone."

"Of course you won't," Rosa said.

Impulsively I reached for her hand. "I hope we'll be great friends," I said.

"I should think so," said Rosa.

"And you must help me."

"Help you?" said Rosa. "I can't imagine you needing much help—at least not from me. You're ever so capable, but as for me—well, I've always had people taking care of me, like dear Miss Twinkleton and funny old Mrs. Tisher, and as a result I'm afraid I don't know how to take care of myself."

"There's so much I don't know," I told her, "so much no one ever taught me. I'm terribly ignorant of how I should behave. You must keep me from making mistakes."

She looked at me in astonishment. "A silly little goose like me?"

"Oh, you aren't," I said. "Why do you say such a thing?"

"That's what Eddy says about me."

"He must have been teasing," I said. "I'm sure he loves you very much."

She sighed. "Yes, I suppose he does. It's naughty of me to suggest otherwise. And I'm sure I'm quite as much to blame as he is if we sometimes get on each other's nerves.

Only you see Eddy and I have known each other most of our lives. He's like a brother. We never had the opportunity to fall in love properly. Do you know what I mean?"

I wasn't sure I did, but I encouraged her to explain.

She sighed again. "It's so hard for both of us, you know—this arrangement our fathers made. Everybody knows about it. The girls here at the school tease me something awful. They make a fuss over Eddy every time he comes."

"What's so bad about that?" I asked. I didn't dare tell her how much I envied her engagement to Edwin Drood.

"We quarrel," she said. "We're never together ten minutes at a time without one of us starting a quarrel. I promise myself ahead of time not to annoy him, but I just can't seem to help myself."

I reached for her hands. She was so very young. I would be the older sister she had never had. We would help each other.

"Of course I'll be your friend," she said. "And you must be mine. We must tell each other everything. I'll tell you all my secrets and you must tell me all of yours."

I knew I could never tell her how I felt about Edwin Drood. "Are you sure you want to tell me all your secrets?" I asked.

"My secrets are so ordinary," she said. "I'm sure yours are more interesting. You must tell me what it was like to grow up in Ceylon. And you must tell me what it's like to have a brother. I've only had Eddy, and while he's like a brother, he isn't really a brother. And you must tell me if you've ever been in love."

"I haven't," I said quickly. Then I added: "I may be older than you, but I've never been engaged."

Rosa sighed. "Oh, it's not as exciting as everyone seems to think. It's really rather tiresome."

"Edwin is very handsome," I suggested.

"I suppose he is." Another sigh.

I thought about how she had fainted that evening. "Can I ask something personal?" I said hesitantly.

"Of course."

"Mr. Jasper—"

She tensed. "What of him?"

"What happened tonight?"

"What do you mean?" She looked away and bit her lip.

"Why did you faint?"

"I got nervous, I suppose."

"I think it was more than that."

"What more could it be?"

"Mr. Jasper," I said.

A shudder ran through her.

"He's in love with you, isn't he?"

"Don't say that!" She snatched up her pillow and clutched it to her. "Some nights I'm afraid to go to sleep for fear I'll dream of him."

"Is he so frightening?" I asked.

She nodded vigorously. "I can't bear the way he looks at me! I hate his eyes. I hate the way he watches my hands when I play, and my lips when I sing. I hate the way he strikes the chords of the piano, as if he's speaking to me, whispering to me, dreadful things . . . ."

"Has he told you he loves you?"

"Not in words. He never says anything. That's the awful part. He doesn't have to say anything. I know what he's thinking."

"Like tonight?"

"Yes, except it was even worse tonight. It was as if he touched me." She shuddered again. "You won't tell anyone, will you? Eddy adores him. It would kill him to know. If it weren't for Eddy, I'd stop taking lessons from him, but I don't know how to tell Eddy, so I keep on going. Oh, you can't imagine how afraid of him I am. I dread going to music lessons and use every excuse I can think of to avoid them. I don't even like to leave the Nuns' House because sometimes he's lurking about."

I remembered how she had been frightened on the way back to the Nuns' House from Minor Canon Corner. "That's what frightened you as we were walking back tonight, wasn't it?"

"Yes, I thought he was there."

"Well, he isn't going to hurt you now that I'm here."

"You will help me, won't you?" Rosa said. "But Eddy mustn't know. Promise me that."

"All right," I said. "I promise."

"Oh, you're so strong," she said. "I wish I could be like you."

"You can," I said. "You just have to believe you can."

"Oh, I couldn't," she said. "I'm ever so. . . . Eddy's right. I am a silly little goose."

She opened her mouth and yawned then the way a child yawns and stretched her arms.

"We ought to go to bed now," I said.

"Poor Helena. You're probably all tired after your journey from London, and here I am keeping you awake."

"I don't mind," I said.

"Then will you sit with me while I'm falling asleep? If you don't, I'm afraid I shall dream about Jasper."

"All right," I said. "I'll wait until you've fallen asleep."

She snuggled down among her blankets and wrapped her arms around her pillow. Within five minutes she was soundly asleep. I looked at her lying there so innocently. She looked far too young to be a bride so soon, but at least marriage would put her safely beyond the clutches of her music teacher. In the meantime I would find a way to protect her from his attentions.

I blew out the candle, slipped back to my own room, and lay down in my narrow bed. I was tired from the long ride and the excitement of the evening, but sleep came slowly. When at last it did, I dreamed of walking through the streets of Cloisterham on the arm of Edwin Drood. He pointed out the houses as we passed. In the distance I could see the cathedral tower. From time to time he turned his head and smiled at me, and I smiled back at him.

2

The next morning when Rosa and I went down to breakfast the table was all abuzz. The heads of twenty girls turned to look at us as we entered the dining room.

"Whatever's happened?" asked Rosa.

"Haven't you heard?" the nearest girl said. "Miss Landless's brother threw a bottle of claret at Mr. Drood." They all looked at me.

"Neville?" I said. "You must be mistaken." But my heart sank. I knew only too well Neville's temper. In Ceylon he had come home bruised and bloody more than once.

"No, I heard he threw a knife," said another girl. This was even worse. Oh, please, I thought, don't let it be true.

"Maybe it was both," suggested a third girl. "A bottle of claret and a knife." Some of the girls around her laughed.

"Oh, for goodness sake," Rosa said. "Who started this silly rumor? Miss Landless and her brother only arrived last evening. And when we last saw Eddy and Mr. Landless, there was nothing amiss between them."

"It was later," said a girl with auburn hair. "At Mr. Jasper's rooms."

At the mention of Jasper's name, Rosa glanced anxiously at me. "I'm sure Mr. Landless would never do such a thing," she said, "although Eddy can be very provoking at times. I'm sure it's just a misunderstanding. Whatever have they got to quarrel about?"

"You," the girl with auburn hair said, and the table burst into giggles.

Rosa blushed. "Oh, you're all just teasing me."

"Oh, no, it's true," a girl with freckles said. "I heard the cook tell the maid. Mr. Landless said he admired you and Mr. Drood said he had no business admiring you, and then Mr. Landless threw a bottle of claret at him."

"A knife," insisted the girl on the other side of the table.

"A decanter," said the girl beside her.

"I'm not listening to another word of this," Rosa declared, clapping her hands over her ears.

It was very difficult to get through breakfast with the buzz continuing about us. Rosa tried to introduce them to me, but I could hardly concentrate on names when my thoughts were all revolving around Neville and Edwin Drood. I hoped the rumor was wrong. Of all people to quarrel with, why did Neville have to quarrel with him? I knew I had no hope of a future in which Edwin played a part, but still I did not want my brother to be at odds with him. What in fact had happened? After breakfast Miss Twinkleton lectured us about the evils of spreading rumors but made no mention of either of the two young men who had been the subject of so much speculation at the breakfast table. When the lecture ended, I asked to speak to her privately. She took me to her sitting room.

"Please, I want to visit my brother and find out what's happened," I told her.

"I think that's hardly necessary," she said. "I understand your concern, but there's some perfectly simple explanation, I daresay. I don't believe for a moment your brother did anything wrong. He seemed a most respectable young man when I met him last night. I'm sure he would want you to begin your studies this morning, as no doubt he is beginning his with Mr. Crisparkle."

I did not like to oppose Miss Twinkleton so early in our acquaintance. I realized it might make her think I was obstinate and headstrong. However, I was determined to see Neville. "He's my brother," I said. "As orphans we are alone in the world. We only have each other."

Miss Twinkleton's locks trembled. "I quite understand that; however, you must realize patience is a virtue young women should cultivate. Proper young women don't go rushing out into the street because of something they've heard."

"Please," I said, "I must go to him. I can't possibly concentrate on my studies until I find out if there is any truth in this story that he and Mr. Drood have quarreled." I didn't care if she thought badly of me for my defiance. I assumed I was not a prisoner at the Nuns' House. There were no locks on the doors. I was free to leave if I wanted, with or without her permission.

Perhaps she saw my determination. She heaved a sigh and gave up the argument. "Very well. Go if you must. But I'm sure it's quite unnecessary."

. . .

Although the walk to Minor Canon Corner was short, I felt better when I arrived. Perhaps it was the brisk autumn air or the tolling of the cathedral bell. Even the ivy growing on the walls of the parsonage gave me comfort. Surely in such a world there could not be much amiss.

Mr. Crisparkle was flushed and a little out of breath when he answered the door. He had not yet finished fastening his clerical collar, which was perhaps why he looked so flustered. "I've just been boxing," he said. I must have looked perplexed. "Shadow-boxing," he explained. "I do it in the morning. Keeps the body and mind in shape." He poked the air with his fist to illustrate.

"I've come about my brother," I said. "Is it true he and Edwin Drood have quarreled?"

"I'm afraid it is," he said. "Jasper came by earlier to return your brother's hat. He said the quarrel was bad indeed. Had he not been there, the two young men might have come to blows."

"What does Neville say?"

"He denies nothing." Mr. Crisparkle sighed. "I fear he's off to a bad start, especially with Mother. She didn't approve at all of the condition in which he came home last night. There's nothing wrong with drinking in moderation, but your brother went too far. I fear he has some vices to overcome."

"I grant that my brother has a passionate nature," I said, "but drunkenness is not one of his vices."

Mr. Crisparkle did not argue but led me into the sitting room, a small room with a rocker by the fire and a calico cat curled up in front of it. There was a picture on the wall of the Sermon on the Mount and a small portrait of a rosy-cheeked boy on the mantel which I suspected was Mr. Crisparkle as a boy. Mr. Crisparkle left me alone while he went to summon Neville. I didn't have long to wait. Within minutes Neville burst into the room full of righteous indignation.

"I don't know what you've heard," he said, "but it wasn't my fault. Drood provoked me. I never meant to quarrel with him."

"Is it true you threw something at him?"

"No, never. But he was insufferable."

"Come sit down and tell me everything."

He glanced at the chair distractedly but made no move to sit down. "If you'd been there . . . ." He didn't have to finish his sentence. I knew what he was thinking. If I'd been there, it wouldn't have happened. He would have held himself in check. The wildness in him would have stayed at bay.

"Start at the beginning," I said.

He paced the room like a caged animal. "We were walking away from the Nuns' House. I took offense at something he said."

"At what?"

Neville hesitated. "It was the way he spoke about Miss Bud, if you must know. It irked me. He's so far beneath her. The idea that he will marry her when he doesn't appreciate what good fortune he has but treats her as casually as if she were his sister—it's so unfair."

"Then it's true," I said. "Rosa was the cause of your almost coming to blows."

"I couldn't help myself," he said. "I couldn't bear to hear him speak of her so lightly."

"It's not your place to defend her against the man she intends to marry," I said. Poor Neville. He had no right to fall in love with Rosa, nor I with Edwin Drood. They were both as hopelessly beyond our reach as the stars in the sky. Still I knew how he felt.

"She's like no one I've met before," he said. "A fairy, an angel. And to think she will belong to that cad."

"If you got to know him," I said quietly, "I'm sure you'd find he's not so bad as you think. He seemed like a very nice young man that night we met him at Minor Canon Corner."

Neville stopped in his tracks. "You defend him? You take his side against me?"

"Of course not." Neville was in no mood to be reasoned with. I knew him well enough to know I would have to let his anger run its course. He did not want to hear that Edwin Drood might have some good qualities. I would have to be careful or he might guess that I was half in love with his adversary. "What happened next?"

"Mr. Jasper interrupted us."

"Oh?" I said, surprised. "Mr. Jasper was there?" I remembered how Rosa had cried out as we walked from Minor Canon Corner to the Nuns' House. She had thought Jasper was lurking in the shadows, following us.

"He was out for a walk I guess," said Neville. "He invited us back to the Gate House for a hot stirrup."

"And the quarrel continued? Jasper didn't try to stop it?"

"I don't remember exactly." Neville frowned and put his hand to his forehead as if to clear his thoughts.

"How much did you drink?" I demanded.

"Only the one stirrup . . . I think."

28

"What else do you remember?"

"I don't know. It's all so muddled. I keep seeing this picture of Rosa."

"Rosa? She wasn't there."

"No, but there was a portrait of her on the wall."

"Rosa Bud?"

"Yes, and Drood continued his infuriating arrogance—it was more than I could bear—his carelessness toward her—and his insulting manner to me."

Neville flushed, his hands clenched. "I wanted to kill him."

"What did he say?" I asked, reaching for his hand. "What did he say that upset you so much?"

"I can't tell you. I won't repeat it."

"But you remember?" I wondered if it was only in his overheated imagination that the insult existed. I could not imagine the charming young man who had sat beside me at dinner the evening before insulting anyone.

"God, yes. He insulted me. It was cause enough to fight."

I unclenched his fingers, as I had so many times before. "Oh, Neville, you must control yourself," I reminded him. We're strangers here. You can't fight every man you disagree with."

"Does she know?" he asked in a tone of despair.

"Who?"

"Rosa, of course. Rosebud." He spoke her pet name as if it were the name of a saint.

"Everyone in Cloisterham knows."

"I don't care about everyone in Cloisterham," he declared. "I only care about her. Will you ask her to forgive me?"

"It's Mr. Drood you should ask forgiveness of," I said. "He's the one you quarreled with."

"Never," he said vehemently.

I did not understand what had happened between the two young men, but I did understand that Neville regarded Edwin Drood as his rival and bitter enemy. I would not be able to confide my own foolish yearnings for Drood to my brother. It would just add to his outrage. I could only hope that time would blunt his anger, and that when Rosa and Edwin married and left for Egypt, an event that might be only months away, he would soon forget them, and eventually I would too.

When I relayed Neville's message to Rosa, she forgave him at once. "Goodness knows," she said, "I've often wanted to throw something at Eddy myself. If your brother had thrown something at him, it would have served him right. I'm sure he deserved it." After that, we avoided the subject of the quarrel. No doubt Rosa wished to spare my feelings, as I did hers.

The next afternoon her guardian Mr. Grewgious arrived from London. He met with her behind the closed doors of Miss Twinkleton's private sitting room. When they emerged, she introduced me to him. He was older than our Mr. Honeythunder, an odd-looking man, tall and bony, all awkward angles, but with a kind face.

"So you are the young woman from Ceylon I've heard so much about," he said. "I hope England is proving agreeable to you."

"It is," I said. "Although I wonder if I shall ever get used to the cold and damp."

"Well, you must bundle up and take care not to catch a chill," said Mr. Grewgious. "I'm sure the esteemed headmistress will watch over you, just as she has so admirably done over Rosa." Miss Twinkleton was standing close enough to hear his remark and gave him an appreciative smile.

The visit from Mr. Grewgious seemed to lift Rosa's spirits.

"Is it all arranged then?" I asked her after Mr. Grewgious was gone and we were back in our room.

"What?"

"Your marriage."

"Oh, yes. I guess it is."

I wondered what Mr. Grewgious had said to so alter her mood.

"When will it be?" I asked.

"In May," she said. "And then we're off to Egypt in the summer."

Since only last night she had not wanted to go to Egypt, I marveled at the change that had come over her. Looking at her at that moment, I could not help but feel keenly the difference in our prospects. Not that I envied her Egypt. But I envied her Edwin Drood, with his charming smile and pleasant disposition. What I would have given to be in her place! I would have gone to the ends of the earth if I could have gone with someone like him.

Later that night as Rosa was brushing her hair she suddenly turned pensive. "Do you think it is more important to honor the wishes of one's dead parents or to follow one's heart?" Before I could answer, she added, "I know what you would do."

"And what would that be?" I asked, looking up from the novel I was reading.

"You would follow your heart."

"Oh? Are you so sure?" I was amused by her certainty.

"I am," she said. "You would not be stopped by old promises. You would know at once what should be done and do it." She snapped her fingers for emphasis.

She made me sound so formidable that I had to smile. I was not nearly as sure that I would find such a choice simple to make. I had never been faced by such a choice. If my parents had arranged a marriage for me, would I have refused, especially if it were their dying wish? I supposed it would depend on who the young man was. If I knew I could not come to love him, why then I probably would not honor the arrangement. But if he were Edwin Drood, well, in that case there would have been no conflict between the promise and what my heart desired. But I could not tell her that, and I did not want my feelings for Edwin to color my advice to her. I knew I must be careful what I said. I was her friend, and she trusted me.

"Sometimes it's not so simple," I told her. "It's better to think things through carefully instead of acting impulsively."

"I shall," Rosa declared. "I shall be ever so careful."

On that note our conversation ended, and in the week that followed neither of us referred to the subject again. I did not want to influence her choice. The rest of the girls assumed that the date of the wedding was moving rapidly closer. I did not let Neville know that Rosa might not marry Edwin Drood after all. I was afraid to rouse hope in him where there might be none. After all, Rosa had never suggested she was in love with Neville. As for myself, I tried not to think about what it might mean to me if Rosa broke her engagement to Edwin Drood.

During this time I resolved to make as much as I could of my opportunity to learn. I worked hard at my classes at the seminary and Rosa did her best to teach me what she knew. In addition, Neville shared with me what he was learning from Mr. Crisparkle, so that I was benefiting from two directions at once. Although I did not have much more freedom in Cloisterham than I had had in Colombo, I was allowed to take walks with my brother. I looked forward to these outings with a fervor. There was much old architecture of interest in Cloisterham, but Neville felt uncomfortable under the curious eyes of other pedestrians. He preferred the less frequented areas near the river, where there were lonely open stretches and old ruins. One chill afternoon we were walking a favorite route deep in conversation when we spotted Mr. Crisparkle nearby walking on an embankment.

He waved to us and we waved back. Then he made signs to indicate that he would join us if we wished, and we waved again to convey our willingness. Soon he came clambering down the embankment to us.

"I see you are taking the air," he said as he arrived red-cheeked and a little out of breath. "Very invigorating, isn't it?"

"Helena doesn't like being cooped up at the Nuns' House all day," said Neville. "She begs me to come by and rescue her on a regular basis."

"Actually I'm glad I ran into the two of you," Mr. Crisparkle said, looking from Neville to me and then back again. "There is something I wanted to say and perhaps here we can talk more freely than in another place."

By *another place* I assumed he meant Minor Canon Corner, where his mother might chance to overhear what was said. She had taken a dislike to Neville after that first night when he had come home less than sober.

"I refer of course to your quarrel with Edwin Drood," he said, his face growing serious.

I felt Neville's arm stiffen and hoped he would not say anything rash. Mr. Crisparkle had been very kind to take him in, and I had no idea what would happen to us if he changed his mind. We would be thrown back upon Mr. Honeythunder's largesse, and I suspected that was in decidedly limited supply where we were concerned. The next arrangement he made for us might not be nearly so agreeable as Cloisterham. He might even send us to different places, and I did not want to be separated from Neville.

Mr. Crisparkle turned from Neville to me. He had very pleasant blue eyes I noticed. "Miss Landless," he said, "I have noticed that you and your brother have a very close relationship."

I acknowledged that we did.

"Then I ask you to use your influence to help end this unpleasant business. As I have told your brother, I think he should apologize to Edwin Drood. He has steadfastly refused."

"I cannot force him to do something he does not want to do," I told Mr. Crisparkle.

"Surely he would listen to you. He speaks so highly of you."

"He speaks highly of you as well," I said. "And yet you have not persuaded him."

Mr. Crisparkle heaved a deep sigh and tried another tack. "I am deeply concerned about the bad reputation he now has in Cloisterham. It is quite unfortunate that the altercation occurred, but not too late to make amends if your brother would but apologize."

"I won't apologize," Neville said. "I'm not sorry. Drood was insolent. Let him apologize."

"There you go again," Crisparkle said. "Look how you're clenching your hands. It's a most deplorable habit."

I held firmly to Neville's arm. I knew he would not strike Mr. Crisparkle, but I sought to restrain his anger. He had never told me what Edwin had said that night which so incensed him and because mention of his adversary never failed to arouse his temper, I did not like to refer to it.

"I can't help it," Neville said. "I could not stand by and let him speak slightingly of Miss Bud."

"Miss Bud?" said Mr. Crisparkle, surprised.

"If you had heard him, sir, you too would have come to her defense."

"I think not," Mr. Crisparkle said.

"I admire her," Neville said boldly. It rang in the cold night air like a challenge.

"The young lady's about to marry Edwin Drood," Mr. Crisparkle said.

"I love her," said Neville, undeterred, "and Drood is unworthy of her."

"I did not realize—" Mr. Crisparkle frowned.

"Nevertheless, you must master your feelings. In a few months she will marry Drood. Have you told anyone else about this? Does Rosa know?"

Neville shook his head. "Only Helena knows."

Mr. Crisparkle glanced at me. "Rosa doesn't know?"

"No," I said.

"Then no one must know. Promise me. You must not tell anyone."

We both promised, Neville more reluctantly than me.

"And you must apologize," he told Neville, "even if young Drood is partly to blame. Perhaps I can arrange a meeting. I think he is coming again soon. If he will meet you halfway, will you apologize? Surely you see it's not good to have all Cloisterham whispering about you?"

Neville stared moodily at the river through the gathering dusk. What did he care of what Cloisterham thought of him?

"Surely your sister agrees with me?" Mr. Crisparkle said, glancing at me for support.

I hesitated, knowing how Neville hated the idea of apologizing to Edwin Drood. He still felt outraged by what had passed between them. I could almost hear the angry arguments flashing through his brain like lightning in a stormy sky. Nevertheless, if a reconciliation could be accomplished, I was in favor of it. "I would like him to be friends with Drood, if that is possible," I admitted.

"There, you see?" said Mr. Crisparkle. "Your sister agrees."

"Oh, very well," Neville said. "I'll apologize. But only if he meets me halfway."

"Fair enough," Mr. Crisparkle said, rubbing his hands together. He looked out at the river and then he looked back at me. "Miss Landless, how is it that you and your brother turned out so different? He lacks your admirable self-control."

"We had an unhappy childhood," I said. "I needed self-control to survive. Perhaps Neville needed rage."

"Well, rage will only get him in trouble now," Mr. Crisparkle said. "He would be wise to let you be his guide. You are his better half. Neville, you should strive to be more like your sister. Learn how to get that temper under control. Practice self-restraint. And now you should be taking her home. It will be getting dark soon. Miss Twinkleton will be worried."

We said good-bye to Mr. Crisparkle and turned back toward Cloisterham then.

"He's right, you know," I said as we walked back toward the houses of Cloisterham and its old cathedral. "You do need to control your temper. It will get you in trouble one day if you don't."

"I can't help it," said Neville, scowling. "It's my nature, I'm afraid. I feel things more strongly than other people do. I will not abide a slight. I am every bit as good as Drood. He has no right to act as if he is better than me. It galls me no end to be asked to apologize when he is the one at fault."

"Nevertheless, you must make an effort to get along," I said. "Mr. Crisparkle was very good to take you in. If he decides to give up on you, what will become of us? At least here in Cloisterham we have each other. If we are thrown back on the mercy of Mr. Honeythunder, I fear what may happen to us."

"How disagreeable it is to be dependent on strangers!"

Neville said. "I can't wait until I'm able to make my way in the world."

"Are you unhappy with Mr. Crisparkle?" I asked.

"No, of course not. He's an excellent tutor. And I know I'm very fortunate he agreed to take me on."

"Then surely you will not do anything foolish to alienate him."

He sighed. "All right, I'll try to behave myself."

We walked a few minutes in silence. We were back in the streets of Cloisterham now. The street lamps were lit and light spilled from the windows of the houses we passed.

"There is one more favor I want to ask of you," I said as I saw our time together would soon be gone. Always our walks ended too soon.

"What favor?" he asked.

"You must be more discreet about your feelings for Rosa," I told him.

"I can't help it," he said. "I love her."

"How can you love her?" I said gently. "You hardly know her."

"It doesn't matter," he said. "I knew the minute I saw her. She is the sweetest, most exquisite creature I've ever met."

"But she is betrothed to Edwin Drood," I reminded him.

His face darkened, and I was afraid I had stirred up the bitter feelings again.

"I can't stop loving her," he declared. "Don't ask that of me."

"Well, then you must conceal your feelings better," I said. "You ought not have burst out like that in front of

Mr. Crisparkle. Surely you knew he would disapprove."

"I don't care if he disapproves." Neville let out a deep sigh. "You don't understand. You've never been in love."

I felt wounded by his words. I wanted to protest that I too knew what it was like to fall in love. I was tempted to tell him about my feelings for Edwin Drood. In the past we would not have kept such secrets from each other. But something had changed between us. I did not feel he would understand. He was too opposed to Edwin Drood and I was afraid of what hurtful things he might say. In the past he would have guessed my feelings, but he seemed to have no inkling at all. Perhaps that was because we lived under separate roofs now and our time together so meager. Perhaps it was because his own heart was so full of Rosa that he could not see into mine. In any case, I said nothing and felt a new loneliness when we said good-bye and I retreated into the confines of the Nuns' House.

Within a few days it had been arranged that Edwin and Neville would meet and reconcile. Mr. Crisparkle had spoken to Mr. Jasper, who in turn had written to his nephew in London. Edwin, it seemed, was quite agreeable to a reconciliation and had suggested it be done as privately as possible—just he and Neville to dine with Mr. Jasper on Christmas Eve. Mr. Crisparkle was delighted at his success. But Neville dreaded the event. As for myself, I didn't like the idea that there would be only the three of them. What if the conversation took the same turn as on the previous occasion? The presence of John Jasper in no way reassured me. I felt a deep mistrust of him. Neville had been drunk that night, and possibly Edwin Drood had too. Why had Jasper allowed the two young men to overindulge? Why had he not steered the conversation into calmer waters? No, I did not trust Jasper. He had already showed himself to be a dubious mediator.

Adding to my unease was the knowledge that on that same day the engagement between Rosa and Edwin would become official. At the Nuns' House all the girls were breathless with anticipation. Rosa was a great favorite with them, and her relationship with Edwin was a subject of much speculation since it set her apart from them—soon to be a wife though she was but sixteen.

Rosa was nervous as she prepared for Edwin's arrival. She decided on a yellow dress, then changed her mind to a blue. She frowned at her hair and kept asking me to run downstairs and check the time on the mantel clock. Then, determined to avoid the awkwardness of Miss Twinkleton's supervision, she posted me by the window to watch in case he arrived early. At last she was ready. She looked very pretty with her golden curls, blue eyes, and flushed cheeks. I thought Edwin could not fail to adore her. As if on cue, he appeared across the street. I had not seen him since the night I had met him at Minor Canon Corner. He was just as handsome as I had remembered. At that moment I would have given much to be Rosa.

She hugged me impulsively before she flew out the door. "Wish me luck," she said. Then I was left alone with my book about the Peloponnesian War lying in my lap. I looked out the window again. Edwin did not cross the street right away. He merely stood there looking up at the windows of the Nuns' House. I drew back, afraid he would see me. A carriage rolled past him. At last he walked purposefully toward the Nuns' House. I watched the top of his hat until he disappeared from view below me.

Rosa must have been ready at the door. Almost at once they reappeared, Rosa clinging to his arm. I watched them cross the street and sit side by side on a bench under a bare elm tree. Would he propose at once or would they talk a while? It seemed strange to think that I was about to witness a proposal. They had both always known their lives were leading up to this moment, but now it had come. I hoped they did not spoil it by quarreling. I envied Rosa, but I did not wish her ill. If I could not have Edwin Drood, then I was glad she could.

They must have sat there and talked at least fifteen minutes. Time and again I picked up my book and tried to read, but my mind kept straying to the couple on the bench. Then I noticed that I was not the only one watching them. Farther down the street someone stood in the shadow of a tree. He was barely visible, yet I knew at once that it was Edwin's uncle and guardian, John Jasper, the choirmaster. The realization made me shiver. I did not think it was concern for his nephew that led him to spy on them. I thought of Rosa's fear of him. She was the reason he lurked there. He wanted her for himself. Soon, however, she would be safely beyond his reach.

I glanced back at the two lovers just as they stood up. Rosa flung her arms around Edwin's neck and they kissed. It's done, I told myself. They are engaged. Henceforth, I must banish Edwin from my thoughts just as Neville and John Jasper must banish Rosa from theirs.

I prepared myself to meet Rosa with a warm smile and congratulate her when she came back to our room.

"Oh, don't say a word," she said as she burst into the

41

room, her cheeks pink from the cold air. "It's a secret. I can't tell you yet."

I could not imagine why her engagement to Edwin should be a secret, but I didn't press her. To every girl who popped her head in to ask, she said the same. It was a secret. We must be patient. But she was happy now, her eyes were bright, she smiled more, the weight of worry had lifted, and I could think of no other reason than that Edwin had proposed and she had accepted. Now that she had made her decision, she could stop worrying about whether it was the right thing to do.

Later that same evening Neville appeared to take me for our customary walk. It was a dreary overcast night and the air was chilly. The brightly lit windows that we passed only served to make us feel our outcast state more acutely. I wished that Neville and I were going to spend the evening together around a cheerful fire with friends, but it was the night appointed for him to dine with Jasper and Edwin Drood. I could tell the coming dinner weighed heavily on his thoughts, although he avoided talking about it. He walked with a large staff gripped in one hand.

"What is it for?" I finally asked.

"Hiking," he said. "I thought I might go on a walk to see more of the countryside."

This surprised me. He had never before mentioned an urge to go on a hike. "When?" I asked.

"Tomorrow."

I wondered at the suddenness of his outing. Had he planned it for a while and kept it secret from me? I doubted that. Knowing Neville, it was more likely an impulse. The question was why did he want to go. I doubted that he really wanted to explore the countryside.

"Do you go alone?" I asked, wondering if Mr. Crisparkle might be accompanying him. I would not worry about him if Mr. Crisparkle was watching out for him.

"Yes, I'm going alone," he said.

"But it will be Christmas," I objected, distressed at the idea that he would be alone and at the mercy of inclement weather.

"It would be a good time for me to go away," he said. "I'm not good company. It's awkward for everyone when I'm about. If I'm invited, then Drood can't be. And if I'm not invited, then you're not invited. And if we are, he's not. Don't you see how awkward it is? Besides, I promised Mr. Crisparkle not to let Rosa know my feelings, but if we are in the same place, I'm not sure I can hide them. No, it's altogether better for everyone if I go away for a while. Besides, it will give me a chance to think."

"But alone?" I repeated, still not convinced.

"It will do me good," he said firmly.

I saw his mind was made up. "How long will you be gone?"

"Two weeks."

Two weeks seemed like a long time, but I did not argue. I knew it would be useless. "What does Mr. Crisparkle say about your plan?"

"He approves. He is completely in favor of it."

"Then let me go with you," I urged. "We could explore the countryside together. You know I'm strong. I could walk just as far as you. I wouldn't hold you back."

"I will be sleeping under the open sky," he said.

"I don't mind sleeping under the open sky," I insisted.

"Helena, please. I need time alone to think."

I saw that I was not going to change his mind. "Write to me," I said.

"Every other day." He planted his staff for emphasis.

"What wood is it made of?" I asked, eyeing the staff again. It seemed quite formidable.

"Ironwood."

"Isn't it heavy?"

"Well, yes, it's heavy. Mr. Crisparkle said I ought to have found something lighter."

A wave of anxiety swept over me. What if something happened to him when I was not there to help him? What if he injured himself? I didn't want him to go, but I didn't know what I could say to change his mind. Besides, he said he wanted time alone, and if that were the case, I ought to let him have it. I took a deep breath and pushed aside my qualms. "I'll miss you," I said. "Please be careful."

"In a fortnight I'll be back," he said, "and you'll see my jaunt did me a world of good."

While we talked, the wind was growing stronger and we could see flashes of lightning in the distance. We turned back and took a shortcut through streets we usually avoided. We had just rounded a corner when Neville suddenly stopped. Ahead of us a young man was bending over an old beggar woman who sat on the pavement. I recognized Edwin Drood at once. He was talking to the old woman and didn't notice us. Neville and I retreated. Neither of us said a word. I knew Neville did not want to speak to his nemesis. Silently we skirted the street where we had seen Edwin Drood and continued on our way to the Nuns' House. Neville said nothing until we were at the gate.

"I wish I didn't have to go there," he said, glancing down the street at the Gate House, an ancient brick structure that straddled the street and provided living quarters on one side for Mr. Tope, the Chief Verger at the cathedral, and his wife, and on the other side for John Jasper. "I have a strange feeling about it."

I did too, but I told myself it was the coming storm which made me feel uneasy. "Soon it will be over," I said, patting his arm.

He looked glum as he walked away. I lingered at the gate and watched him walking up and down in front of the Gate House, steeling himself to go in. Twice he passed it. At last he entered the dark doorway of the stairs and disappeared. I stared at the doorway for several minutes, strangely reluctant to turn away. I don't know what I expected. Did I think Neville would reappear and wave to me, reassure me that all was well? I had the urge to follow him, just as I had when we were children. But now we were children no more. I had to let Neville go where he must go and hope that he would come safely back to me.

3

That night a storm raged. Long after Rosa went to bed, I huddled in a blanket at the window watching the street, hoping to see Neville on his way back to Minor Canon Corner. I was still by the window the next morning when I was awakened by a knock on the door. A pretty auburn head poked in. I recognized Miss Ferdinand.

"The cathedral was damaged last night," she said. "It was struck by lightning."

Rosa and I hurried to dress. When we went downstairs a dozen girls were clustered at the windows. We joined them and saw that indeed the hands of the cathedral clock were broken off. Some intrepid repairmen were crawling on the roof to assess the damage, and a cluster of people had gathered below to watch them. I saw Mr. Jasper run up to the group hatless and with his coat unbuttoned. He was gesticulating wildly.

A minute later Miss Ferdinand burst into the room. "Edwin Drood is missing," she announced breathlessly.

"And they're saying Miss Landless's brother may have murdered him."

"Nonsense," Rosa said. "That's ridiculous."

They all looked at me. I knew at once what I must do. I was not about to sit around waiting for Miss Twinkleton to give me permission to go out. I turned and headed for the door.

"Where are you going?" Rosa asked, rushing after me. She caught my arm. "Helena, you can't just walk out. It isn't allowed."

"I have to find out what's happened," I told her.

"Miss Twinkleton won't like it."

"I don't care. I have to know."

"Well, at least put on a wrap. You'll catch cold."

Rosa's anxious face made me pause. I realized she must be just as concerned as I was. "I'm sure Edwin is all right," I said, squeezing her hand. "It's probably just a silly rumor."

At that moment Mrs. Tisher, a widow employed by Miss Twinkleton in a vague capacity as assistant, appeared, attracted by the commotion. She saw me with my hand on the door latch and uttered a small cry. I threw the door open before she could stop me.

The cold air rushed at me as I stepped outdoors. I hurried down the walkway and out the gate. By the time I reached the small crowd of people gathered in front of the cathedral, they had formed a circle around Jasper.

"My poor boy, my poor boy," he moaned, wringing his hands. It seemed strange to see him so distraught. His clothes looked as if he had slept in them and his hair was windblown.

"I'm sure he'll turn up," said Mr. Crisparkle, trying to comfort him.

"What's happened?" I asked Mrs. Tope, wife of the Chief Verger. She was a neat tidy woman of middle age. I had never spoken to her before, but she had been pointed out to me by Neville on one of our walks.

"Haven't you heard?" she said. "Edwin Drood has disappeared."

"Perhaps he is just out for a morning walk," I suggested.

"He never came home," Jasper burst out as if he had heard me. "My poor boy never came home." His wild eyes fell on me as if he had just noticed my presence. He pointed at me. "Your brother—" he said in an agitated voice. "Where is your brother, Miss Landless? Can you tell us that?"

All heads turned to look at me. I stood a little straighter, conscious that I had rushed out of the Nuns' House without a shawl or bonnet. It made me feel more exposed to their eyes.

"He's gone on a walking tour," I said, trying to sound like it was the most normal thing in the world for my brother to do.

"Aha!" Jasper cried, as if I had admitted Neville's guilt.

Mr. Crisparkle was suddenly beside me. "Miss Landless, you shouldn't be here. Come. Let me walk you back to the school." He put my hand on his arm and held it firmly.

"Neville is innocent," I said as we walked away. "They accuse him unjustly."

"No doubt you are right. It is just a misunderstanding."

"We must drag the river," Jasper shouted behind us. "We must find my boy."

"Perhaps Mr. Drood has gone back to London," I said to Mr. Crisparkle.

"Perhaps."

I stopped. "Surely you don't believe that Neville did what they say?"

"We all know they quarreled," he said, again taking my hand on his arm and urging me back toward the Nuns' House. "All of Cloisterham knows it. That your brother has a violent temper—"

"He's no murderer," I said.

We were now out of earshot of the crowd at the cathedral. "They have sent after your brother," said Mr. Crisparkle. "He can't have gone far. They will bring him back. Perhaps he can shed light on this unfortunate business."

By noon there was still no word of Neville, and Edwin Drood was still missing. I worried that both might have met with foul play. Everyone said they had left the Gate House together. This was what Jasper maintained. They had gone to look at the river, although the storm was already underway. The thought that the two of them might have fallen into the river struck icy terror in my heart. Had they quarreled again? Had they fallen into the river locked in a fatal embrace? Or had one slipped and the other followed after in a vain attempt at rescue? Such were the thoughts that haunted me. I longed to hear that both Neville and Edwin were alive and safe.

There was no one to whom I could turn for comfort, not even Rosa, for she had shut herself up in Miss Twinkleton's sitting room. As evening approached, I became so desperate to talk to Rosa that I watched for Miss Twinkleton to leave her rooms and slipped in as soon as I saw her come out, cross to the dining room, and disappear through the doorway. Rosa was curled up on the settee with a book, but she dropped it as soon as she saw me and sprang up to hug me.

"Are you all right?" I asked.

"I feel like I can't cry another tear," Rosa said, her eyes red and swollen. "I expect any moment to hear it was all a big misunderstanding. That Eddy got miffed and returned to London or is just doing this to tease me. Of course I don't really believe that." She dabbed at the corner of her eye with a handkerchief.

"My poor darling," I said.

"But here I am, being so selfish, as usual. I'm sure you're just as frantic about your brother as I am about Eddy. Eddy is like a brother to me, you know. We've known each other all our lives."

"They will be found," I promised. "Both of them."

"It doesn't seem possible that anything could happen to Eddy. Only yesterday I talked to him. And finally all was right between us. After so much misunderstanding, at last we were in agreement."

"They will find him," I said. "People don't just vanish."

"I must tell you something," Rosa said, turning her innocent blue eyes on me. "Eddy and I are not engaged. Please forgive me for not telling you at once, but I thought Mr. Grewgious should be the first to know. I've sent him a letter. Now he knows, and so I can tell you too."

"Not engaged? But yesterday . . . ." I remembered how Edwin and Rosa had hugged as I watched from my window. I had been so certain they would marry now.

"Yesterday we agreed not to get engaged," she explained patiently. "We both knew it wouldn't work. We would have been miserable as husband and wife. We quarreled all the time."

"And Edwin?" I said.

"He agreed completely."

"But I thought your marriage was all arranged," I said, still stunned by her revelation.

"We did too. But then Mr. Grewgious made us see that we both had a choice. When he came down that week in November, he told me I must decide, and when Eddy went to talk to him in London, he made Eddy see too that we mustn't get married just because our parents wanted it. It must be because we want it. He made us see the importance of making the right decision. You know, marriage is a very serious step." Her lip trembled.

"It is indeed," I murmured.

"I knew you would understand," Rosa said. "I didn't like keeping it a secret from you, and I'm glad now you know. Only I'm so worried about Eddy that I can't think straight."

"I know," I said, holding tightly to her hand. I remembered how Edwin had said he would like to show me about Cloisterham. And then I tried to block out the thought. It seemed disloyal to take any pleasure in the fact that they had broken their engagement. What did it matter now if he was not alive and safe? Rosa had told me her secret, but I could not tell her mine.

In the afternoon Neville was brought back by a small band of townsmen who had gone in pursuit of him. They took him to the house of Cloisterham's mayor, Mr. Sapsea. As soon as I heard, I rushed there to be with him, but a bespectacled man at the door would not let me in. He said Neville was being questioned. After a few minutes Mr. Crisparkle came out to talk to me.

"He maintains his innocence," Mr. Crisparkle said.

"You must help him," I said.

"I will do all I can. But it doesn't look good."

"My brother didn't kill anybody," I insisted.

"But I'm afraid appearances are against him. Everyone knows he quarreled with Edwin Drood. Everyone has heard about his quick temper. And then—although I know it's not fair—he is a stranger in our town, while everyone knew Edwin Drood and took an interest in the courtship of the two young lovers. Then there is also Drood's connection with Jasper, whose devotion to his nephew is well known. Jasper is so frantic about his nephew's fate that the whole town aches with sympathy."

"They still haven't found anything," I said. "Drood might still be alive."

"If he is," said Mr. Crisparkle, "where is he? The last person to see him alive was your brother, and your brother once before was angry enough—he said so himself—" Here Crisparkle lowered his voice to a whisper. "Angry enough to kill him."

"He didn't do it," I said. "He wouldn't have."

"I hope you are right," Mr. Crisparkle said.

It was another hour before Neville emerged with Mr. Crisparkle by his side. He looked terrible. His clothes were soiled and torn. He had a cut over one eye and a bloody cloth bound around his head. Worse was the look of abject misery in his eyes.

"What have they done to you?" I asked, dismayed.

"I fought them," Neville said, "the men who were sent to bring me back. They came up on me with no explanation. I thought they were going to rob me. And so I fought. If they had just explained themselves, I would have cooperated, but they didn't."

I walked silently beside Neville and Mr. Crisparkle as they made their way to Minor Canon Corner. Jasper had argued to have Neville sent to jail in Mayfair, but Mr. Crisparkle had persuaded the Mayor to let Neville return to Minor Canon Corner in his custody. Once we were safely in his house, Mr. Crisparkle tactfully withdrew so Neville and I might talk alone.

"How is Rosa?" Neville asked as soon as the door of the parlor had closed.

"She's quite well," I assured him.

"I didn't kill him," Neville said. "Will you tell her that?"

"You didn't quarrel again?" I asked anxiously.

"No, we made up at Jasper's over dinner, just as planned. We both may have drunk too much—"

"Neville!" I could not believe that after the unfortunate outcome of their previous encounter they had indulged again.

"There were toasts," he explained. "It would have been rude to refuse. And each time our glasses were empty, Jasper wanted to make another toast, and so they must be filled again. And the drink seemed strangely potent, so that the room spun around as if I had drunk more than I thought I had."

"Just like the other time," I said, remembering.

"Yes, I guess it was," Neville agreed. "But we didn't quarrel. We were quite friendly in fact. I began to think Drood was not so bad. He seemed quite sincerely sorry that he had been offensive on that previous occasion. He said it was a fault of his and that he just can't help it popping out. He said it's why he quarrels so much with Rosa."

His face darkened. "I still think he's not good enough for Rosa, but for her sake, I would not have hurt him."

"I believe you," I said. "What happened next?"

"We left together. It was late and both of us were a little drunk. The wind was wild and there was lightning in the sky. We decided to walk by the river and take a look at it. It was a fiercesome kind of night."

"And did you go down by the river?"

"Yes, I can remember that, the water all abroil and the wind whipping around us, although it's all kind of hazy, like something I dreamed."

"And you parted on good terms?"

"We did. I give you my word."

"And you returned then to Minor Canon Corner?"

"I did."

"And he?"

"He was on his way back to the Gate House."

"What happened to him?"

"God knows," Neville said. "It's like he vanished into thin air."

It was difficult that evening to sit through dinner with all the whispering. Even between Rosa and me there was an uncomfortable barrier, both of us aware that Neville was suspected of murdering Edwin. I did not believe for a minute that he had, but I feared the very sight of me might be a painful reminder to her. Nor was there anyone to whom I could turn for comfort—no one knew how I feared for what had become of Edwin, and I was alone in believing in my brother's innocence. Nightfall came and there was still no sign of Edwin Drood.

I slept fitfully that night, and in my dream I was standing by the river in a storm with Neville, crying out Edwin's name.

The next morning I was called out of history class by Mrs. Tisher. "Miss Twinkleton wants to see you," she said, and lowering her voice added: "I think it's about your brother, Miss."

Alarmed, I hurried down to Miss Twinkleton's sitting room.

"My dear, I'm afraid I have bad news," she said. "I've just received a message from Mr. Crisparkle that your brother's been taken to the Mayor's house again. Something has been found."

"What?" My stomach dropped. I was terrified she would say 'a body.'

"I don't know," she said, straightening the blotter on her desk. "But I thought you might want to go to him."

I thanked her, grabbed a shawl, and rushed across the street to Mr. Sapsea's large and imposing house. This time I was admitted at once. The room to which I was led seemed full of men. Some were sitting and some standing. Mr. Sapsea was at the center of the room talking to a man I didn't know. Neville was seated in a chair with two townsmen standing on either side guarding him. He had a clean bandage wrapped around his head. When he saw me, he nodded but didn't smile. It pained me to see him treated like a prisoner. I started toward him, intending to say something encouraging, but almost at once Mr. Crisparkle was at my side.

"Have they found Edwin?" I asked, relieved to see a friendly face.

"No," Mr. Crisparkle said in a low voice, drawing me a little apart, "but we have found evidence that he met with an accident."

"What kind of accident?" I studied his face for some clue.

He lowered his voice so that only I could hear. "Last night I walked to Cloisterham Weir. No one searched there because it was two miles above where Neville and Edwin went to look at the river. I'm not sure what drew me there. It was dark and I couldn't see much. I decided to go back in the daytime. I didn't sleep well. I dreamt I was searching Cloisterham Weir for Edwin's drowned body. As soon as it was morning I went back. Among the timbers I noticed a small glint, something that caught the rays of the morning sun. I swam to it. It was Edwin's gold watch on a chain. His initials were on the back."

"You think he fell in and drowned?" I asked.

"I don't know what to think."

"Perhaps he threw his watch into the river," I suggested, trying to think of an explanation that would leave the possibility that he could be alive.

Mr. Crisparkle shook his head, and my heart sank. "He wouldn't have. It belonged to his father. I fear he has come to an unfortunate end."

"But you found no body," I pointed out, not willing to give up.

"No. I kept diving, hoping to find him, but only turned up a shirt-pin on the muddy bottom. I fear that too is his."

His watch and shirt-pin. Would he have thrown in both? It didn't seem likely.

The man to whom Mr. Sapsea was talking turned out to be a jeweler who had been sent for to identify the watch.

"Yes, I recognize it," he said, turning the watch over in his hand. "The last time I saw it, it was in the possession of young Edwin Drood. I wound it myself at twenty minutes past two in the afternoon on the day he disappeared and it doesn't look as if it's been wound again."

At that moment Jasper arrived looking white and haggard. People stepped back and made a path for him. He took the watch from the jeweler in his trembling hands and someone handed him the shirt-pin. "Yes, they are my poor dear boy's," he said. Then he looked straight at Neville. "You killed him!" he said in a terrible voice. "And you will pay for this. If it's the last thing I do, you will pay for this."

Everyone began to talk at once. They all seemed to think it was definite now: Edwin had been murdered—the shirt-pin and the watch were proof. And they were convinced Neville had done it. Neville looked around him miserably, all the fight gone out of him.

"Do something, can't you?" I begged Mr. Crisparkle.

I don't know if he heard me, but he quickly stepped between Jasper and Neville. "We are all deeply concerned about the fate of your nephew," he said to Jasper, "but we must not let our feelings so cloud our reason that we rashly rush to judgment. I admit that appearances are not good. That Edwin Drood met with foul play seems likely, from the discovery of his jewelry in the weir. Still there is no body and hence no evidence that a crime has been committed. You cannot convict a man of murder on the basis of a quarrel. Suspicious appearances are not enough. You say he had Edwin Drood's blood on his staff, but how do you know it was not his own blood, spilled when our zealous townsfolk grappled with him in their attempt to apprehend him? He was the last to see Edwin Drood alive, as he freely admits, yet that is not proof he killed Edwin Drood. He insists on his innocence, and I believe him. Would you have it on your conscience that you convicted a man who may be innocent?"

The others present considered this. Neville was taken to a small room to await the decision, and they let me wait with him. I was grateful to be away from his accusers, especially Jasper. A burly townsman stood guard at the open door, as if Neville might make a reckless break for freedom, but Neville sat with his head bowed in his hands, looking crushed by the world.

"You must not lose heart," I said, trying to comfort him.

"You are the only one who believes I'm innocent," he said.

"Not the only one. Mr. Crisparkle believes it too."

"He's been very good to me. I don't deserve it. I've been only trouble for him."

"Neville," I said gently. I tried to pull his hands down, but they would not budge.

"I'm not like you," he said. "You always were the good one."

"What choice did I have?" I said. "I had to be good to survive."

"I should never have been born."

"Don't say that." I put my arms around him and we rocked together. "Without you where would I be? What would I do? Who could I talk to?"

I knew Neville's black moods and that I must sit by him and help him through. I dreaded the thought of him alone in a prison cell left to his own dark thoughts. Once in Ceylon he had been thrown into a dark and filthy cell for having been involved in a fight with an Indian. He had tried to hang himself with his shirt. The black thoughts had been too much, and I had not been there. I didn't want that to happen again.

For two days the townspeople searched for Edwin Drood. They dragged the river and combed the banks. Their lanterns could be seen on the river at night. A Lost notice was nailed to a lamppost on High Street with Edwin Drood's name on it. But the fate of Edwin Drood remained a mystery.

Mr. Grewgious arrived at the Nuns' House at midday on the second day of Edwin's disappearance. Miss Twinkleton ushered him into her private sitting room, where Rosa had been staying ever since they found the watch and shirt-pin. A little later Mrs. Tisher stuck head into French class to say I was wanted.

In the sitting room I found Rosa in tears and Mr. Grewgious looking quite helpless. She was clutching a huge handkerchief, which must have been his. Miss

DEANNA MADDEN

Twinkleton hovered over her, urging her to have some tea and biscuits. I went straight to Rosa and held her.

"It's my fault," Rosa sobbed.

"It's not your fault," I told her.

"Most certainly not," Mr. Grewgious said.

"I should have warned Eddy."

"How could you have known?" Miss Twinkleton said. "You're not a fortune-teller."

"I should have told him, but I didn't and now he's dead. Oh, it's too much to bear."

"Miss Landless," Mr. Grewgious said, turning to me, "have you any idea what she's trying to say?"

I looked up at the tall angular kindly-faced man, who was clearly perplexed. "She never told Eddy about his uncle."

"Jasper? What about him?"

I hesitated, wondering if I should tell. After all, it was Rosa's secret, not mine. I could feel her shoulders shaking and made up my mind. Why should I protect John Jasper? "Mr. Jasper is in love with her."

Mr. Grewgious frowned. "Did he say he was?"

"He didn't say he was," I admitted, "but I noticed it our first night here. It was the way he looked at her. Rosa was so upset she cried."

"Is this true?" Mr. Grewgious asked her.

Rosa nodded vehemently, the handkerchief pressed to her nose. "I couldn't tell Eddy."

"I'm not sure what this has to do with the young man's disappearance," Mr. Grewgious said.

"I was afraid of him," Rosa said.

"Edwin Drood?"

"His uncle. I don't think he wanted me to marry Eddy."

"You have suspicions about him?"

"I do." Rosa started crying again.

Miss Twinkleton reached out and patted her shoulder, then offered tea again.

"We should have told him we weren't going to marry," Rosa said, "but Eddy said he couldn't bear to disappoint his uncle, and I said since you were coming down, we could let you break the news, and he was so relieved. But if his uncle had known, maybe Eddy would still be alive."

"Oh, my goodness," Miss Twinkleton said and began to fan herself.

"Now, now," Mr. Grewgious said. "Let's not jump to conclusions." He turned back to Rosa. "If what you say is true, Jasper has been deceiving a lot of people. He has convinced all of Cloisterham that he dotes on his nephew."

"And that my brother is a murderer," I added.

Mr. Grewgious scowled and shook his head. "Could it be possible? I confess I don't like the man. There is something about him not quite right. However, I fear that no one will believe it." He shook his head again. "No, for now we must be cautious. We will wait and watch."

"But I can't possibly take singing lessons from him anymore," Rosa protested.

"Of course not."

"He shall not give lessons to my pupils ever again," Miss Twinkleton declared.

"Let's not be too hasty," said Mr. Grewgious. "We mustn't let him know we suspect anything. Therefore, I suggest you let him continue as before, but without Rosa as a pupil. You can say she is too upset for singing lessons."

"He shan't go near her," said Miss Twinkleton, putting an arm around Rosa protectively.

Mr. Grewgious reached for his hat. "And now if you ladies will excuse me, I will do exactly what the missing young man wanted me to do—inform his uncle that the engagement had already been broken off that night before said young man disappeared. Then we will wait and watch."

4

In the end they did not charge Neville. So long as there was no body, there was no certainty that a crime had been committed, yet all of Cloisterham thought he was guilty, and Neville could not walk the streets without being stared at and whispered about. The entire community shunned him. It was almost as bad for me, but I was determined not to let them beat me down, and I ventured out anyway. Poor Neville, however, could not bear it. He stayed in his room at Minor Canon Corner as if he were still under house arrest and could only be persuaded to leave it under cover of darkness. To make matters worse, Mr. Crisparkle's old mother objected to his presence in the house and so Neville could not appear at dinner but had to take his meals in his room. Mr. Crisparkle was torn between wanting to placate his mother and wanting to aid Neville. It was clear Neville could not continue to stay at Minor Canon Corner and disturb the old lady's peace of mind. Nor was there any other suitable shelter for him in Cloisterham since everywhere he went he was regarded as a murderer. As a result, Mr. Crisparkle decided that Neville should take lodgings in London, where he could continue his studies. I did not like being separated from him, but Mr. Crisparkle promised that I could join him within a few months when the term ended.

Neville's new rooms were in the Staple Inn, a moldering old building in Holborn which also housed the law office and living quarters of Mr. Grewgious. Mr. Crisparkle took me there shortly after Neville had moved in. One had to climb up several flights of creaking stairs to reach the garret where Neville now lived. There were sloping ceilings, heavy wood beams, and only a little furniture. The sunlight streamed in from a small window that looked out upon London rooftops and chimneys beyond a cracked and smoke-blackened parapet where a few bedraggled sparrows hopped. It was very like a prison cell, and my heart sank at the idea of Neville being confined in such a place. But there were books—thanks to Mr. Crisparkle—and I began to think what I could do to make the room more cheerful when I moved in. Neville had an unhealthy pallor due to spending so much time indoors. Even here he avoided the sunlight and the eyes of people, only going out at night to roam the London streets. Mr. Crisparkle had taken it upon himself to watch over Neville and be a friend to him. He traveled to London once a week to visit Neville and help him in his studies. It was as often as he could manage, given his duties at the cathedral. In between times there were Mr. Grewgious and his clerk Mr. Bazzard downstairs, whom Neville could turn to if he needed anything.

When the end of the term came, I was sorry to leave the Nuns' House, especially since it meant leaving Rosa.

She had become like a sister to me. We both had tears in our eyes as we said good-bye.

"You must write me at least twice a week," she said. "You must tell me all about London and what you are doing."

"I doubt I shall be doing much except watching over Neville," I said.

"I wish we could be closer," Rosa said. "I will miss you ever so much. How will I stand it here all by myself?"

"You have Miss Twinkleton," I said.

"Ah, dear Miss T. What would I do without her?"

"And maybe Mr. Crisparkle could bring you for a visit. It isn't so far." I glanced at Mr. Crisparkle, who at that moment was waiting for me by the omnibus.

Rosa shook her head. "I don't think I could. It would remind me too much of Eddy."

There was nothing I could say to that, except to hug her again and promise that I would write often. Once on the omnibus, I leaned out the window and waved to her until she was out of sight.

Mr. Crisparkle made some polite remarks about the scenery we passed, but since we were not alone on the omnibus, neither of us mentioned Neville, though I'm sure he was uppermost in both our thoughts. On the train we had a compartment to ourselves and could talk more freely.

"I must admit I'm very relieved you will be with your brother," Mr. Crisparkle said as he sat across from me. "I worry about him."

"So do I," I confessed.

"He has suffered terribly over this business."

I agreed. "He feels that everyone suspects him. It is an intolerable burden. It weighs him down."

"I hope you will be able to raise his spirits."

"You are very good to help him," I said.

"I am trying to make amends."

"For what?" I could not imagine anything for which Mr. Crisparkle needed to make amends. He had been nothing but helpful ever since our arrival in Cloisterham.

"For the way Cloisterham has treated him."

Yes, there was that, although it was certainly not Mr. Crisparkle's fault. "You believe in his innocence?" I asked.

"Completely. I didn't at first I admit. The evidence against him looked bad. But he was so insistent in his denials, and then too, having gotten to know Neville, I know his heart to be good. While his temper may carry him away, his conscience I think would force him to acknowledge the deed. If he had killed Drood, he would have confessed. He doesn't have the kind of temperament that can live with guilt. Then too there are other things that do not add up."

"Such as?"

Mr. Crisparkle leaned forward in spite of the fact that there were only ourselves in the compartment. "If he was the murderer which the town takes him to be, why did he not hide himself? He had announced that he would go off on a walking tour, and he did. It was no great difficulty to find him and bring him back. That is not the plan of a murderer."

"But you do think Edwin Drood was murdered?"

"I'm afraid so. The shirt-pin and watch I found at the Weir make that fairly certain. I have thought and thought, and the only possible explanation is that which Jasper suggested—that the murderer wished to remove all identification from the body. When the body is found, we may not know it is Edwin Drood because there may be no way to identify it."

"And if he was murdered," I said, "who was the murderer?"

"Perhaps we will never know," he said. "Perhaps it is one of those mysteries never meant to be solved."

"But if it is never solved," I said, "Neville may never be able to hold his head up again."

"There I look to you to help him."

I met Mr. Crisparkle's gaze steadily. I did intend to help Neville but perhaps not in the way he envisioned. "If Edwin Drood was in fact murdered, someone murdered him," I said, "and I intend to find out who."

He looked at me in alarm. "Oh, really, Miss Landless, you mustn't. This is a matter for the authorities."

"The authorities are only too ready to blame my brother for the crime. If they do find Edwin Drood's body, they will charge Neville with murder. It is only for want of a body that he is now free."

"I understand your concern for your brother," he said. "I am concerned too. Still I urge you not to do anything rash that would compromise his position further—or yours."

"Our position, Mr. Crisparkle, could not be much worse," I pointed out.

"I am urging you as one who cares for your brother's welfare *and yours*, not to do anything reckless. I know you care deeply for your brother, and you would not want to hurt his cause."

"I do not intend to hurt his cause," I said. "But I cannot stand by and let him be accused unjustly."

"What is it that you mean to do?" he asked uneasily.

"Find out what really happened that night."

"And how will you do that?"

"I will find a way. I will ask questions. I will do whatever it takes."

"And you will not be dissuaded?"

"I will not."

"It could be dangerous," he said.

"I'm not afraid."

He sighed. "I don't approve of your plan. I think it is ill-advised and quite likely dangerous, but if you really are determined to pursue this, let me help you."

"How?" I said.

"I'm sure you will think of something," he said with a rueful smile. "You are a most resourceful young woman, and if you are determined to do this, why then do it you will."

I felt as if I had just achieved some kind of victory, but what it was, I wasn't really sure.

I did not tell Neville about my intent to find out the truth about what happened that night. He was too distressed already. My first concern was to chase the gloom from his attic rooms and to see that he was not alone. Almost the first thing I did when we arrived was to open a window to let in fresh air. To my surprise I found a green arbor had miraculously appeared where before there had been only a small bare ledge leading to a crumbling parapet.

"You have a garden!" I exclaimed. It seemed like

something out of the *Arabian Nights*. He had rubbed a magic lamp and there it was—a garden among the blackened rooftops. I scrambled out onto the ledge in delight. The trailing vines were bean plants and among them flowers peeked shyly out.

"They belong to my neighbor, Mr. Tartar," Neville explained, sticking his head out the window. "He strung them across from his window ledge." He pointed to the left, and I saw there an even wilder growth of bean plants and indeed they stretched across the narrow gap between the two buildings like a leafy bridge.

At that moment a tall sunburnt man wearing a seaman's cap emerged from the next door lodgings and stepped carefully among the bean plants and flowers with a watering can.

"Is that Mr. Tartar?" I asked Neville.

"So it is," said Neville. Then he raised his voice. "Mr. Tartar, come meet my sister."

Mr. Tartar came to the edge of the parapet and then easily leaped the distance between the two buildings, as if he had not been several floors above the ground. He pulled off his hat and shook my hand. He was a young man still in his twenties, with blue eyes blazing out of a sun-bronzed face. He beamed at me and looked thoroughly delighted.

"Extraordinary!" he said, looking from me to Neville and back again. "You and your brother are spitting images."

"We're twins," I said.

"Extraordinary," he repeated.

"Do you often jump across like that?" I asked, glancing over the edge of the parapet. "It looks quite dangerous."

"Not a bit," he said. "It keeps me in shape."

"He was in the Royal Navy," Neville said. "He's used to climbing rigging."

"Well, your bean plants are quite wonderful," I said.

"I'm trying to adapt to dry land," Tartar explained, "but London is such a close and cramped place. My plants help me breathe."

"Would you like to come in, Mr. Tartar?" I said, for it seemed strange to be standing on the ledge talking to a stranger.

He accepted the invitation with obvious pleasure and ducked after me through the open window into the small room where we had our table and chairs. With three of us in the room, we seemed nearly to fill it. But small though it was, it was pleasant enough with its new curtains and a gay cloth spread over the table.

"So you and Neville are friends?" I said.

"Aye," he said. "I thought he could use a friend. I couldn't help noticing how cooped up he was."

"It was very kind of you," I said.

"Perhaps you can persuade him to take more breaks from his studies," Mr. Tartar said. "It's not healthy to be always indoors."

"I go out at night," Neville said. "I don't like the day. I have my reasons."

"My brother recently endured an ordeal from which he has yet to recover," I explained, not wanting our visitor to think Neville rude.

"So he told me, and I shall not pry."

"I was accused of murder," Neville said bluntly.

For a moment there was an awkward silence.

"It's a serious charge," Mr. Tartar observed.

"My brother is innocent," I said, so there should be no misunderstanding.

"I can believe that," Mr. Tartar said.

"Why?" Neville demanded. "How do you know I'm not a murderer?"

Mr. Tartar looked at him thoughtfully. "Because you have not the look of a murderer." I liked him for that answer.

"And can you always tell by the look?" Neville persisted. "Don't you think it's possible to deceive other people—make them think you're harmless when in fact you're not?"

"Maybe so," Tartar agreed, "but I don't think you are one of those either."

"I have a terrible temper," Neville said. "It sweeps me away sometimes." He seemed determined to make Mr. Tartar see him in a bad light.

"That's unfortunate," Tartar said. "Still, many men have tempers and only a few of them ever kill." He took a deep breath. "Who may I ask are you accused of murdering?"

I was afraid Neville was going to say it was none of his business. "A young man we met in Cloisterham," I said. "They quarreled. Neville was the last person to see him alive."

"But the night it happened, we parted amicably," Neville said.

Tartar nodded, then tilted his head to one side and narrowed his eyes. "And how was he murdered, if I may be so bold as to ask?"

"We don't know," I said when Neville stayed stubbornly silent. "The body was never found."

"Then in fact there may have been no murder?"

"If Drood's alive, where is he?" Neville demanded. "Why doesn't he come forward?"

"They found his watch and his shirt-pin," I said. "Everyone thinks he was drowned."

"Ah, but he might have been drowned and not been murdered," Tartar said. "Have you thought of that?"

"Even if it happened like that," I said, "Neville would still be blamed. The town is convinced of his guilt."

"We are outsiders," Neville explained. "We arrived in Cloisterham only a month before Drood disappeared."

"We grew up in Ceylon," I added.

Tartar gave me a quick look. "So your brother told me. I've been there."

"You have?" I said, surprised.

He nodded. "And I know how cold and dark London must look to you after that. I told your brother I'll be his friend . . . and I'll be yours too, if you want." He extended his hand, and I shook it, a great leathery warm hand, and then Neville shook it too, and we all grinned at each other as if we had reached some kind of understanding.

When Mr. Tartar climbed back out onto the ledge, I felt glad to know that Neville had found a friend like him.

Soon Mr. Crisparkle returned from conferring with Mr. Grewgious, whose offices were also in the Staple Inn, his windows visible from our front windows. For the next few hours Mr. Crisparkle worked with Neville on his lessons and I listened and followed. Mr. Crisparkle tactfully included me and tried to make sure that I too understood.

These lessons were far more difficult than what I had encountered at Miss Twinkleton's, where mathematics and science were not even part of the curriculum, nor were Greek or Latin or philosophy. It made me wonder about the quality of education I was receiving at that establishment.

"You mustn't fault Miss Twinkleton for that," Mr. Crisparkle said when I asked him about this. "Miss Twinkleton's young ladies are expected to marry and so have no need of those subjects. Neville, on the other hand, will need to make his way in the world."

"It seems unfair, doesn't it," I asked, "that so much knowledge should be withheld from young women?"

"I suppose it does," he said. "But are you sure the young women mind?"

I had to admit that they probably did not, but I thought I minded. Difficult though Neville's lessons were, when I learned them I felt a sense of accomplishment that I did not feel at Miss Twinkleton's.

As it grew dark Mr. Crisparkle asked Neville if he was ready to walk with him to the train station. Neville said he was.

I went into my room to fetch my hat and shawl, expecting to accompany them. When I returned, they both looked at me with obvious discomfort.

"Oh, Miss Landless, you can't—" Mr. Crisparkle began, then stopped, embarrassed.

"Surely ladies also can walk?" I said. "I walked in Cloisterham and so surely I can here too."

Mr. Crisparkle looked at Neville for help.

"It would be better for you to stay here," Neville said, not meeting my eyes.

"Surely it would not be improper if I had two men as escorts," I said.

"It could be dangerous," Mr. Crisparkle said. "London is not Cloisterham."

"Then it is dangerous for you as well."

Both of them avoided my eyes. I wondered what they were not telling me.

"Mr. Crisparkle wishes to speak with me privately about a certain matter," Neville said.

It sounded plausible, and yet I did not believe him. For some reason they did not want me with them.

"Very well," I said, sitting down again. "I will wait here."

Mr. Crisparkle looked relieved.

"Don't wait up for me," Neville said as they went out the door. "I may be quite late. I usually walk about until I thoroughly wear myself out."

I watched them from the window as they set off together under the gaslights. I did not like being excluded. If I had been a man, they would not have left me behind. It was very frustrating to so often be left out of things because I was a woman. For a while I read, but time passed slowly. I was reluctant to go to bed because I knew I would find it impossible to sleep. The old building sighed and creaked and groaned. A dozen times I thought I heard furtive footsteps on the stairs. I would look up from my book, my ears straining. A dozen times I went to the window and peered out into the dark night for a glimpse of Neville's returning figure. Finally, well after midnight by the tolling of the clocks, I fell asleep.

5

In the weeks that followed I was to learn that Neville frequently went on these late night jaunts but always he insisted on walking alone. I had the feeling that he was hiding something from me, and that hurt me because we had always been so close. I was sure he did not frequent any of the inns or brothels. And yet I was just as sure that there was something he was not telling me.

My suspicions were confirmed one day while I was visiting Mr. Grewgious in his office to thank him for all he had done for my brother. Mr. Grewgious had been called aside by his clerk Mr. Bazzard to attend to some business and I was waiting for him to return when I looked out his window and noticed a man in the second story stairwell of the building across the street. I could not see the man clearly because his face was shadowed by his hat, but there was something familiar about him. He did not seem to be in any hurry, for he was still standing at the window when Mr. Grewgious returned fifteen or twenty minutes later.

"I see you are admiring our view," Mr. Grewgious said, removing his hat. "I'm afraid it's not much of a view."

"I see someone across the way is admiring *this* view," I said.

Mr. Grewgious sat down at his desk and picked up a pen. "Yes, the stairwell opposite does seem to attract people wanting a view."

"He seems strangely familiar," I observed.

"Does he?" said Mr. Grewgious.

"I can't think who he reminds me of."

"Mr. Jasper perhaps?"

Just then the man leaned forward for a second and I glimpsed his face. It was indeed Mr. Jasper. "Why is he here?" I asked. "Why is he standing in the stairwell across the street?"

"He's watching," Mr. Grewgious said.

"Watching what?"

"Watching who comes in and who goes out a certain door."

"You mean the door to this building?"

"It would seem so."

"What does he want?" I said, trying to see Jasper more clearly. He had stepped back into the shadows again.

"Come away from the window," Mr. Grewgious said. "It's not certain that he knows we've spotted him. If he's going to watch, it's better that he places himself where we can see him. Don't you agree?"

"Does Neville know?"

"Neville knows. Neville knows and leads him a merry chase through the streets of London by night."

"Neville's late night walks!" I said. "That's why he won't let me go along. Mr. Crisparkle knows too?"

"Yes, he does."

"We must do something," I said, growing more alarmed the more I thought about it. "It isn't good for Neville. What does Jasper mean—to push him to the brink of madness?"

"Perhaps," Mr. Grewgious said.

"He must be stopped."

"How can we stop him?"

"But Neville is innocent," I protested. "Jasper has no right to pursue him."

"You must calm yourself," Mr. Grewgious said. "We have our eye on Mr. Jasper. As long as he watches us so openly, we can watch him as well."

"How long has this been going on?" I asked.

He shrugged. "A few months."

"The whole time Neville's been here?"

"I'm afraid so."

"But what of his duties in Cloisterham?"

"He travels between London and Cloisterham. I presume his duties get done."

"So part of the time he is not watching Neville?"

"We think there are other watchers, men hired by Jasper for the times he must be absent."

"Couldn't we move Neville?" I suggested.

"We could, but for now he's probably safest here."

"Do you think he might be in danger?"

"Perhaps."

"But why? Why won't Jasper leave him alone?"

"Cloisterham would say Jasper has been driven mad by grief over his nephew's disappearance, that he blames your brother, that he intends to get revenge."

"And what would you say?"

Mr. Grewgious sighed. "I say we should watch him."

"Do you think Jasper is mad?"

"Possibly."

"Do you think he killed Edwin Drood?"

"It doesn't matter what I think. What matters is what can or cannot be proved in a court of law."

"Rosa thinks . . . ."

He held up a hand to stop me. "Rosa has no proof."

"Then we must find proof," I said.

"It's not that simple. The authorities have already investigated. Unfortunately all the evidence points to your brother."

"There must be something else, something they didn't find."

Mr. Grewgious looked thoughtful. "Perhaps there was something else."

"What?"

He pressed the tips of his fingers together and nodded his head as if he were thinking. "Something small," he said cryptically. But that was all he would tell me. Then he called for Bazzard, and I understood that I would be interfering with work if I stayed longer, so I took my leave and went back upstairs. Neville was studying at the table in our garret rooms when I walked in.

"Why didn't you tell me Jasper is following you?" I demanded.

"Is he?"

"You know he is. I saw him from the window in Mr. Grewgious's office. Why didn't you tell me?"

"I thought it would be better if you didn't know."

I sat across from him. He looked so pale and tired. "I thought we shared everything," I said. "No secrets."

"Have you no secrets from me?" he asked, glancing up from his book.

I wondered if he had guessed my feelings for Edwin Drood and felt myself coloring. "We must find out what happened that night," I said firmly.

"And how are we to do that?" Neville asked.

"By going over everything that happened."

"Don't you think I've gone over it a hundred times already?" Neville said. "Don't you know I dream about it at night?"

I did indeed. I had heard him cry out often enough and run to his bedside to comfort him just as I had when we were children. It pained me to think of all the nights he had woken alone in a cold sweat with no one to turn to before I moved to London. I knew how distressed talking about that night made him, but I wanted to understand what had happened.

"Please," I said, "tell me again what you remember about that night. Maybe if we go over it again, we will notice something we overlooked before."

"Honestly, Helena, I don't think it will do any good."

"Please!"

He sighed. "Oh, very well, if you insist." He leaned his elbow on the table, head in hand, as if his head hurt and closed his eyes. "I didn't want to go," he said in a glum voice.

"I know." I remembered how I had urged him on and wished we could turn back the clock to that awful night and do it all differently. If we could move back to that moment in time, I would tell him not to go. I remembered how the coming storm had seemed to hint of something terrible approaching and Neville had had a dread upon him which proved all too prophetic.

"You arrived first," I reminded him.

"The door was unlocked so I went in."

"How long was it until Edwin arrived?"

"Not long. Maybe fifteen minutes."

"What did you do while you waited?"

"Looked about."

"Did you notice anything unusual?"

"No, everything was like before."

"Then Edwin Drood arrived."

"Yes. I remember hearing the clock chime."

"So why was he late?"

"He didn't explain. But he did say he'd had a curious experience."

"Did he seem upset?"

"No, not upset, but like he had something on his mind. I thought that later too."

"You didn't quarrel?"

"No, I was determined not to be provoked. I didn't want to disappoint Mr. Crisparkle. He so badly wanted us to make up."

"And you apologized to Drood?"

"I did."

"And he apologized to you?"

"Yes. I've told you all of this before."

"When did Jasper arrive?"

"Perhaps after another fifteen minutes."

"Did he explain why he was late?"

"He said he'd gotten into a conversation with Mr. Sapsea."

"What happened next?"

"Dinner arrived. We sat around and talked until near midnight. And then Edwin and I walked down to the river to watch the storm come in. After that, I walked back to Minor Canon Corner and he to the Gate House."

"Whose idea was it to go down to the river?"

"Mine, no maybe Edwin's. I don't remember. I guess we both thought we needed a bit of a walk to clear our heads."

"What was the conversation about at dinner?"

"Nothing important. Just small talk. Edwin talked about Egypt. I talked about Ceylon. Jasper . . . ."

"Yes?"

"I don't remember," Neville said, shaking his head. "It was six months ago."

"And then you and Edwin walked down to the river?"

"Yes."

"What did you talk about?"

"I don't remember. It's all very hazy."

"The drink—"

"Wine has never affected me so strongly before," Neville said. "Except that other time."

"Both times it was Jasper's wine that affected you so strongly."

He opened his eyes and looked at me. "What are you suggesting?"

"Perhaps he added something to the wine."

Neville looked at me blankly. "Like what?"

"I don't know. A drug."

"You've been reading too many novels," he said.

"Just think about it," I urged. "Twice it happened. Both times under similar circumstances. You say you didn't drink much and yet you were drunk. Who poured the drinks?"

"Jasper, of course."

"And did he also become drunk?"

"I don't think so." Neville frowned. "I can't remember. What are you getting at?"

"Perhaps Jasper purposely drugged both of you."

"Why would he do that?"

I took a deep breath. "When Edwin left you, he said he was returning to the Gate House, didn't he?"

"Yes, he did."

"Suppose he did return to the Gate House."

"But Jasper says he didn't."

"Suppose Jasper is lying."

Neville looked perplexed. "Why would he lie?"

"To throw all the suspicion on you. Think about it. Why was all of Cloisterham so ready to condemn you? Wasn't it because they already believed you to be dangerous? And why was that? Because of your quarrel in November with Drood. Jasper made sure everyone knew you had quarreled. He told everyone you were dangerous. Don't you see?"

"But he was only looking out for his nephew because he doted on him."

"Are you sure?"

Neville shook his head. "Helena, your imagination is carrying you away. God knows, I hate the man. He has made my life a hell. But I have never doubted his devotion to Drood. He worshipped the ground his nephew walked on. You should have heard them go on about each other."

"Did you know that Jasper is in love with Rosa?"

Neville stared at me.

"It's true. That night at Mr. Crisparkle's after dinner when he played the piano and she sang, remember how upset Rosa became? I guessed his secret then and later I heard it from Rosa's lips."

"Rosa told you that?" He stared at me. "Why didn't you tell me?"

"She told me in confidence."

"You think he killed Drood to get Rosa for himself?"

"I do."

Neville stood up, nearly knocking over his chair. "We have to tell someone."

"It would do no good," I said. "It's not proof he killed Drood. Cloisterham will still see him as their respected choirmaster, and you will still be the distrusted outsider. You fit their idea of a murderer more than he."

"It's hopeless then, isn't it?" Neville said, dropping back in his chair and clutching his head in his hands.

"We must look for proof," I said. "Something that Cloisterham can't ignore."

"What?"

"I don't know. But somewhere I feel certain there is proof. You mustn't give in to despair. The day will come when you will be vindicated. I promise."

I had no idea how I was going to help Neville, but I was determined to. For the rest of the day I mulled it over and it was still occupying my thoughts the next morning as I sat by the window vainly attempting to read a book. I had just read the same passage twice over when I thought I heard someone call my name. Laying aside my book, I climbed out among the flowers and bean plants. Next door on Mr. Tartar's ledge stood Rosa Bud in a pink hat and pink dress, looking like a rose come to life in Mr. Tartar's garden.

"What are you doing here?" I exclaimed, delighted to see her.

"Mr. Tartar kindly let me borrow his garden so I could talk to you," she said.

"Is he there?"

"No, he wanted to give us privacy. Oh, you should see his rooms, Helena! They're ever so wonderful. All so tidy and neat with little cubby holes and compartments and nooks for everything. I've never seen anything like it."

"How do you know Mr. Tartar?" I asked.

"I don't," she said, visibly blushing. "We only just met. But Mr. Grewgious knows him, and he went to school with Mr. Crisparkle, and he saved Mr. Crisparkle's life once."

"Saved his life?"

"Saved him from drowning."

"I can't imagine Mr. Crisparkle in danger of drowning."

"It was a long time ago," Rosa said, "before Mr. Crisparkle learned to swim. In fact, he said that was why he decided to learn to swim."

"Are you alone?" I asked, wondering how private our conversation was.

"Mr. Crisparkle is here too," she said. "That is, he's inside."

"Why did he not bring you up to our rooms?" I asked.

"Because your rooms are watched. My guardian and Mr. Crisparkle thought it was better for me not to be noticed."

"Yes, it's true, I'm afraid. We're watched." I thought of Jasper lurking in the staircase of the building across from the Staple Inn. How fortunate that he only had a view of the doors and not of the back of the building, else he would have seen us then.

"How is your brother?" Rosa asked.

"Low in spirits." I glanced back, wondering if I should call Neville from the other room.

"I'm sorry to hear that."

"It still weighs heavily on him."

"As it does also on me."

"And yet time helps to heal the wound."

"Yes, it does," agreed Rosa.

"It is wonderful to see you again. Even if we have to call to each other from roof to roof."

"Actually I'm here for a reason," Rosa said. "I have something to tell you about Mr. Jasper."

"Mr. Jasper!" I said, surprised. "What about him?"

"He came to see me at the Nuns' House. He asked me to marry him."

"Never!" I said. "You couldn't!"

"He said he would give up his pursuit of the murderer if I consented to be his wife."

"You mean Neville. No, Neville wouldn't want you to do that. You must not consider it."

"And he said if I didn't agree, he would harm you and Neville."

"He threatened us?"

"Yes, he did."

"Me as well as Neville?"

"Because you are my friend, dear Helena, and he has got it into his head that Neville is a rival."

That could explain why he was watching Neville so closely and why he followed Neville at night. Maybe revenge was not his motive; maybe jealousy was. He had killed Edwin Drood, and he might kill Neville too if he thought my brother stood in his way. He had threatened me merely because he wanted Rosa. He knew her tender heart might lead her to agree to a marriage she would otherwise have spurned.

"You turned him down of course."

"I could never bear to be touched by him." She shuddered.

"Oh, you must resist him," I said. "You mustn't give in to his demands."

"That's why I've run away," Rosa said. "I couldn't stay in Cloisterham another minute while he was there."

"So you've come to Mr. Grewgious for help."

"He always knows what to do. Dear Mr. Grewgious— whatever would I do without him?"

"But where will you live?" I knew she couldn't very well stay with Mr. Grewgious. It would not have been proper.

"I don't know. But I'm sure Mr. Grewgious will think of something. Meanwhile I'm staying at Furnival's." Furnival's was a respectable inn down the street.

"Oh, if only you could stay there," I said, "and I could see you often."

"I'm afraid that cannot be," Rosa said, "since you are watched."

I knew she was right. "Yes, we must take no chances."

"You must be careful," Rosa said. "I couldn't bear it if something were to happen to you or Neville. Mr. Grewgious wanted me to tell you what had happened, so you would know the danger."

"I'm not afraid for myself," I told her, "but for my

brother I am. Jasper turned the people against him in Cloisterham, and he might try to do the same here."

"What's to be done?" Rosa said. "Mr. Grewgious said to ask you. He thinks you're ever so clever and said you might have a plan."

"Well, not a plan exactly," I said. "Just an idea."

"An idea is exactly what we need," said Rosa. "What is your idea then?"

"These days Neville sees very few people and very few people see him. Jasper has tried and failed to turn Mr. Crisparkle against him and knows he should stay clear of Mr. Grewgious. However, Mr. Tartar is an unknown. Jasper may attempt to approach him. Therefore, I suggest Mr. Tartar, if he is willing, be open and often in his contacts with Neville, so Jasper might try to warn him off. Then we could see what Jasper is about."

"I'll ask," Rosa said and ducked inside. Soon she was back. Mr. Tartar, waiting outside the door, had been called in and consulted. "He would be only too happy to oblige," Rosa said. "He is a most obliging sort of man." She glanced shyly back at his window, and I wondered if he was standing there.

Just then I thought I heard Neville stirring. If he came out of his room, he would hear us talking. It seemed better for him not to know Rosa was so close at hand. He might react recklessly and put her in danger of being noticed by our watcher.

"I did do the right thing by turning him down, didn't I?" Rosa asked anxiously, referring to Jasper.

"Of course, you did," I said. "We would not for a minute want you to give in to his wicked demands."

"And will you tell Neville all that I've told you?"

"I will."

"And will you ask him not to hate me?"

"Hate you? There's no danger of that."

"I'm so sorry he has been made to suffer for Eddy's disappearance. Will you tell him that?"

I assured her I would. She blew kisses across the open air, and I did too. Then she disappeared within, and I was alone again. I had the urge to rush downstairs and over to the next building so I could see her again. There was so much to say, and we had had so little time. But of course I couldn't do that so long as Jasper might be watching. I mustn't do anything to place Rosa in danger.

I had hardly climbed back in the window when Neville came into the room. "I thought I heard voices," he said.

"You did," I admitted. "I was talking to Rosa."

"Rosebud? Here?"

"She was in Tartar's garden."

"How could that be?" He stuck his head out of the window and looked quickly about. "I don't see her."

"She's gone now. She was only here briefly. Mr. Grewgious thought if she used Mr. Tartar's garden it would give us an opportunity to talk without Jasper noticing."

"Why didn't you call me?" he said. "You know how I feel about Rosa."

"That was precisely why I didn't call you," I said. "I was afraid you couldn't talk to her without revealing your feelings."

He groaned. "Perhaps I couldn't. Was she well? What did she say? How did she look? Did she ask about me?"

As soon as he paused for breath, I told him all that Rosa had told me.

6

By way of Mr. Grewgious, we learned that Rosa was safely tucked away in a house in Bloomsbury Square belonging to a widowed relative of Mr. Bazzard's by the name of Billickin. Miss Twinkleton had agreed to come to London to be Rosa's companion for the month, while her young ladies were on summer break. I couldn't see Rosa of course, but I was glad to know she was safely out of Jasper's reach.

Soon Mr. Grewgious and Mr. Crisparkle began to wonder if I should not be moved as well. They worried that having me near Neville might put me in danger too. However, I would not hear of being moved. If being at the Staple Inn was a danger for me, then even more so it was a danger for Neville, and my place was at my brother's side. Besides, I was not going to abandon him to his melancholy moods. I worried that he was as much a danger to himself as Jasper was to him. Mr. Grewgious and Mr. Crisparkle gave up their attempt to persuade me but warned us to be always on our guard. They urged Neville to take his walks in daylight, but they knew as well as I that he would not. Only the darkness could hide him from the eyes of men. The darkness was his friend. Moreover, he seemed to gain a perverse pleasure from leading his watchers through the labyrinthine London streets at night. It was a dangerous game of cat and mouse that left him bright-eyed and exhilarated when he returned home before dawn to throw himself upon his bed, exhausted, to sleep at last.

It was three nights after Rosa had appeared in Tartar's garden that Neville began to pace restlessly in his room like a caged animal. I recognized the signs. They invariably preceded his forays into the night. As I anticipated, within a quarter of an hour his door flew open and he stood before me in his coat and hat.

"Don't try to stop me," he said.

I put down my book and reached for my shawl. "I'm coming with you."

"It's too dangerous," he objected.

"I won't let you go alone," I said, determined to accompany him since I knew it would be useless to try to dissuade him.

"No!"

"Then I'll follow you." I could be as stubborn as he.

He looked as if he were going to make a rush for the door. I wrapped my shawl about me, ready to follow. He knew I would do it.

"You can't go," he said. "You must realize that. Women don't walk the streets at night, at least not respectable women. It's dangerous."

"Then I'll change my clothes," I said. "I'll borrow clothes from you. We'll look like two young men. Surely two young men are safer than one?"

"For God's sake, Helena, it's me he wants, not you."

"Remember how we roamed the streets of Colombo together?" I told him. "I wore your clothes and no one knew I was a girl."

"It was a children's game."

"The streets of London are no more dangerous than the streets of Colombo. Remember that time a man with a scimitar chased us most of the way home?"

Neville sighed and threw himself down on a chair. "Be quick then."

I didn't wait for him to change his mind. Within five minutes, I stood before him dressed in his own clothes, my hair hidden beneath one of his hats.

"Well?" I asked, turning around for him to get the full effect. I was very pleased with myself. I thought no one would guess I was a woman, at least not if they passed me on a dark street at night.

Neville gave me a skeptical look. "You really think you're going to fool people dressed like that?"

I glanced down at my trousers and boots, or rather his trousers and boots. "I don't see why not. Besides, people see what they expect to see. If they expect to see a man, they see a man."

"If anyone finds out I let you do this, they'll blame me, you know."

"Oh, stop worrying," I said. "No one will find out."

I may have sounded brave, but I was holding my breath as we went down the narrow stairs from our attic rooms. I was afraid of meeting anyone who might recognize me. When we were finally out the door, I heaved a sigh of relief and I think Neville did too. The street outside was empty except for a few passersby. I looked around nervously, wondering where our watcher might be. Neville started down the street at a brisk clip, and I had to hurry to keep up with him.

It was completely different to be out in the streets of London at night. The night sky was thick with clouds and no stars could be seen. The buildings loomed in the darkness around us like brooding monsters. We passed through narrow gas-lit streets, down crumbling flights of steps, past soot-blackened buildings. Occasionally we passed other walkers like ourselves, as well as beggars, prostitutes, and sailors. I tried not to stare, but it was all so new and exciting. I was seeing parts of London that I would never have seen otherwise. It was incredible how free men were to roam and no one thought it odd. No one gave me a second glance. I began to understand why Neville so often went walking at night.

For a while I thought we were not being followed, but as we drew nearer to the river I heard footsteps behind us. We turned and doubled back, but our watcher was elusive, and then I wondered if I had only imagined the footsteps behind us.

"Is he there?" I asked Neville in a low voice.

Neville nodded.

"Is it Jasper?"

"I don't know. It might be one of his spies."

"Have you ever seen them?"

"Not up close. They're too clever for that."

We crossed another bridge. Below us the water shone like oil. A clock chimed. In the distance I thought I heard a scream, but it might have been just the screech of an owl or the yowl of a cat.

Neville pulled me into the shadow of a wall. "Watch now," he whispered.

For several minutes there was nothing. Then two men stole across the bridge like moving shadows.

"Two of them?" I asked, alarmed.

"I've never seen two before," Neville admitted.

They started in our direction, and Neville pulled me by the arm. "Let's go," he said.

Our watchers were not so careful now to keep out of sight. Each time we looked back, there they were, and it seemed to me that gradually they were growing bolder, closing the gap between us.

"What will we do?" I said. We were far from the Staple Inn and safety.

"You shouldn't have come," Neville said. "I ought not to have let you."

"And how would you have fared against two alone?" I said. "Surely it's better for them to see you're not alone?"

We had for so long been walking briskly that I was now a little out of breath. And then, quite suddenly, our pursuers were gone. We turned several corners and hurried down alleyways, glancing behind, but they seemed to have given up the chase.

"Let's go home," I urged. "They're gone now."

"Don't be so sure," Neville said.

Hardly had he spoken than we rounded a corner and found ourselves face-to-face with two rough-looking men, one with a scar down the left side of his face, gripping a length of pipe in his hand. Neville stepped in front of me and blocked the blow with his upraised arm. Instantly he was locked in a scuffle with the man with the scar. The other man's fist shot out and caught me in the face. The blow knocked me to the pavement, dazed. My hat lay beside me and my hair fell down.

"It's a woman!" the man said in surprise. He stood uncertainly, looking down at me. He had a brutal-looking face and a hulking body. Then he turned his head tensely and looked down the street. "Someone's coming."

The scuffle stopped. The other man got up. "Let's get out of here."

"What about her?"

"Leave her."

They loped off down the street. I crawled to where Neville lay face down, unmoving. I struggled to turn him over. He moaned but didn't open his eyes. In the moonlight I saw a gash on his temple. Then I heard footsteps crunching on the pavement and looked up to see someone approaching. In the dark I could see only a shadowy outline.

"Neville," I said. "Neville, wake up." My fingers were trembling as I lifted his head onto my lap. "Please don't die," I whispered. "You mustn't."

I glanced up desperately at the man, who was nearer now. I hoped he was not a thief or cutthroat. "Please help us," I begged.

He stopped. Then cautiously he drew nearer.

"My brother is hurt," I said. "Will you help us?"

The stranger squatted beside me without a word. I saw with surprise that he was a Chinaman. He looked no older than Neville and I. Judging by his clothes, I thought he might be a dockworker or a seaman.

"We were attacked," I explained. "Two men attacked us."

He reached out and touched Neville's arm. Neville

moaned again. He pushed Neville's hair back and examined the gash on his temple.

"I'll pay you," I said desperately.

"Where do you live?" he asked.

"Staple Inn, in Holborn." I felt wildly grateful that he spoke English.

He shook his head. "Too far."

"Could you get help for us then?" I said, afraid he might walk away. "Find a policeman?"

"No policeman," he said. His answer confused me. Did he mean there were no policemen nearby or was he refusing to get a policeman?

Before I could ask, he reached under Neville and scooped him up, though he was about the same size as Neville. I picked up my hat and followed him down the street. I wasn't sure where we were. Neville had taken us down so many alleyways in the maze of London streets. But I didn't think we were headed in the direction of Holborn. We were going toward the waterfront.

"Where are you taking us?" I asked anxiously.

The young Chinaman didn't answer. I wondered if he could be leading us into even more trouble. I remembered stories I had heard of women abducted in London and sold to slave harems in the East. I didn't feel any more reassured when we rounded a corner and came upon a row of squalid shanties. He carried Neville to one of these and we climbed the narrow stair that led to the door.

"Knock," the young Chinaman told me.

I hesitated, then knocked. I thought I heard movement inside, but the door stayed closed.

"Again," he said.

I knocked again, and then a third time.

After the third knock, the door opened a crack, and an old hag peered out. "What do you want?" she asked in a hoarse croak.

"Open up," the young man said. "It's me, Jack."

She looked at me suspiciously as she opened the door a little wider.

"What's this?" she asked, looking at Neville in his arms.

He didn't answer but pushed past her. Inside was a small dingy room lit by a single candle. In the center of the room was a sagging bed on which lay a sleeping dark-skinned man, one arm flung out in a gesture of abandon. The Chinaman lay Neville gently beside him.

"Is he drunk?" the old woman asked, moving the candle closer and peering at Neville.

"My brother and I were attacked," I said. "He's been injured."

She looked at me then. "A woman, are you, dearie?"

Since she could see I was, I didn't bother to answer.

The Chinaman pushed the sleeping man farther from Neville. His action awoke the man, who reared up, looking quite fierce, then sank back down, mumbling. I noticed several long-stemmed pipes sitting on a stand by the bed and understood. We were in an opium den. They had places like this in the backstreets of Colombo. I had heard about them, but I had never seen one before. I wondered if these people would rob and murder us. There was still time for me to turn and run, but I didn't want to leave Neville at their mercy.

"Why did you bring them here?" the old woman asked querulously.

The young Chinaman ignored her and held the candle closer to examine Neville's gash.

"My brother needs a doctor," I told her. "We must send for a doctor."

"I have a business to run," she said. "What will my customers think—a man lying here bleeding to death?"

"They will pay you," the Chinaman said.

"Yes, we'll pay you," I said desperately.

The old woman tilted her head to one side, turning this over in her mind. "You have money to pay?"

"Not with me," I said, "but I can send for it. Do you have some water and cloths to wash his wound?"

Mumbling to herself, she limped about the room, fetching a bowl of water and some rags for me.

"Can someone go for a doctor?" I asked again.

"Jack," she said, nodding toward the young Chinaman. "He brought you here. He can go for the doctor."

Without a word Jack turned and slipped out the door. I hoped he was indeed going for a doctor and not abandoning us to the old woman, whom I did not trust.

The gash on Neville's temple had stopped bleeding. I tried to wash it as gently as I could.

Meanwhile, the other man who lay on the bed was muttering in his sleep. The old woman moved closer, listening.

"Is he all right?" I asked.

"Oh, he's just fine. My stuff is good. I know how to mix it to give the good dreams. They come to Princess Puffer when they want good dreams."

"Princess Puffer?"

"That's what they call me."

"Do you live here?"

"Where else would I live?"

"Have you any family?"

"Not anymore," she said. "There's only me now. I got no one to take care of me but meself."

"My brother's all the family I've got," I said. "I don't see how I could go on living if anything happened to him."

She made a sound like "ah" or "ha" which could have meant anything—agreement, disagreement.

Neville moaned softly. I wiped his face but he didn't open his eyes.

Beside him the dark man stirred.

"Waking up, are you, dearie?" the old woman said, reaching out a claw-like hand and touching his arm.

He sat up and looked around the room with dazed eyes. He was an Indian, a seaman by the look of his clothes. He didn't seem surprised to find himself sharing the bed with Neville.

"How was the journey?" the old woman asked him. "Did Princess Puffer give you good dreams?"

The man stumbled to his feet. He stared at me for a minute.

"Never mind, never mind," the old woman said, tugging him by the arm toward the door. "Don't forget your knife."

He stopped near the door and plucked up a knife from the floor. After he was gone, the old woman sat down on a rickety wood chair.

"I always take their weapons away," she explained. "It's not safe to leave them armed. They might hurt somebody. I make a good mix, but you never know what the dream will bring. There's some what have dark corners in them where you wouldn't want to go, dearie. No indeed."

I shivered and tried not to think about those dark corners as I held Neville's limp hand. The old woman rocked and crooned to herself in the shadows. She might have been a witch and Neville and I the lost orphans in a fairy tale who had wandered into her clutches. I thought about the men who came to this dark little room to smoke her pipes and surrender to opium dreams. But she did not strike me as a sinister figure. She was merely an old woman whose life had been hard. I watched her pick up one of the pipes and light it with a match. She was taken by a fit of coughing. "My lungs are dreadful bad," she muttered when the coughing had subsided, "but what's a body to do?"

I felt pity for her as we sat there in that small dingy room and waited for help to come. I lay my head down on my arms beside Neville and must have slept. The candle had gone out when I was awakened by a sharp knocking at the door. The old woman muttered as she roused herself and went to see who it was. She admitted the young Chinaman and a bespectacled man with a bag whom I took to be a doctor. He glanced about the room with distaste before approaching Neville.

"We were attacked," I said.

The doctor merely nodded. He did not seem to care what had happened to us. I wondered if the young Chinaman had explained our situation to him. I did not want him to think we were patrons of the opium den. I was suddenly aware of how odd I must look, my hair loose and dressed in Neville's clothes. What must the doctor think?

"He's my brother," I said, hoping that would lessen his disapproval of us.

He made no indication that he heard me but bent scowling over Neville's gash.

"You washed it?" he demanded.

"Yes."

He lifted Neville's eyelids. Then he turned his attention to Neville's right arm. Neville moaned as the doctor moved it and his face contorted.

"His arm is broken," the doctor said.

"But he'll be all right?" I asked anxiously.

"His arm will be all right," the doctor said. "Let's hope he has a hard head."

Then, while Princess Puffer rocked, and the young Chinaman squatted beside her, I watched anxiously as the doctor set Neville's arm and bandaged his head.

"If he wakes up, he's going to be in pain," the doctor said. "Give him this." He handed me a small dark vial.

"What is it?" I asked.

"Laudanum. Only a few drops, mind. And only if it's necessary. You don't want to make him a slave to it." He looked again about the room, at the old woman rocking in the corner and the young Chinaman squatting near her. His eye fell on the pipes.

"Not very suitable surroundings," he said, turning to me, "but it could be dangerous to move your brother while he's unconscious. You'd better wait until he wakes."

"What about my customers?" the old woman demanded. "I got to make a living, don't I?"

The doctor glanced at me. "I'm sure the young lady and gentleman will pay you."

"Yes," I said, "of course."

When the doctor had gone, I asked the old woman for paper, a pen, and ink. After much rummaging in an old basket in the corner, she brought forth a soiled and crumpled scrap of paper, a quill, and ink. I wrote a note to Mr. Grewgious to let him know where we were and asked him to please send money. I hesitated before I handed it to the young Chinaman, wondering if he would be able to deliver it. Would he know Holborn? Could he read the address? In case he could not, I read it to him. He took it in his hand and looked at it. I couldn't tell from his face whether he could read or not.

"Can you find it?" I asked.

Without answering, he folded the paper and tucked it in one of his pockets. Then he opened the door and vanished into the night.

The time passed slowly as we waited for the Chinaman to return. After what seemed like hours, there came a sharp rap on the door. The old woman shuffled to it and opened it a crack.

"Oh, it's you," she said. "You've come at a bad time. You'll have to come back later."

"I want it now," a man said. "Don't make me wait, old woman."

A chill ran through me. I knew that voice. I would have recognized it anywhere—Jasper. He had tracked us down. I looked at Neville lying swathed and unconscious on the bed and then I looked frantically about for a weapon and snatched up an iron poker from the corner.

"Come back later," the old woman repeated. "I've no room for you."

"I tell you I need it now," Jasper said impatiently. "Let me in."

I thought he was going to force his way in and I tightened my grip on the poker.

"Go away," the old woman said, holding firm to the door. "I can't give you any now."

"You say no?" Jasper said angrily. "To me?"

"I only say later," the old woman said. "Come back later. Come back when it's dark."

There was a tense moment of silence. "All right, when it's dark," he said. "But you'd better have it ready, old woman, or you'll be sorry."

The old woman closed the door. She saw the poker gripped in my hands. "Oh, you'd fight him, would you?" she said, amused. "Not him, dearie. You wouldn't want to fight him."

"He was looking for us," I said.

She looked at me curiously. "For you? Why would you think that?"

"The men who attacked my brother were working for him."

"Were they now? And could you prove that in a court of law?"

"No," I admitted.

"He's a wicked man all right," she said, "but I don't think he was looking for you."

"Then what did he want?" I asked.

She chuckled. "A pipe. He come for a pipe. Same as all the rest."

"He smokes opium?" This surprised me. Edwin's doting uncle? The choirmaster who sang in the cathedral? What would the people of Cloisterham think if they knew? Here was proof that he was not the respectable man he pretended to be when he walked the streets of Cloisterham.

"Aye," she said, "and he'll be back, and next time he

won't be so easy to get rid of. If you fear for your brother, he ought to be moved."

"But you heard the doctor. It wouldn't be safe."

"Safer somewhere else than here," the old woman said, rocking once more and regarding me thoughtfully through narrowed eyes.

I looked at Neville lying asleep on the bed, his arm in a sling, his head bandaged. He had been hurt taking a blow aimed at me. I knew I must not let Jasper find him.

"And what have the two of you to do with that man?" the old woman asked.

"He blames my brother for the death of his nephew."

"I see," the old woman said and began coughing. "And is your brother to blame?" she asked when the fit of coughing had subsided.

"No, of course not. My brother never hurt anyone."

"And yet there was a death . . . ?"

"Yes, but Neville had nothing to do with it."

She held up her hand, as if to stop me. "A nephew, you say."

"Yes, a nephew."

"And what might be the name of this nephew?"

"Edwin Drood," I said.

"Not Ned?"

I looked at her, wondering why she would ask. She was an odd little woman. "No," I said.

"Maybe a nickname?" she suggested.

"I don't know."

"What did he look like, this nephew?" she asked, her eyes almost closed.

"He had blond hair and very blue eyes." I didn't add that they were the bluest I'd ever seen.

She nodded. "And he was a handsome boy and kind?"

"Yes," I said, "he was handsome and kind."

"That's him," she said, rocking. "I knew it was him."

"You knew Edwin Drood?" I asked, wondering if the old woman was a little crazy. How could she have known him?

"I was there," she said knowingly. "I saw him. He gave me three and sixpence. He was a handsome boy, and kind all right. He took pity on an old woman who needed a bit of help."

"You were in Cloisterham?" I asked, not knowing whether to believe her.

"I was," she said firmly, nodding and rocking.

"When?" I asked.

"On Christmas Eve last."

The night Edwin had disappeared. It seemed too incredible to be true. Perhaps she knew something that would throw light on Edwin's fate. "You saw him?" I said, excited now. "Was it after midnight?"

"Nowhere near as late as that," she said. "Much earlier. Round about dark."

I felt disappointed. That would have been before the dinner. Even if she had been in Cloisterham and seen him, it would not mean she had been the last person to see him alive.

"What were you doing in Cloisterham?" I asked.

"Went to find a needle in a haystack," she said cryptically. "I went to warn him."

"Warn who?" I said. "Edwin?"

"Ned," she said.

"Warn him about what?"

"That something awful was going to happen."

"How did you know?"

"I have my ways," she said, tapping the side of her nose. "I hear things that others never hear. I know secrets what would make your blood run cold."

"You warned Edwin?"

"I asked the young gentleman if his name were Ned—it was Ned I was looking for—and when he said it weren't, I asked if he had a sweetheart, for I knew Ned had a sweetheart, but he said, no, he hadn't a sweetheart. I told him he was lucky, for it was a bad night to be Ned."

My thoughts were in a whirl. I believed her now. She had been in Cloisterham and saw Edwin on the day of his murder. She had tried to warn him. If only he had heeded her!

"That was the night he disappeared," I said. "No one has seen him since."

"And no one will," the old woman said, rocking.

"How can you be so sure? Do you know what happened to him?"

"Maybe." She smiled and rocked. She couldn't possibly know, I told myself. I should stop asking these fruitless questions. But I couldn't stop.

"Did his uncle murder him?"

"If he did, he'll pay for it," the old woman said. "He'll pay dearly. I'm not agoing to let him get away with it. Not this time."

I had no idea what she meant. Perhaps she was crazy. Perhaps she had only dreamed she was in Cloisterham while smoking one of her opium pipes. I watched her rocking and smiling, smiling and rocking. Suddenly I felt very sleepy. I yawned and lay my head down beside Neville's. I told myself I would only rest a bit, not fall asleep, but I must have fallen asleep at once because I remember nothing more until morning.

7

Morning was well advanced when the young Chinaman returned with Mr. Grewgious and his clerk Bazzard. Mr. Grewgious looked about the room with a grim expression, taking in the long-stemmed pipes, the ugly walls, Princess Puffer in her chair, and Neville on the sagging bed. Bazzard shook his head and sighed deeply.

"I didn't expect to find you and your brother in such surroundings," Mr. Grewgious said with disapproval in his voice.

"We had no place else to go," I explained. "We were attacked by two men."

Mr. Grewgious held up his hand to stop me. "This young man has told me everything I need to know. Now we must consider what to do about your brother."

"We must move him at once," I said. "Before Jasper comes back."

"Jasper?" he said, frowning. "Has Jasper been here?"

"We have had the bad luck to come to one of his haunts."

He turned to the old woman. "Is this true?"

She shrugged. "I have many customers. I don't ask their names."

Mr. Grewgious looked thoughtfully at Neville lying unconscious on the bed. "If we take him back to his rooms at the Staple Inn, he will again be watched and will again be in danger. I propose we move him to a new location—hide him away where he will be safe. What do you think, Bazzard?"

"Just what I was going to recommend," Bazzard assured him. "My thoughts exactly."

"Do you know of such a place?" I asked.

"I believe I do," Mr. Grewgious said.

"And I believe I do too," Bazzard added. They looked at each other and smiled.

The young Chinaman and Bazzard carried Neville to the carriage they had waiting outside. Then Mr. Grewgious counted out some coins for the old woman, who seemed well pleased, and some more for the Chinaman, who silently pocketed them.

Mr. Grewgious then gave instructions to the driver and we were off. Neville's bandaged head lay in my lap, and I did my best to protect his broken arm. On Mr. Grewgious's orders, the carriage moved slowly, but still the ride was bumpy over the cobblestones, and whenever we turned a corner I had to brace to keep Neville from rolling to the floor. After we had rattled through the London streets for a while, Neville let out a groan. He opened his eyes and looked up at me with a bewildered expression on his face.

"Helena!" he whispered. "Is it you?"

"Sshh. Don't try to talk," I told him.

"Where are we?"

"On our way to safety."

"What happened?"

"We were attacked."

He reached one hand up to his head, touched the bandages, and winced. "Who attacked us?"

"Two men. Thugs hired by Jasper most likely. Don't you remember?"

"No," he said, closing his eyes. "I remember nothing."

"We were walking—"

He groaned again.

"Are you in pain?"

"My arm—" he said.

"Your arm is broken."

"Where are we going?"

"Mr. Grewgious is taking you someplace safe."

He closed his eyes again. During the rest of the ride, I watched Neville's pale face, his eyes clenched tightly and his hand gripping mine. I tried to will my strength into him to help him bear the pain. Meanwhile, I thought about our plight and what we should do. Clearly Jasper had to be stopped. I was sure that he had been responsible for the attack on Neville and me. As long as Neville was alive, he was not safe from Jasper. We could leave England perhaps and live abroad, but what if the shadow of what had happened in Cloisterham followed us wherever we went? No, we needed to stop Jasper. And to do that we needed to know what had happened to Edwin Drood that fateful night. Somehow there had to be a way of finding out.

The carriage finally stopped on a street of cramped old houses. Neville and I waited in the carriage while Mr. Grewgious and Bazzard knocked on the door of a house that looked almost exactly like the others. It was answered by a maid, who ducked inside and was soon replaced by a large-sized, severe woman whom I took to be the head housekeeper or the lady of the house herself. This personage looked at our carriage skeptically. She appeared to be opposed to taking us in. However, Mr. Grewgious and Bazzard kept talking until she relented.

Then Neville was gently lifted out of the carriage and carried into the house. Once inside, Bazzard and the carriage driver navigated their awkward burden up the narrow and winding stairs to a second-floor bedroom, followed by Mr. Grewgious and myself.

Just as we were passing one of the rooms, a door flew open and to my surprise there stood Rosa. She stared at me equally surprised, then sprang forward with a small cry and hugged me. Her eyes widened as she saw Neville through the open bedroom door being laid upon a bed, his arm in a sling, and his head bandaged.

"What happened?" she cried in dismay.

"We were attacked by some men sent by Jasper," I said.

"You as well? You aren't hurt?"

"No, I'm fine, but Neville has a broken arm and a nasty gash on his head."

Behind her Miss Twinkleton appeared looking very flustered. "Oh, dear," she said at the sight of Neville. "The poor young man." And then she saw me. "Miss Landless, is that you?" Her voice was full of shocked disapproval.

I had forgotten that I was still dressed in Neville's clothes and no doubt my hair was quite wild by now. "Yes, it's me," I said, vainly attempting to smooth my hair down. I wondered if she would expel me from the seminary. Probably she had never seen one of her young ladies in trousers before. I left her staring after me and followed Neville into the bedroom where he now lay. Light trickled in through a grimy window. A coverlet had been drawn back and he lay on the sheets looking deathly pale.

Rosa stood beside me, clutching my hand. When Neville opened his eyes and saw her, he smiled. "Is it really you?" he whispered. "Or am I dreaming?"

"Poor Neville," she said, reaching for his hand. "Who did this to you?"

He closed his eyes again.

"He isn't going to die, is he?" she asked in alarm.

"No, the doctor said he should recover," I told her. "But he's in a lot of pain." At that moment, as if to prove me right, Neville moaned piteously. "Could he have a small glass of wine?" I asked. "The doctor gave me some laudanum to give him for his pain."

Rosa immediately sprang for the door to fetch a glass of wine. In her haste she nearly knocked down Miss Twinkleton, who stood in the doorway wringing her hands. "Oh, dear, was there no place else you could take him?" she asked Mr. Grewgious. "I really don't know if I approve. It's not quite proper, you know—a young unmarried woman and a young unmarried man under the same roof."

"Nonsense," said Mr. Grewgious. "They're in different rooms. And the young man is no threat to anyone in his condition. My ward's safety is just as important to me as it is to you. I'd never have brought him here if I thought it was improper. Besides, I didn't know where else to take him. I couldn't very well leave him lying in an opium den, could I?"

"Oh, dear, no!" Miss Twinkleton said, looking as if she

were about to faint at the mention of opium dens. "Is that where he was?"

"He did not go there of his own volition, of course," said Mr. Grewgious.

"Of course." She began to fan herself with her hand, but his answer seemed to reassure her somewhat.

The landlady, now introduced to us as Bazzard's cousin Mrs. Billickin, looked at Miss Twinkleton with disdain. "The gentleman's right," she said firmly. "This is a respectable house. I don't see anything improper in letting a room to a young lady and another to a young man. And no one's going to tell me different."

Rosa must have flown down the stairs, for she was back almost at once with a glass of wine. She held Neville's hand while I measured the laudanum.

Together we helped him drink it.

"He should sleep now," I said. "The laudanum will ease the pain but it will also make him sleepy."

We all tiptoed out of the room.

"Might I ride back with you?" I asked Mr. Grewgious as I followed him down the stairs.

He turned and looked at me in surprise. "I thought you would want to remain here with your brother."

"I need to change my clothes," I said.

"You could borrow some of mine," offered Rosa, who was right behind me.

"And you think they would fit me?" I asked, smiling. I was a good head taller than Rosa.

"I hadn't thought of that," Rosa said, clapping a hand over her mouth to stifle a giggle. "Of course they wouldn't, not anymore than yours would fit me."

I couldn't tell her it was more than the fact that her

clothes wouldn't fit me that made me determined to return to the Staple Inn. A plan had gradually been forming in my mind during our carriage ride and now I was eager to put it into action.

"I could have Bazzard bring your clothes to you," Mr. Grewgious said, regarding me. "I don't think you should go back to your rooms. It's not safe."

"Jasper did threaten you as well as Neville," Rosa reminded me. "And all because I wouldn't consent to marry him. This might not have happened to poor Neville if I had—"

"No—" I stopped her. "You could not give yourself to such a man. Neville would not want it, nor would I. It's unthinkable."

"But if anything should happen to you—" Rosa said, tears welling in her eyes.

"I will be careful. I promise."

Before I climbed into the carriage, Rosa hugged me.

"Take care of Neville for me," I said. "I'll come back as soon as I can."

"I will care for him as if he were my own brother," Rosa assured me.

Mr. Grewgious helped me into the carriage and then he and Bazzard climbed in after me. Rosa waved her handkerchief as we rolled away.

I thanked Mr. Grewgious again for coming to our rescue.

"It was very good of you," I said.

"Nonsense. I did what anyone would do," he said.

"He's a good man," Bazzard said. "It's a privilege to work for him."

"The privilege is mine," Mr. Grewgious insisted. "I'm

fortunate to have working for me a man of such prodigious gifts." They bowed their heads slightly to each other.

"Mr. Honeythunder would not have," I said. "Nor would our stepfather."

"Precisely," said Bazzard.

"I'm an old bachelor," Mr. Grewgious said, "and my life would seem quite pointless if I didn't make myself useful from time to time."

For a while we rode in silence, each wrapped up in our own thoughts. As we neared the Staple Inn, I could see that something was on Mr. Grewgious's mind. Several times he had cleared his throat as if preparing to speak, then changed his mind. He glanced at me and then out the window. Finally he took off his hat.

"Perhaps—" he said, frowning at it. "Perhaps you would like to borrow my hat?"

I stared at his hat for a minute, uncomprehending. Bazzard stared at it too. Then I realized why he was offering it. With my hair down, anyone who saw me would know I was a young woman, but if I tucked my hair under his hat, when we arrived at the Staple Inn any watcher would see Mr. Grewgious alighting with a young man, maybe even mistaking me for Neville.

"Of course you'll want to return to your brother once you've had time to pack up your belongings," Mr. Grewgious said. "And once your brother is well enough to be moved, we'll have to find another place for him. Mrs. Billickin's boarding house was all I could think of on the spur of the moment, but Rosa and Neville are both being sought by Jasper. I think we ought to spread out our pieces to make the game more difficult for him."

"Just what I was thinking," said Bazzard.

"Can't we stop him?" I asked.

"How?" said Mr. Grewgious. "By stooping to the same low tactics he uses? I think there's no legal way to stop him."

"Next time Neville might not be so lucky," I said.

"That is why we must put him in a safe hiding spot where Jasper can't find him," Mr. Grewgious said. "We must outwit our opponent."

"What then? Are we to spend our lives hiding from him?"

Mr. Grewgious looked at me sternly. "You aren't planning to do something foolish I hope?"

I pretended that something out the window had caught my eye. I had no intention of telling him about my plan. I knew he would try to talk me out of it.

"You are in danger as well as your brother," Mr. Grewgious said. "Don't think that Jasper will behave like a gentleman."

"I don't expect kinder treatment because I'm a woman," I informed him.

"My dear, don't underestimate him. He's a desperate man. We don't know what he's capable of."

"I'll be careful," I promised.

Mr. Grewgious nodded. "See that you are."

When we arrived at the door of the Staple Inn, any watcher would have seen a tall angular man without a hat and two other men with hats disembark from the carriage. We were soon inside so there was little time for closer observation. Mr. Grewgious then insisted on climbing with me to Neville's attic rooms to assure himself that no one lurked there in wait for me.

I thought this an unnecessary precaution, but when I put the key in the lock, to my surprise I found the door already unlocked.

"What is it?" Mr. Grewgious asked, noticing my hesitation.

"Nothing," I said quickly. "We forgot to lock the door when we went out."

"Are you sure?" he asked with a frown. "Might someone have broken in?"

The truth was that the door had been locked when we left. I had locked it myself. But it would only alarm Mr. Grewgious more if he knew that. Then he might not leave me alone there, and to carry out my plan, I needed to have time alone.

Mr. Grewgious entered the rooms with me and went from room to room, peering in the wardrobe and under the beds and looking suspiciously out the window at the bean garden, as if a prowler might lurk there. At last, satisfied, he left me with the stern injunction to call him if I felt uneasy.

"I'll be fine," I told him. "I'll lock the door."

"All right. Tomorrow we will find a safer place for you," he said.

When he was gone, I took a bath and made myself some tea. I was glad he had searched our rooms. At least I didn't have to worry that someone was hiding there. All the same the door had been unlocked. I asked myself what that might mean. Had someone broken in while we were gone, and if so who, and for what purpose? The banknotes in the upper bureau drawer had not been taken. Nothing was disturbed. Or was it? Was the miniature of our mother sitting exactly where I had placed it on the bureau? I wasn't sure.

I pulled out our trunk and began to pack it. I remembered how I had packed it in Ceylon and wondered if it was our destiny to move from place to place. In the middle of my packing, I was startled by a rap at the window. Tartar was there—he had jumped from his ledge to ours. I hurried to open the window and let him climb in. It had begun to rain and he was wet.

"Are you all right?" he asked anxiously.

"I'm fine," I assured him.

"Mr. Grewgious told me what happened." He looked at my trunk. "You're leaving?"

"Mr. Grewgious doesn't think it's safe for us to stay here," I told him.

"Where will you go?"

"I don't know."

I looked at him standing there, his face and shirt wet, and imagined him on the deck of a ship with the wind blowing through his hair. The dark cramped room we stood in, in the midst of a sprawling crowded city, seemed an odd setting for such a man. It occurred to me that perhaps he felt as lost in London as Neville and I.

"If you need a place to go—" he began.

"Mr. Grewgious will take care of us," I assured him.

Suddenly I stopped and all other thoughts fled from my mind. I stared at the bottom of the drawer I had just emptied. Where was the red sari that had belonged to my mother? Besides the miniature, it was all I had left to remember her by. I turned quickly and searched among the clothes I had just packed.

"What is it?" Tartar asked, watching me.

"My mother's sari," I said. "I can't find my mother's sari."

"Perhaps it's in another drawer," he suggested.

"No, I always keep it there." I dumped the clothes, searching wildly. I couldn't lose it.

"Let me help," Tartar said. "What does it look like?"

"A red silk sari." I was on the verge of tears.

We searched for several minutes.

"It must be here somewhere," Tartar said.

I was trying not to believe that an intruder had taken it. Why the sari and not the banknotes? And why hadn't I put the sari in a safer place? Why couldn't the thief have stolen something else?

"We'll find it," Tartar said. Then he stopped and looked quickly around. "Is anything else missing?"

I shook my head. "I must have misplaced it." I didn't want to tell him the door had been unlocked. I was afraid he would stay. I knew what I must do and I had to do it alone.

We searched several more minutes, on the floor, behind the bureau, even pulling out the drawers. I was more composed now.

"You're probably right," I said. "It will turn up later."

"So you leave in the morning?" Tartar asked.

"Yes, in the morning."

"Will you be all right here alone?"

"I have Mr. Grewgious downstairs and you within shouting distance. I think I'll be safe enough."

"You could have been hurt last night," he said.

"But I wasn't."

He smiled. There were small wrinkles at the corners of his eyes. "I'll miss you and your brother."

"We won't be far away," I said. "We'll still be in London."

"London's a big place."

"I think we'll meet again," I said. "You'll have to come visit Neville and me once we're settled, and Rosa."

"Miss Bud?" he said. "Will she be there too?"

"At least I hope she's nearby," I said.

"Well, then I'll have to drop by for a visit," he said, "once you're settled."

We shook hands then, and he left the way he had come.

After he was gone, I searched again for the sari and tried to think if anything else was missing. It seemed strange that only that had been taken.

Finally the trunk was packed, except for some clothes of Neville's which I put into a small bag. Then I took off my dress and donned a shirt, trousers, and a jacket of Neville's. With a pair of scissors I cut my hair short enough to be bound at the back like a man's and my transformation was complete. I sat down and wrote a note for Mr. Grewgious:

Dear Mr. Grewgious,
Don't think me ungrateful for all you have done for my brother and me. I have had to go away for a while to see to certain matters. Please know that I am safe, and take care of Neville.
Respectfully,
Helena Landless

This done, I took one last look around the room, picked up my small bag, and then slipped out. I carefully locked the door. It was night now as I crept down the stairs, pausing to listen at every landing. When I reached Mr. Grewgious's door, I slipped my note and the key under it, hoping he would not find them until morning.

Then I let myself out of the Staple Inn into the murky night, one more shadow in a city of shadows.

8

It was mid-morning when the omnibus rolled into Cloisterham. The sun was shining on the cathedral tower, the birds were twittering, and the cathedral bell was pealing. I took my small bag and set off for the Travellers' Twopenny, where I knew I could get a bite to eat and find a cheap place to stay. Located in a narrow back lane, it was a two-story wooden structure that had seen better days. The porch sagged, the fence wanted mending, and the windows panes were thick with grime. On the porch sat a grubby little boy of about eight or nine who jumped up as I approached. "Carry your bag, sir?" he asked. I hesitated, knowing my funds were limited. However, he looked more in need of a half-penny than I was so I let him carry it.

"Do you work here?" I asked.

"I do when I ain't working somewheres else."

This struck me as an amusing answer coming from one so young. I was about to ask him what else he did when he told me.

"You need a guide?" he asked as we mounted the stairs.

"A guide?"

"To the ruins," he explained.

"I'm not sure," I said. "Maybe."

"Well, if you do, just look for Deputy."

"Deputy?"

"That's me." He grinned and I saw his front teeth were missing.

"All right. I will."

"You from London?" He gave me a sideways look.

"Yes," I said.

"What's your name then?"

"Poker." On the omnibus I had decided, since I had to have a name, to call myself Poker. It seemed apt because I was in Cloisterham to poke about, so to speak.

"You don't look like you're from London," he said skeptically.

"Where do I look like I'm from?"

"I don't know," he said. "But not from there."

"Well, I am," I said. "Where are you from?"

"I'm from here. Leastways this is all I remember. Who knows, maybe I'm from London too. Maybe I'm a gentleman and just don't know it."

"Who takes care of you?" I asked.

"I take care of meself," he said. "Just like the other boys what work here."

"And are there many of them?" I asked.

"Six," he said. "And we're all called Deputy, but the others aren't as good at ruins as I am."

"How old are you?" I asked.

"Don't know."

"Have you been working here long?"

"Long as I can remember. And this ain't my only job."

"It's not? What else do you do?"

"Stonin' for one thing."

"Stonin'?" I had no idea what this was.

"Mr. Durdles pays me to see he gets home. When I find him out late, I stone him until he gets home. I don't know what he did before he had me to watch after him."

This sounded like a strange arrangement to me. "Who is Mr. Durdles?" I asked.

"He carves monuments for dead people," said Deputy. "He knows just about everything about dead people in Cloisterham. He's what you might call an expert on it."

Since I was in search of information about someone who was presumably dead, I wondered if Mr. Durdles could help me. It was worth a try. "I'd like to meet him," I said. "Could you arrange that?"

"Sure," said Deputy. "For a price of course."

"Of course."

"I also run errands for Mr. Datchery," said Deputy.

"And who is Mr. Datchery?"

"He's a retired buffer getting by on his means."

"What sort of errands?"

"It depends. Sometimes he wants to see something, and he asks me to take him, since he's new to Cloisterham. And sometimes he just pays me to keep my eyes open and listen."

This was very intriguing. "And what sort of things do you see or hear that are worth paying for?"

Deputy looked around as if to be sure no one would overhear. "He likes me to watch Mr. Jasper," he said, dropping his voice.

"Who is Mr. Jasper?" I asked.

"The choirmaster."

"And what do you watch him doing?"

"Coming and going, and who he talks to, and what he says, only I don't let him catch me at it, 'cause I don't want to get picked up by my neck again and half choked to death."

"He did that to you?"

"Tried to kill me, he did," said Deputy, tilting his head to right and then to left so I could see his neck. All I could see was that it was in need of a good wash. "Someday I'll get him with a stone in the back of his head. See if I don't."

"Why did he pick you up by the throat?"

"No reason. Said I'd been following him, but I hadn't—not that time. But he was hopping mad. If Durdles hadn't been there, he might have killed me."

I had not been in Cloisterham an hour and already I had stumbled upon this boy who could tell me so much. However, I would have to be careful if I wanted to conceal my true identity. Until I knew more about the man named Datchery who was paying him to spy on Jasper, I would have to be very careful.

I pulled out a half-penny and handed it to him. Then I pulled out another.

"What's that for?" he asked, eyeing it.

"To see the ruins."

He grinned at me again, showing the large gap where his teeth were missing.

After I had deposited my bag with the proprietor of the Travellers' Twopenny and made arrangements for a room, Deputy took me to High Street, and I admired the old buildings as if I had not seen them before. We passed the Gate House, where Jasper lived and where the man Datchery was renting a room from Mr. and Mrs. Tope. We passed the Sapsea residence, with its head of Mr. Sapsea's father over the door and the Nuns' House. I had no fear of one of the young ladies or Miss Twinkleton herself looking out and seeing me because it was summer and the young ladies had all gone home and Miss Twinkleton was in London watching over Rosa. Besides, even if they had looked out, they would only have seen a young man looking around at the sights, for I was wearing Neville's clothes now. When we passed Minor Canon Corner, however, we kept to the other side of the street. I didn't want to run into Mr. Crisparkle, who might recognize me in spite of my disguise. As we approached the cathedral, Deputy pointed out the cemetery to me, which was encircled by an iron railing. There was an assortment of tombstones, some old and broken, some new, some well-tended, some that looked long neglected.

The cathedral looked very imposing as we drew nearer. I leaned back my head and gazed up at its massive gray square tower against the sky. "Can we climb the tower?"

"What for?" Deputy asked.

"I bet it has a good view."

He shrugged, clearly not interested in views. "It's locked, but Durdles might let you go up. He's got a key."

"Have you ever been up there?" I asked.

He shook his head. "You want to see inside?" he asked.

The double doors stood open, so I said yes. The interior of the cathedral was dim, musty smelling, and eerily silent. There was a high ceiling and light filtered in through stained glass windows.

"It's old," Deputy said. "Real old. Durdles says it's full of old dead bodies, monks and bishops and nuns and whatnot, especially down in the crypt. They're buried in the walls and under the floors. Durdles knows how to find them. He says maybe he'll teach me."

"How does he find them?" I asked, curious.

"Like this." The boy put his ear to the stone wall as if he was listening. Then he took an imaginary hammer and chisel and tapped.

"I think I would like to meet Mr. Durdles," I said.

"Can't right now," Deputy said. "I have an appointment."

"With whom?" I asked, amused.

"Mr. Datchery. Have to see if he wants me for something."

"Go on then," I said. "Don't let me keep you. I can find my way about on my own."

After Deputy had dashed off, I wandered about the streets of Cloisterham, then took our old route down to the river. I stopped near the ruin of an old monastery and looked out at the sails on the river. I missed Neville and wished he were there with me. With no one to talk to, I felt very alone. I wondered if it had been a mistake to leave London without telling anyone where I was going. I hoped they didn't worry about my disappearance, and that they didn't guess what I was up to.

One of the advantages of my new identity as Poker was that it was so much easier to walk in trousers than in skirts, and I could go wherever I wanted without having to be escorted by a man. In the afternoon I walked to

Cloisterham Weir, where Mr. Crisparkle had found Edwin's watch and shirt-pin. I sat down on a rock near the weir and wondered if Edwin Drood had died in this spot. If so, what could have brought him to such a place on that stormy night? Had he been dead or alive when his jewelry was taken from him? Had he lost his footing near the weir and fallen in or been murdered as he stood gazing at the waters of the weir? If he had fallen in, where was his body? No, the only explanation seemed to be the one that had already been suggested by Jasper and others. The murderer had deliberately tossed Edwin's jewelry into the weir so that his body could not be identified. Poor Edwin. He had just disappeared. Now he would never marry Rosa or travel to Egypt or do any of the other things he had planned to do.

When I returned to the Travellers' for supper, there was still no sign of Deputy, so I wandered out again on my own. When I had been one of Miss Twinkleton's young ladies, I was not allowed to go out alone after dark. In London it had been too dangerous to walk after dark, even with Neville as my escort. But now, dressed as a young man, I could wander about as I pleased. It was wonderfully liberating. However, I didn't forget why I was there. I tried to retrace the route Edwin and Neville took that night from the Gate House to the river. Neville had shown me the exact spot where they had stood watching the storm come in, and then they had wandered back, parting near Minor Canon Corner, Neville's destination. It was not much farther to the Gate House.

As I stood across the street from the Gate House, I contemplated the lighted windows of Jasper's rooms. Had Edwin returned that night and been murdered by his uncle? If so, what had Jasper done with the body? Or had Edwin never made it back, as Jasper claimed, and if so, what had happened to him? It was almost as if the storm that night had swallowed him. Aside from his watch and shirt-pin, no trace of Edwin Drood had been left behind.

The next morning I rose early to attend morning service at the cathedral. I was about to leave the Travellers' when I saw a scrawny old woman hobbling out the door ahead of me. I could hardly believe my eyes. It was Princess Puffer, the old woman from the opium den, and at her side was Deputy. This was very strange, I thought. What was Princess Puffer doing in Cloisterham? The sleepy cathedral town seemed an unlikely place to ply her trade. Was her visit in some way connected to Jasper? As they were headed in the same direction I was, I followed, keeping a discreet distance behind them.

It was a beautiful morning in June, the sun shining down on us, the birds singing with abandon, the breeze rustling in the elm trees. The destination of my quarry proved to be the same as mine—the cathedral. I waited until they had disappeared into the cool, shadowy interior before I entered. Then I took a seat in an empty pew in the back, not wanting to draw attention to myself. The congregation was small. Some of them looked familiar and some didn't. I didn't see Princess Puffer right away. She too seemed to be trying to avoid attention. She had placed herself deeply in shadow behind a pillar. Soon the choir bustled in, made up of boys of different ages and heights and several men, including John Jasper and Septimus Crisparkle. The organ commenced to play and the service began. The two men stood side by side, the dark head beside the blond. Looking at Jasper, I wondered how he could make the transition from the man who lurked on London's streets and sought oblivion in an opium den, to this pillar of the community, the choirmaster of Cloisterham. When he sang, his face looked as innocent and good as the boyish face of Mr. Crisparkle beside him. They looked like grown up versions of the sweet-faced boys they sang with. It made me wonder how much we ever really know of the people around us. We think they are what we see and yet they may lead secret lives quite different from the public selves they show others.

The choir was singing the Morning Prayer. *When the wicked man turneth away from his wickedness* . . . . And there was Deputy, I saw with surprise, not with Princess Puffer, but peering through the bars of the door of the choir. My eyes swept the room again, taking in the small congregation scattered about the pews, and came to rest on the shadow where Princess Puffer watched. I saw her clench her fist at the choir. I doubted it was their singing that called forth such a gesture. More likely it was the one man among them whom she knew, John Jasper. Of course he couldn't see her there behind the pillar. Then she clenched both fists. What did it mean? Was he something more to her than a customer who paid to smoke her opium? Why was she there? Certainly she had not traveled all the way from London just for the morning service. London had no dearth of cathedrals. No, she had some other purpose for being there, and somehow that purpose involved Jasper. She had come here to see him but not be seen by him. I decided I would find out what she was up to.

When the service was over, I lingered to give others the chance to leave first. When I finally stepped out into the sunshine, I saw a man I didn't know talking to Princess Puffer. He was unusual looking, an older man with a quantity of white hair under his hat and startling black eyebrows. His clothes showed him to be a man of some means. I could not imagine why someone like him would know Princess Puffer, or why she would know him. He didn't look like one of her customers.

I wondered what they were talking about but dared not risk going too near. Soon enough they were done talking. Princess Puffer hobbled away just as Deputy sauntered around a corner of the building.

"Halloa, Dick!" he cried.

"Halloa, Winks!" the white-haired man responded.

"Halloa, Poker!" Deputy called to me.

The man turned to look at me. It was too late to duck back into the cathedral. There was nothing to be done but step forward and be introduced.

"Datchery," the man said as he shook my hand. "Dick Datchery—a retired buffer trying to live on his means. I'm trying out this lovely old town to see if I want to retire here. I understand you're a stranger too?" He leveled cool grey eyes at me from under those disconcerting black eyebrows and seemed to ask who are you and what is your business in Cloisterham?

"Henry Poker," I said, trying to sound as casual as he. "I'm here for the ruins." I was grateful to Deputy for suggesting the ruins as a reason for my visit. It provided a convenient explanation for my presence in Cloisterham.

"I'm surprised one so young has an appreciation for things so old," Datchery said cheerfully.

I was careful to meet his gaze straight on. I suspected that if I did not, he would guess at once that I had something to hide. Besides, I wanted to learn who he was and what had brought him to Cloisterham. "I understand you've found lodgings," I said.

"As a matter of fact, I have," said Datchery, "very architectural ones at that—at the Gate House. Are you acquainted with it?" Those grey eyes studied me again.

"Yes, I believe it's that odd building just off High Street that straddles a street. As a matter of fact, I was thinking of sketching it." I thought this last was a stroke of inspiration. People interested in old buildings ought to sketch them.

"Were you?" His eyes never wavered. It was most disconcerting.

I wanted to ask more about his lodgings at the Gate House, but I couldn't think of any way to ask without making him suspicious. I doubted very much that someone as reclusive as Jasper would rent him rooms. So he must have rented from the Topes on the other side, in which case he had planted himself where he could see every movement that Jasper made. Jasper could not enter or leave his rooms without being subject to observation. Was this a mere coincidence?

"I believe you are staying at the Travellers'?" Datchery said, still coolly regarding me. No doubt Deputy had given him that piece of information. I wondered what else Deputy had told him about me.

"I am."

"I prefer the Crozier myself, but I can understand how a young man like yourself might prefer the economical advantages of the Travellers' Twopenny. Will you be staying in Cloisterham long, Mr. Poker?"

"I'm not really sure," I said. "It depends."

"On the ruins?"

"Yes, on the ruins."

He smiled. "We must have dinner sometime."

"Yes," I said, vowing that I would not if I could help it. There was no telling how much he would be able to trip me up over a dinner. Under such scrutiny I had no idea how long I would be able to keep up the pretense that I was a man. Perhaps he had already seen through my disguise. I did not know who he was, but he was certainly not just a buffer looking for a place to retire. His presence in Cloisterham was no accident. In fact, it seemed likely he was there for the same reason I was—to find out what had happened to Edwin Drood. He too was watching Jasper. I didn't envy Jasper with someone as hawk-eyed as Datchery camped outside his door.

"Haven't you got something to do?" Datchery said to Deputy.

The boy's grubby palm shot out and Datchery dropped a coin in it. They both looked down the street at the receding figure of Princess Puffer, and then Deputy took off at a run after her. So, I thought, you are also curious about the old woman and you are using Deputy to find out about her.

I tipped my hat to Datchery then and went to look at the tombstones in the little cemetery nearby. Enclosed by a wrought iron fence, the cemetery was located in the shadow of the cathedral. I had noticed it before but never bothered to examine it more closely. Now I roamed idly among the tombstones, reading the names inscribed on them. This was a place Neville and I had not visited during our stay in Cloisterham, preferring to ramble in the open countryside. I was not really expecting to find anything useful to my search, so it was with a shock that I came upon a sarcophagus inscribed with the name of Edwin Drood. I stared at it, wondering how it could be.

"I see you are admiring our monuments," said a voice outside the fence.

I turned to see Mr. Sapsea, the mayor, regarding me. He had just emerged from the morning service. I remembered only too well the last time we had met—when Neville had been accused of murdering Edwin Drood. I just hoped he didn't recognize me.

"Yes, they are very interesting," I said.

"You might wish to look at that one," he said, pointing with his walking stick to the largest monument.

I saw there was a long inscription engraved on it with his own name, Mr. Thomas Sapsea, prominently displayed in the middle. I supposed he was one of those persons who prepare for their own demise well in advance of the occasion, for although he was around sixty years of age and a trifle corpulent, he appeared to be in good health. On looking closer at the inscription, I saw in fact it was the tomb of Ethelinda, whose name was engraved in small letters at the top of the inscription.

"I composed it myself," Mr. Sapsea said with evident pride.

I read hurriedly through a lengthy statement to the effect that Ethelinda, wife of Mr. Thomas Sapsea, auctioneer, etc. (here it listed his various occupations, of which there were many), had looked up to her more worldly husband, and asked if the reader could do the same, or *if not, with a blush retire.*

"My wife," he explained. "I confess I am the author of those lines."

"You are a master of words," I said politely. "A poet perhaps?"

"Well, I must confess I have written a few odes." He nodded, pleased. "You are a most astute young man. What may I ask is your name?"

"Henry Poker," I said, holding out my hand. "I have come to Cloisterham to study the tombs and ruins."

"Have you?" he said. "Splendid. So few young people today appreciate the past. They all seem to want to run off to London to seek their fortunes. It's very reassuring to run into a sensible young man for a change."

I wondered what he would say if he knew I was actually a young woman and in fact the sister of a young man he had been ready to condemn for murder. I decided to take advantage of this chance meeting to gain some information if I could. "Perhaps you could tell me about that tomb," I said, pointing at the sarcophagus that bore the name of Edwin Drood.

"Certainly. What do you wish to know?"

"Who was Edwin Drood?"

"He was a faithful servant of her Majesty. Helped to build the empire. Built buildings, roads, bridges, that sort of thing in India."

I doubted that the Edwin Drood I had known would be described in such a fashion. I assumed this was someone else by the same name. However, the coincidence was remarkable. I wondered if the deceased could be a relative. "Do you know how he died?"

"Of a fever, I believe. Although many said it was of a broken heart. He lost his wife, you know. Pretty young thing. They said he never got over it. I can understand that. I feel much the same about my own Ethelinda, which is why I wanted her to have an appropriate monument. A fitting monument is very important, you know."

"The name seems familiar," I said. "Edwin Drood, that is."

He hesitated and glanced about him. Was he concerned that someone might overhear? Then he leaned forward and lowered his voice. "Perhaps you heard about his unfortunate son of the same name, who died some six months ago. Murdered. It was in the London newspapers at the time."

"Murdered!" I feigned shock. "How?"

"Drowned. Robbed too no doubt. But such crimes are not typical here. You'll find Cloisterham as safe as the next town, and a great deal safer than London. You have nothing to be afraid of. See here, you seem like a very respectable young gentleman. If you want to quote that inscription I wrote, you're welcome to it. Just be sure to say I wrote it. The name is Sapsea. S-A-P-S-E-A."

I assured him I would probably quote him and would be sure to spell his name correctly. Then, seeing I was unlikely to steer the conversation back to Edwin Drood or his father, I took my leave of the Mayor and went on my way.

That afternoon I went in search of Stony Durdles, the local stonemason, whom Deputy had told me about. I wasn't sure what I would learn from him, but Deputy had said he knew more about the cathedral and its hidden secrets than anyone else in Cloisterham. I had to find him myself since Deputy was not around. Princess Puffer had left the Travellers' Twopenny, presumably to return to London, and I wondered if Deputy had been instructed to follow her into the city. At least I knew one thing Datchery did not know. I knew what Deputy would find in that back lane in Shadwell. But Datchery would soon know it too, and when he did, he would also be quick to guess Jasper's secret vice. I wasn't sure that got us any closer to knowing what had happened to Edwin Drood. Nor did it explain why Princess Puffer had followed Jasper to Cloisterham and shaken her fist at him in the cathedral. Well, I would let Datchery pursue Princess Puffer. Meanwhile, I would find out if the stonemason knew anything that would help throw light on the events of that awful night.

I didn't have to search far to find the house of Mr. Stony Durdles. Several passersby helpfully steered me in the right direction. Everyone seemed to know the backstreet where he lived in an old unfinished stone house. I recognized it as that of a stonemason the moment I saw it. In front of the house was a clutter of tombstones, urns, broken columns, and sculptures of angels and children, all in various stages of completion. Four dusty-looking journeymen were at work among the debris, chipping away at the stone with hammers and chisels. They looked at me curiously as I made my way through their handiwork.

"I'm looking for Mr. Durdles," I said.

One of the journeymen pointed toward the open door of the house with his chisel. "He's in there."

The door was open but I hesitated to enter without being invited to do so by the owner. I tried to peer into the interior but could make out nothing in the darkness.

"Mr. Durdles!" I called out.

"Who wants him?" a surly voice responded from within.

"Poker," I said. "My name's Poker. I'd like a word with you if you wouldn't mind."

I could hear someone moving about, but several minutes passed before anyone appeared. The man who stepped out blinking into the light was covered with a fine dust that made him resemble the stones around us. It coated his hair, his eyebrows, and his clothes from his yellow neckerchief to his boots.

"You don't look like you're in mourning," he observed, squinting at me with bloodshot eyes. "And you're too young to be thinking about a stone for yourself."

"I didn't come to order a stone," I said. "I came to ask if you'd show me about the cathedral. Deputy tells me you know more about it than anyone else in Cloisterham."

"Deputy does, does he?" he said, looking around as if he expected to see the boy.

"That's right. The boy who works at the Travellers' Twopenny."

He looked back at me. "What do you want to know about it?"

"I understand you have a talent for finding hidden remains there."

"I've found a fair amount. You interested in dead monks and such like?"

"Whatever you can show me," I said. "I'd be most grateful."

He scratched his chin thoughtfully. "You're interested in seeing the crypt, I suppose."

"Yes, I am."

"And the tower too maybe."

"Why not? Do you recommend the tower?"

"That's what the others asked to see."

I tried to sound casual. "What others?"

"Mr. Jasper for one. Mr. Datchery for another. You know them?" He seemed to ask the question out of simple curiosity, not suspicion. It didn't appear to matter to him whether I knew them or not.

"I've met Mr. Datchery," I admitted cautiously.

Durdles nodded. "He wanted to see the crypt and the tower."

"Then I'm sure I would like to see them too."

"By night or by day?"

"What do others prefer?"

"Others prefer by night."

"Then night it is."

"You ain't afraid of ghosts?"

"Are there ghosts?" I asked.

"Some say there are."

"What do you say?"

"I say there are a lot of dead people there."

"I'm sure you're right," I agreed.

"I haven't ever *seen* a ghost," he said, leaning closer and lowering his voice. At such close quarters I could not help noticing the smell of alcohol on his breath.

"Well, I've never seen one either," I told him.

"But maybe I *heard* one once."

This was interesting. "You heard a ghost?"

He nodded. "I heard something that no one else heard. I asked a lot of people the next day and no one but me heard it. Wouldn't you call that a ghost sound?"

"What did you hear?"

"A kind of cry. A scream maybe. And then a howl of a dog. A most awful lonesome sound, like someone died."

"When was this?"

"Christmas Eve a year ago."

"Christmas Eve!" I repeated.

He looked at me narrowly. "That's right."

"Wasn't it Christmas Eve when Edwin Drood was murdered?" I asked.

"Wasn't *that* Christmas Eve," he said. "It was the one afore it." He was looking at me carefully now. "Did you know the young man maybe?"

"No," I said. "I've just heard about how he was murdered."

Durdles nodded. I couldn't tell if he believed me or not. I would have to be more careful. I had nearly given myself away.

"When would be a convenient time to see the crypt and the tower?" I asked.

He considered. "Come tonight if you want. Tonight's as good as another. I'll be here."

"All right," I said. "I will."

9

It had been dark about an hour when I left the Travellers' and walked the short distance to Durdles' house. Once there, I made my way through the clutter of unfinished monuments and blocks of stone that lay like so many ghostly sentinels guarding his entry. I had to rap at the door several times before he answered it. He blinked at me as if he had no idea who I was.

"Poker," I reminded him. "You said you'd show me the cathedral tonight."

"Did I?" he said. "Well, just a minute." He disappeared back inside. I could hear him moving about, making assorted bumping, clattering, and thumping noises. After what seemed a very long time, he returned, carrying a small bundle and an unlit lantern. I wondered what was in the bundle but didn't want to appear nosy.

"Would you like me to carry something?" I asked.

He looked doubtfully from the bundle to the lantern and then back again. After much deliberation, he handed me the lantern.

As we started on our way, I could smell alcohol on his breath and wondered if he were in fit condition for our excursion. But being eager for it myself, I made no objection and pretended not to notice when he bumped up against a fence, collided with a tree, or mistook a bush for a path. I was grateful for the moonlight or he might have run afoul of even more objects.

Our route took us down the back lane, past the Travellers' Twopenny, through the Monks' vineyard, and then past the cozy lighted windows of Minor Canon Corner. When we reached the cathedral, we did not head for the main entrance but skirted the massive stone structure until we came to a neatly tucked away side door. After much fumbling in his pockets, Durdles pulled out a key and unlocked the door.

Once we were inside, he locked the door again behind us. Then we descended some stone steps and found ourselves in the crypt, a dark musty room of arches and large pillars. A little light filtered in through low windows and cast shadows on the floor. There was an odor of damp, mold, and decay.

"A long time ago there used to be a monastery here, you know," Durdles said, "and there was a convent. Several hundred years ago they buried their monks and abbots and nuns and abbesses and whatnot hereabouts, some of them in the walls and some under the floors. There's a lot of old ones sleeping down here."

The cold damp and the thought of the ancient dead around me made me shiver. "It gives a person a strange feeling, doesn't it, to be surrounded by the dead?"

"I feel more at home down here than I do up there with the living," Durdles said. "Down here it's peaceful."

"Lonely too," I added, looking about uneasily.

"That may be," agreed Durdles, "but it's lonely up there too."

I looked at him curiously. He was a strange man to prefer the company of dead people. Reaching down to the base of a pillar, he pulled a dusty bottle out of the shadows and uncorked it. He offered it to me, but I declined. He shrugged and took a big gulp.

"I notice you didn't bring along anything for thirst," he said, wiping his mouth on the back of his hand. "Climbing up and down steps can make a body thirsty."

"I suppose it can," I agreed.

"Now take Mr. Jasper," he said. "Do you know Mr. Jasper?"

"The choirmaster," I said.

"That's right. When Mr. Jasper come to see the crypt, he brought along a little something."

"Did he?" I asked. "What did he bring?"

"A bottle."

"I see. And should I have brought a bottle too?" I asked.

"No, no matter," he said, waving his hand to dismiss my question. "I'm better off drinking this. It may be cheap, but it doesn't rob me of my wits."

"And what Jasper gave you did?"

"All I know is I fell asleep down here and when I woke up I'd been asleep several hours. It ain't a good place to sleep. It makes me ache something awful to sleep down here in the cold and damp. It gives me Tombatism."

"Rheumatism?" I suggested.

"Nah, tombatism. Don't catch it anywhere but in the tombs."

"And what was in the bottle that Jasper brought with him?"

"Wine," he said.

There it was again—Jasper's wine. So Neville and Edwin had not been the only ones affected by it.

"When did Jasper come here with you?" I asked.

"About six days before Christmas Eve last year."

In other words, about six days before Edwin Drood disappeared. Was there a connection? Why was Jasper skulking about the cathedral? Why drug Durdles?

"And this is where I was when I heard the ghost cry."

"The Christmas Eve before."

He nodded and took another swig. "Some of the town boys were throwing stones at me and I come in here to get away from them. I sort of fell asleep and it woke me up when I heard it. Awful sound. I didn't stick around after that."

I shivered involuntarily. It was a strange story. I wondered what he had heard, but I suspected that if I had been awoken by such a sound in such a place, I too would not have stuck around to investigate.

"Was Deputy one of those boys?" I said, remembering that Deputy had said one of his jobs was to stone Durdles.

"They're terrors, those town boys. Wild as little savages. But you can't blame them. They got no one to teach them better. Orphans every one of them. Travellers' gives them a place to sleep at any rate and sees they don't starve. Yep, Deputy was one of 'em. One of the wildest of the lot. He used to stone just about anything. Whether it moved or not made no difference to him. And so I made a pact with him, told him I'd pay him a halfpenny to stone me home if he found me out late. He took to it right off.

We both benefited from it. He made sure I got myself home when I was half a mind to lay down and sleep on the damp ground in the churchyard and I gave him a purpose in life."

"The arrangement seems rather hard on you," I observed.

"No matter," he said. "The thing is, before I took that boy in hand, he had no purpose, and now he does."

"Mr. Datchery is paying him too," I said, "but not to get stoned."

"Deputy told me." He took another swallow. Then he felt in his pockets again and pulled out another key. We climbed some steps and he unlocked another door. On the other side was a narrow passage, which we followed until we could see the nave itself. Light filtered through the stained glass windows as we crossed to an iron gate, which Durdles unlocked with yet another key drawn from yet another pocket. This gate led to a narrow staircase that wound upward around a stone pillar. Durdles stopped every so often to drink from his bottle. He still clutched his small bundle and I still carried the lantern. When it grew too dark to see our feet, Durdles struck a match and lit the lantern. We continued climbing by its light. Occasionally a cobweb brushed my face. We came to galleries from which we could look down into the nave. After that the staircases became narrower and steeper. Durdles led the way with his lantern and I followed close on his heels. As we approached the top, we could smell the night air. High in the tower above us in a sudden rush of wings some birds took flight. We set the lantern down inside the tower so the wind would not blow it out. Then we stepped out into the night. Overhead the sky was full of stars. Below us winked the lights of Cloisterham, and farther out I could see the dark gleam of the river as it meandered toward the horizon.

It was a wonderful view. I held on to my hat to keep it from blowing off. Durdles was quenching his thirst again. From the angle at which he held the bottle, I surmised it was almost empty. Even after he had replaced the cork, I noticed his reluctance to join me at the edge.

"Are you afraid of heights, Mr. Durdles?" I asked.

"Not particularly," he said, "only I had a peculiar experience here once. I had the odd sensation that I could just step off into space." He inched nearer to the edge and looked over. "It's all right this time," he said. "The ground is down where it's supposed to be. All the same, I can't forget that feeling. It didn't scare me at the time. It was almost like I was dreaming, but later when I remembered, it scared me half to death."

I looked down at the ground. Directly below us, deep in shadow, lay the graveyard. To step off the tower here was to land among the dead. I remembered Durdles had said he felt more at home with the dead than the living and he had just finished off the bottle he had brought with him. Perhaps it was best for him to keep his distance from the edge.

"Had you been drinking that time too?" I asked.

"It was that bottle of wine that Jasper brought along."

"The one that put you to sleep?"

"The very one."

"Did Jasper drink from it too?" I asked.

"He did, but I've such a weak spot for the stuff that I suppose I drunk the most of it."

I suspected that he might in fact have drunk all of it.

Jasper could have pretended to drink from the bottle. He had known Durdles' weakness for drink and taken advantage of it. But for what purpose?

"Would you like a bite to eat?" Durdles asked, untying his bundle and taking out a piece of hard bread. "Or don't you eat either?"

"I eat," I said, suddenly realizing I was hungry.

He sat down where he was, leaning his back against the wall, and I did the same. How free it felt to sit as a man sits and not worry about how to spread my skirts or if they should get dirty. He broke his piece of bread in half and handed half to me.

"I wondered what you had in your bundle," I said.

"I never go anywhere without my lunch," he said. "Never know where I'll be when I want a bit of food."

We chewed our pieces of bread silently. It was almost hard enough to break teeth.

"So, Mr. Potter, do you have family?" Durdles asked.

"I do," I said as soon as I could swallow the piece of bread I was endeavoring to chew.

"That's good. Everybody should have a family. It don't do to be alone in this world."

"No, sir."

"It can be a cold, hard world."

"That it can."

"Sometimes when a man's all by himself, he does things he wouldn't otherwise do."

"I suppose he might," I said.

"Things which if he had a wife and a child, he might not do."

"That's true."

"Things he might otherwise be ashamed of."

"I see," I said, although I did not.

Durdles heaved a mighty sigh. "You seem a well-bred young chap," he said. "I'll bet your mother's proud of you."

"She is," I said after the slightest hesitation, which I hoped he didn't notice.

"And your father."

"Him as well."

"I thought so." He nodded as if he were satisfied.

I looked up at the stars and felt acutely the absence of both my mother and the father I had never known. I didn't tell him that all the family I had in the world was an injured brother lying in a bed in a lodging house in London. At the thought a twinge of guilt shot through me that I was not by his side. With effort I quelled it.

When we were finished eating, Durdles re-tied his bundle and we retraced our steps down the winding tower staircases, through various doors that had to be unlocked and then locked again, until once again we were in the damp crypt.

"Are you the only person with keys?" I said as he unlocked the door which would take us back out into the night.

"That fellow Datchery asked me the same thing," said Durdles. "The Dean's got keys, I told him, and Tope's got keys—Tope's the verger."

"And Jasper?"

Durdles was silent a minute. "I'm not saying he does and I'm not saying he doesn't. All I know is that night when I fell asleep in the crypt, I dreamed I lost some keys. Jasper was there and then he wasn't there and then when I woke up, he was there again, and I had dropped one of my keys. It was lying there on the floor where I had dropped it."

"Do you remember which key it was?" I asked.

"Can't say I do. I was still a bit foggy at the time."

I looked at the floor and imagined a key lying there. Which one had it been? Had Jasper stolen one of his keys, and if so, what had he done with it? Did it have any connection with the murder of Edwin Drood six nights later?

When we were back outside in the night air, Durdles seemed almost sober. "Well, got to say good-night to Evie," he announced and walked toward the little graveyard at the base of the tower. Curious, I followed him. He made his way to a small headstone with the name Evelina engraved on it. For a few minutes he stood in silence looking at it and I stood beside him.

"Who was she?" I asked.

"My wife," he said. "And our little one is there beside her, keeping her company."

I realized then why he felt most at home around the crypt and the cathedral grounds and why he sought comfort in a bottle.

At that moment a small stone flew through the air and struck the ground nearby.

"Take care," he called out. "You'll hit Mr. Poker."

Deputy danced out into the street. "I wasn't going to hit Mr. Poker. Only trying to earn my half-penny."

"Where you been?" said Durdles. "I haven't seen you all day."

"I been to London," said Deputy with a big grin that showed his missing front teeth.

"That's a long way to go," Durdles observed. "You eat anything since morning?"

"An apple I pinched on the omnibus," said Deputy.

"You ought to have more than that—to keep your strength up."

"I suppose I should," Deputy said, "since you put it like that."

"It just so happens I have some victuals at my place," Durdles said. "If you haven't got anything better to do, why don't you come with me and get a bite to eat?"

"All right," Deputy said. "I'll do that."

"Mr. Potter, you want some victuals too?" Durdles asked, turning to me. "It's humble fare but you won't get fed at the Travellers' this time of night."

I was grateful not only for the offer of food but also the opportunity to learn more about Deputy's trip to London, so I accepted his invitation and we all walked back to Durdles' house. The interior was almost as dusty from stone cutting as the exterior. It was an old house with a bare and unfinished look about it. We three sat at a small wood table and Durdles carefully poured a cup of ale for each of us and passed around some hard biscuits and cheese. Once we had had the opportunity to take the edge off our hunger, the conversation turned to the topic in which I was most interested.

"So what did you do in London?" Durdles asked Deputy.

"I was doing a job for Mr. Datchery. He wanted me to find out where Princess Puffer lived."

"And who's Princess Puffer?"

"An old woman who came here from London and then turned around and went back again."

"It's a strange name," Durdles observed.

"It's on account of she puffs opium," explained Deputy, pretending to smoke an imaginary pipe.

"And did you find out where she lived?" asked Durdles.

"In a rat-hole of an opium den." Deputy reached into his shirt, pulled out a grubby piece of paper, and unfolded it. "Look, I drew a map."

Durdles squinted at the paper. "That's a right fine map," he said. "Don't you agree, Mr. Poker?"

I agreed.

"She smokes opium, does she?" Durdles said thoughtfully.

"I already knew she did 'cause I seen her do it at the Travellers'," said Deputy.

"Have another biscuit," Durdles said.

"Okay, I will." Deputy's hand shot out and snatched another biscuit. His mouth opened wide as he bit into it.

"Did you find out anything else?" Durdles asked casually. It was what I wanted to know too, and I was grateful to Durdles for asking, but I wondered why he was so curious. He was almost as inquisitive as Mr. Datchery.

"I did," Deputy said, his mouth still crammed full of biscuit. "I found out that a certain Cloisterham gent what choked me half to death is one of her customers." Deputy grabbed his throat with one hand, rolled his eyes, and stuck out his tongue.

"Jasper?" Durdles said.

"That's right."

Durdles chewed thoughtfully. "So the choirmaster smokes opium, does he?"

"And that ain't all. I found out why Puffer was here looking for him."

"Why?" asked Durdles. "To sell him some of her opium?"

"Not a bit of it," said Deputy. He glanced about as if there might be spies lurking in the room and then leaned close, his face lit by the candle on the table, and whispered, "He murdered somebody."

"Who?" asked Durdles.

"Her daughter!" Deputy sat back grinning, pleased with himself.

"Are you sure?" I asked, wondering why Princess Puffer would go on selling opium to Jasper if this were true. Or why she didn't kill him as he lay unconscious on the sagging bed in her squalid room like the Indian man the night Neville and I had been there.

"Course I'm sure," Deputy said.

"How'd you find this out?" Durdles asked.

"She told me so herself," Deputy said.

"And you believed her?"

"Course I did. Why shouldn't I believe her?"

"'Cause she may not know the difference between what really happened and what she dreamed under the influence of opium."

"You think it's a lie?" Deputy looked disappointed.

"Maybe there never was a daughter. Maybe she only wished she had a daughter. You can't believe anything an opium smoker tells you."

Deputy slumped on his chair. I confess I felt disappointed too. I knew Durdles was right.

"Ask Poker what he thinks," Durdles said, nodding his head toward me.

Deputy looked at me. "Well?"

I saw the old woman in my mind shuffling about the dark and dingy room in the candlelight. What had she said? Something about how she used to have a family but didn't anymore. "I think she had a daughter," I said, and Deputy brightened.

"There, see!"

Durdles looked at me thoughtfully. "If she had a daughter, let's say—just for the sake of argument—and supposing Jasper did murder her, why didn't she go to the police?"

"Who'd believe an old woman who smokes opium?" I said.

"Yeah!" agreed Deputy.

"You need more facts," Durdles told Deputy, "before you go around accusing people. You be careful who you repeat this to."

"I can tell Mr. Datchery, can't I?"

Durdles thought a minute, then nodded. "But I don't approve of him sending you off to London opium dens, and you can tell him that for me. Ain't a fit place to send a boy, not even one as scrappy as you."

"I can take care of myself," Deputy said.

"And I want you to stay away from Jasper," Durdles told him.

Deputy waved the warning away. "He just better watch out or he'll get a stone in the back of his head. I ain't afraid of him."

"Don't you go throwing stones at him neither," said Durdles. "He don't pay you for that service, so don't you give it to him. You keep away from him. I'm not saying he's a murderer. Maybe he never murdered anybody. But if he's done wrong, it'll catch up with him. You'll see. Things have a way of coming out. Don't they, Mr. Poker?"

I think I started when he said my name. Did he know I was not who I was pretending to be? I mumbled agreement, choking on a bite of biscuit, which led Deputy to whack me helpfully on the back. Then it was time to leave, and Deputy and I walked back together to the Travellers' Twopenny.

10

The next morning I got up early and walked to the cathedral. The doors were still locked so I sat down on the steps to wait. At seven Mr. Tope showed up, out of breath and clutching a ring of keys.

"My goodness, you're early, young man," he said as he sorted among his keys. "I don't believe I know you. Are you a stranger here or one of our own youngsters come back all grown up?"

"A stranger," I said, "come to see the ruins."

"Then you must be Mr. Poker," he said, unlocking the doors with one of his keys and pulling them open. "Mr. Sapsea was telling me about you. He said you're writing a book."

"A paper perhaps," I said.

"You made a great impression on the mayor. He's been telling everyone what a remarkable young man you are."

"I see you are in charge of the keys," I said as he thrust them into an inner pocket.

"Yes, just one of my duties as verger."

"Have you ever lost a key?" I inquired.

"Goodness, no," he said, horrified, feeling the keys anxiously.

"You live in the Gate House, don't you?" I said. "Across from Mr. Jasper?"

"I do indeed," he said, looking at me over his spectacles. "However, if you're looking for a room to rent, I'm sorry to disappoint you. We already have a lodger."

"Mr. Datchery," I said.

"Yes indeed Mr. Datchery," he repeated. "A most amiable man."

"He has been fortunate to find such architecturally interesting lodgings," I said.

"That's true," said Tope. "Were you thinking of including the Gate House in your book?"

"I might."

"Then you would probably like to see it more closely. You must come by when you have some free time. I'd be happy to show you around."

I thanked him and told him I would do that.

I watched Jasper throughout morning service. Dressed in his white robe, standing with the rest of the choir, he did not look like a man who might have killed someone. But then neither did he look like a man who frequented opium dens. As I listened to the singing of the choir and the music of the organ surrounded by the ancient walls and stained glass windows of the cathedral, my suspicions of Jasper seemed somewhat unreal. Murder belonged in the backstreets of London and the alleys of Colombo, not in quaint old towns like Cloisterham, where everybody knew their neighbors.

In the early afternoon I wandered up High Street to the Gate House. It was the first time I had passed under its archway. It was a queer old building, straddling a small side street. I knew that Jasper's rooms could be reached by the narrow stair on the right. Across from it was an open door, and as I passed, I discerned Mr. Datchery in the dim interior writing at a desk.

"Mr. Poker, isn't it?" he called out, proving he was as vigilant as I had suspected.

"That's right."

"Are you looking for someone?"

"Mr. Tope's residence," I said, ready with my answer.

"Ah, you have come to the right place, but he has kindly rented me these two fine rooms, so to get to him you need to use the door just beyond that leads to his quarters upstairs."

I thanked him for his help and proceeded to the next door. I wondered if he sat there all day with his door open. If so, Jasper could not come or go without being observed. The thought pleased me. Jasper was learning what it was like to have his movements watched.

"Mr. Poker," said Mr. Tope when he opened his door. "Do come in. Let me show you around our humble abode."

Just inside the door there were hooks on the walls for his ring of keys and miscellaneous tools and household objects.

"How very organized," I remarked.

"Yes, I do like to keep things in their place," he said,

pleased that I had noticed. "If you know where a thing belongs, why then it never gets lost."

"I will remember that," I said.

He led me into a small sitting room crowded with furniture but with pathways running through the room. It seemed a place where things very easily could get lost, but I kept that thought to myself. The little bedroom was likewise tightly furnished but with a pathway leading maze-like to the bed.

"We had to move some of our furniture up here after renting the rooms downstairs to Mr. Datchery," he explained. "It's a bit cramped but cozy, wouldn't you say?"

I agreed it was cozy.

"You must notice the view too," he said.

The little window to which he directed me looked at a nearby wall and at the street below.

"It's a very nice view," I assured him. "You can see the people who pass by."

"Just so," he agreed, clearly proud of his view.

"You must have some tea," Mrs. Tope said as Mr. Tope and I stuck our heads into the little kitchen.

"All right," I said. "I will."

We had our tea in the sitting room, close to the window with a view, although from where we sat we could only see the wall and not the people passing in the street below.

"You have a remarkable property here," I said. "Quite valuable I expect."

"Oh, yes," Mr. Tope said. "There aren't many like this left now. There used to be more but they've been torn down."

"Would it be possible for me to see the rest of it?" I asked.

Mrs. Tope looked at Mr. Tope uncertainly.

"Mr. Jasper has few visitors," she said. "He keeps to himself, poor man. I fix his meals, you know. It goes with the rooms." She nodded at a door behind us. "There's a connecting stair between our rooms and his, which makes it convenient."

I looked at the door but knew it would not be wise to appear too interested.

"I suppose you heard about the disappearance of his nephew last Christmas?" said Mrs. Tope.

"I think I heard something about it," I admitted.

"It had the town in an uproar, it did."

"He was such a nice young man," Mr. Tope said. "Engaged to be married to one of Miss Twinkleton's young ladies. Had all his future ahead of him."

"Mr. Jasper doted on that boy," said Mrs. Tope. "It was an awful blow, his disappearing like that." She lowered her voice, as if someone might overhear. "He was murdered, you know."

Mr. Tope cleared his throat. "Drowned, to be precise. All they found of the poor lad was his watch and shirt-pin."

"Poor Mr. Jasper has been melancholy ever since," said Mrs. Tope, "which is why he might not want to be disturbed, but I'm sure Mr. Datchery, our lodger in the downstairs rooms, wouldn't mind showing you around *his* quarters. He's a retired gentleman who enjoys nothing better than to find someone to talk to. I imagine he's lonely."

"I've seen Mr. Datchery's rooms from the doorway," I said. "I was really hoping to see Mr. Jasper's."

"Well, perhaps Mr. Jasper wouldn't mind," said Mr. Tope. "We'll ask him."

I followed him down the stair and across the little street. We climbed Jasper's stair and Mr. Tope knocked at his door. While we waited, Mr. Datchery appeared below us.

"Not at home?" Datchery asked cheerfully, looking up the stair at us and smoothing his mane of white hair.

"I'm afraid not," said Mr. Tope. "Our choirmaster appears to be out."

Disappointed, I had no choice but to follow Mr. Tope back down the stairs.

"This young man is interested in our Gate House," Tope said when we were outside in the street with Datchery. "He's in Cloisterham to study our architecture and ruins."

"A fine old building," agreed Datchery, gazing up at it in admiration.

"I was going to show him Mr. Jasper's quarters, but I guess Mr. Jasper isn't at home."

"I guess not," Datchery said, still smiling. "However, you can look over my quarters if you'd like, Mr. Poker. Fine old rooms, a little musty, which is only to be expected in an old building, and somewhat lacking in light, which is why I keep my door open."

"Very kind of you to offer," I said, "but I have an appointment I just remembered. Maybe another time."

We smiled at each other genially. I was determined not to spend any more time in Datchery's presence than necessary, and I suspected he knew that.

"Yes, another time," he said. "Anytime. You'll find me sitting here with my door open. For the light."

Tope and Datchery then fell to praising the architecture of the Gate House to each other. Glancing up at Jasper's window as I walked away, I thought I saw someone draw quickly back. So someone was at home. The hunter was becoming the hunted. I wondered how he liked it.

When I got back to the Travellers', I found Deputy waiting for me on the steps.

"Got a message for you, Mr. Poker," he said. "Mr. Sapsea wants you to drop 'round."

"What for?" I asked.

Deputy shrugged. "Didn't say."

"Did he say when?"

"Nope, didn't say that either."

I sighed. "I suppose I should go."

"I wouldn't if it was me," said Deputy.

"And why not?"

"'Cause he's an ass. That's what Durdles says."

"Oh, he does?" I couldn't help smiling.

Deputy broke into a wide grin that showed his missing teeth.

Not eager for another conversation with the pompous mayor, I was tempted to ignore the summons. In all likelihood it had to do with the epitaph he had composed for his wife's monument. Poor woman. I wondered how she had stood being married to such a man. It was evening when I reluctantly decided to see what he wanted. As I walked up High Street, I saw Mr. Crisparkle step out his front door to take the air. Further on I passed the iron wrought gates of the Nuns' House. Then I crossed the street and found myself in front of Mr. Sapsea's old house, which had an imposing figure in the likeness of his father carved above the door. This figure had been the subject of many jokes among the young ladies at Miss Twinkleton's seminary. Old Mr. Sapsea, like his son, had made his living as an auctioneer, and the figure showed him standing at an auctioneer's pulpit with his hammer raised.

The door was answered by a manservant, who showed me into the sitting room, where I was surprised to find Mr. Sapsea in conversation with John Jasper.

"Mr. Poker," he said, "so kind of you to drop by. Have you met my dear friend, Cloisterham's choirmaster?"

"I have not had the pleasure," I confessed.

"We owe a great deal to Mr. Jasper," said Mr. Sapsea. "He has made Cloisterham's choir the envy of the countryside. He is a man of considerable musical ability and also one of Cloisterham's most upstanding citizens. A pillar of the community."

While he was talking, Jasper was silent, staring at me with his dark terrible eyes. I hoped he did not recognize me.

"Would you like a glass of port, Mr. Poker?" asked Mr. Sapsea.

"Thank you," I said, avoiding Jasper's eyes. "I would."

Mr. Sapsea rang for his manservant to bring another glass of port. I had not expected to encounter Jasper, but now that I had, I felt myself torn between curiosity to observe him at close range and an instinct to flee. I felt as if Jasper were trying to bore his way into me and penetrate all my secrets with his gaze. Uncomfortable, I looked away, and my eyes lighted on the large gilt-frame portrait of Mr. Sapsea over the mantel.

"Ah, I see you are admiring my portrait," Mr. Sapsea said. "A good likeness, isn't it?"

"Indeed," I said.

"It was painted by Sir Arthur Warburton. Perhaps you've heard of him?"

"I'm afraid I haven't."

"I'm surprised at that. He's quite well known. I would think coming from London, you would have heard of him. Well, never mind. He's painted many other men of distinction. It only seemed proper that a man of my position should go to the best."

"It's an amazing likeness," I said.

When I dared look back at Jasper, he was still staring at me. "You look familiar," he said. "Have we met before?"

"I don't think so," I said. "This is my first visit to Cloisterham."

"And where do you come from?"

"London," I said.

"What part of London?"

I hesitated only a fraction of a second, being but imperfectly acquainted with the city. "The West End," I said, hoping that would satisfy him. I didn't want to say Holborn, for that might have confirmed his suspicions.

"You have a foreign look about you," Jasper said. "Are you sure you're not from abroad? Italy perhaps?"

"Quite sure," I said.

"You'll have to excuse Mr. Jasper," said Mr. Sapsea. "As you probably noticed, he's in mourning."

Indeed, Jasper was dressed all in black. Perhaps that

was what made him appear so moody, not just the dark burning eyes.

"We were about to start a game of backgammon," said Sapsea, rubbing his hands in anticipation. "It helps Mr. Jasper take his mind off his loss. Would you like to join us, Mr. Poker?"

The idea of spending the evening across a table from Jasper's staring eyes did not appeal to me. "That's very good of you, sir," I said. "However, I'm afraid I can't stay. I must be getting back. I only came by because I received a message that you wanted to see me about something."

"Did you? Oh, yes," he said, "I remember. I wanted to share with you a little poem I tossed off this afternoon. You must tell me what you think of it." He went to his writing desk and from among his papers took up one which he held out to me. It was written in such an ornate script that I could barely read it.

"Might I take it with me to read at leisure?" I asked. "I doubt a cursory reading would do it justice."

"Of course," he said. "Peruse my little gem at your leisure. Find a place where it can speak to you without unwonted distractions and listen to its woodnotes wild."

I took my leave then, and as I did so, it occurred to me that since Jasper would be occupied with Sapsea for the evening, it was an opportune time for me to pay another visit to the Gate House. If I could get into Jasper's rooms, I could search them for clues to Edwin's disappearance.

11

I tried to hatch a plan for eluding the ever-watchful eye of Mr. Datchery, and that in fact turned out to be easy. It seemed Mr. Datchery only kept his door open during the day. Now that it was night, his door was closed, although there was a light at his window. He might have been inside, but it was just as likely that he had taken advantage of Jasper's absence to go elsewhere, or had followed Jasper to Sapsea's house and was even now biding his time until Jasper came out again. Throwing caution to the winds, I climbed the postern stairs that led to Jasper's rooms and tried the door. It was locked. Therefore, I would have to use another route. I hurriedly went back down again and took instead the stair leading up to the Topes' rooms. I knocked on the door softly. No one answered. Nor did I hear any movement within. Holding my breath, I turned the latch and let the door swing open. The sitting room was empty. I moved as quietly as possible across the room to the kitchen, half expecting to find Mrs. Tope there, but the kitchen was also empty. Scarcely able to believe my luck, I went straight to the door that led to the connecting stair. As I had hoped, it was unlocked. I closed the door behind me and felt my way up the narrow stair in the dark. Jasper's door was also unlocked. No doubt it would have been a nuisance to lock and unlock these doors since Mrs. Tope so often used the passage as she served Jasper his meals. The room I found myself in was completely dark so I had to light a match. By its flickering light I saw a small table and four chairs which took up most of the room along with a sideboard. Another door was beyond. I reached it as my match burned out. A lamp burning in the next room threw a dim glow around it but left the recesses of the room in deep shadow. Bookshelves lined the wall. There were several chairs, an Oriental rug, a music stand, and, squatting like a sleeping monster in one corner, a grand piano. Over the chimneypiece was a portrait of Rosa Bud. It was an amateurish work, unfinished, almost a caricature, yet it was clearly Rosa, from the long golden hair tied with a blue ribbon, to the impertinent blue eyes and pursed lips. I thought how it was a pity her picture could not speak and tell what it had witnessed on Christmas Eve when Edwin, Neville, and Jasper had met here for their last dinner.

Besides the door leading to the small dining room, there were two other doors, both of which led to bedrooms. I guessed the smaller bedroom must have been Edwin's when he came to visit. By the dim light from the sitting room I saw a jacket hanging in the press and some shirts in a drawer, but nothing that could tell me about Edwin or his fate. In the other bedroom I found a locked press and a bureau. I opened each drawer of the bureau, hoping to find a key to the press, since Jasper might have locked up anything he did not want someone to find. As I did so, I wondered if Datchery had yet made his way into these rooms. It was a cat-and-mouse game he was playing, and no doubt Jasper was careful to keep his door locked with Datchery watching him so closely. Finding nothing of interest in the drawers of the bureau, I turned my attention to a small book on a stand beside the bed. Opening it, I saw that it was a diary. I took it into the sitting room to look at it under the light. I thought here at last I might find some answers.

October 25, 18--

Tonight my dear boy comes to dine. I must buy some cheese and we will break open that bottle of wine I have been saving. How I look forward to his visit! He brings a breath of fresh air into my otherwise dull life. I can't help doting on him. He is the last of my family. We are the only two left. My kinsman!

11:00 p.m.

In the next room Ned lies sleeping. Ah, the untroubled sleep of the young! I looked in at him just a minute ago and he looked so peaceful, clutching his pillow like a child. I wonder what he dreams about? Oh, the innocent dreams of youth! How I envy him. Tomorrow he returns to London. Back to his engineering studies. He will forget about me, which is as it should be, and I will count the days until he comes again. How will I bear it when he goes to Egypt? If only I could go with him! But that of course is impossible. I will have to learn to live without his visits. My days will stretch before me gray and empty. What will become of me without my boy?

October 27, 18--

My dear boy has gone back to London. I have got up and peeked into his room half a dozen times this evening, hoping to see him there sleeping in his bed. How unsatisfying is a meal eaten alone, even when good Mrs. Tope has gone to such trouble to prepare it. It is always thus when Ned goes away. He fills my life with light by his presence, and when he goes, I am in the dark again. He has no idea how much I depend on him to get through my days. What will I do when he's not here to cheer me up anymore?

Every entry seemed to be about Edwin. When he was not there, Jasper missed him or simply didn't write. As I flipped forward through the pages, I saw Rosa's name and stopped to read more.

November 15, 18--

Little Rosa Bud had her singing lesson this afternoon. She might be quite good if only she practiced. I fear I pushed her too hard. She nearly burst into tears. I forget that she is hardly more than a child. I must try to be more patient next time.

Why was there no mention of his passion for Rosa? To judge by the entry, she was only one of his singing students, nothing more. I moved on to an entry several days later about a dinner with Mr. Crisparkle.

November 21, 18--

Dined at Minor Canon Corner with Mr. Crisparkle and his old mother. Crisparkle suggested I get more exercise to combat my recent bout of low spirits. Old Mrs. Crisparkle recommended a glass of Constantia. How I envy Crisparkle his wholesome disposition. I am sure he sleeps soundly at night.

What does he know of bad dreams? He gets up every morning at the crack of dawn and goes for a swim in Cloisterham Weir. He shadowboxes at home and walks several miles every day. No wonder he sings like an angel. What does he know of dark moods such as I am cursed with? We were born under different stars. No amount of exercise or cold morning dips or glasses of Constantia will cure what ails me. It takes a medicine far more potent.

I turned several more pages, stopping when I came to an entry for the night Neville and Edwin quarreled.

November 28, 18--
This night I saw my dear boy attacked before my very eyes by Crisparkle's new young charge. Had I not been here to stop him, I shudder to think what might have happened. There's something tigerish in young Landless's blood. I fear for my dear boy while he is near. Such hot temper and lack of self-control can only lead to something terrible.

It was disappointingly short. Hoping to learn more, I read on.

December 6, 18--
Crisparkle has persuaded me to write to Ned and suggest a dinner at which young Landless can apologize. At first I thought it was a bad idea to bring the two young men together again, but he has persuaded me that his charge is repentant and sincerely wants to make amends. Reluctantly I have come round and agreed to write to my dear boy and lay the matter before him. I will understand if he refuses. I would not blame him for wanting to stay away from someone who threatened his life.

December 9, 18--

My dear boy has answered. He has consented to Mr. Crisparkle's plan for a reconciliation. He will dine at the Gate House on Christmas Eve. I have conveyed the message to Mr. Crisparkle.

December 23, 18--

Everything is ready. My dear boy will come tomorrow night. I can hardly wait to see him again. Mrs. Tope is making plum pudding.

December 30, 18--

What terrible thing has happened to my dear boy? I fear I will never see him again on this earth. Five days now he has been missing. We have dragged the river and searched the banks and marshes. No sign of him—only his watch and shirt-pin. When I think how we laughed and talked that last night! —how I saw the two young men off with a light heart—never dreaming that I would not see my dear boy again! What a fool I was to trust young Landless. Did he have it all planned? Did he know while he sat at my table and drank my wine that he was going to murder my dear boy? Is he as treacherous as that? Or was it in a moment of rage—some trivial remark poor Ned made—that set him off again? Did he bludgeon my dear boy to death with his ironwood staff? Did he dump his broken body in the river? Who can tell me what happened?

January 7, 18--

I have vowed that my dear boy's death will be revenged. From this day forth I will not talk about this awful deed or rest until I find out what happened to him. The person who murdered him shall pay for his crime. I swear I will bring his dreadful deed to light and he will be punished. My life henceforth will be devoted to his destruction.

This was the last entry. The rest of the pages were blank. For six months Jasper had not written in his diary. And yet he kept it beside his bed. I wondered why. Did he read it before falling asleep? Was it there to remind him of his vow?

I had found nothing in the diary that incriminated Jasper. To the contrary it was full of entries that spoke of his love for his nephew. Even his hatred of Neville was understandable when I looked at it from his point of view instead of my own. I knew only too well that Neville could be hot-tempered. But he had not killed Edwin Drood. Of that I was certain.

Suddenly my attention was caught by a noise. I held my breath, listening. Were those footsteps mounting the postern stairs? I looked around quickly. Where could I hide? Not here, I thought, not in his bed chamber. I must make my way to the dining room and try to go back the way I had come. As I rushed into the sitting room, I heard the distinct click of a key turning in the lock. There was no time to reach the dining room. I fled to the grand piano and crouched in its shadow. The door opened and Jasper entered. He locked the door behind him. I would not be able to slip out that way. I wondered why he was home. The backgammon game ought to have lasted longer.

Jasper pulled off his jacket as he walked into his bedroom. He lit a candle on the stand. From my hiding place I could see him unbutton his shirt. He sat down on the bed and pulled off his shoes.

At that moment I realized I was still holding his diary. I

hoped he wouldn't notice it was gone. Then he was up again, moving to the press. I listened intently, wondering if he were unlocking it. Soon he was back in my field of vision. He sat down on the bed again and by the light of the candle carefully filled a small pipe. I saw a match flare as he lit it. This accomplished, he lay back on the bed, propped on one elbow and began to smoke the pipe.

I suspected that it was not tobacco which he smoked in such a manner, and sure enough I could soon smell the same acrid odor that I had smelled in Princess Puffer's sordid little room. I thought it would be best to wait until he had succumbed to his opium dream before I tried to make my escape. I waited until I heard the cathedral bell toll. Then I crept across the room. I knew I must return the diary to the stand beside his bed or he would know that someone had been in his rooms. I looked at him lying on the bed with his eyes closed and the little pipe beside him on the stand. He looked older and more tired than that night six months earlier when he had sat on my left at the dinner table at Minor Canon Corner. I held my breath as I entered the room and gently lay the diary back on the stand.

At that moment he stirred and mumbled something. It sounded like "Where is it?" There was more, but it was indistinguishable. I hesitated, wanting to flee and yet curious to know if he was dreaming about Edwin Drood. I crept nearer, leaning toward his moving lips, trying to catch the words. He moaned softly in his sleep. Then suddenly his eyes opened and he stared straight at me.

"You!" he said.

I stumbled over one of his shoes in my haste to get away. My heart was pounding as I dashed out of the bedroom and through the dining room door. In the dark dining room I bumped into a chair, but I was too frightened to be cautious now. I found the door to the connecting stair and nearly fell as I groped my way down it. Then I was in the Topes' kitchen. I heard Mr. Tope call out from the bedroom, "Who's there?" Then I was down the stairs and out in the cobblestone street, racing away as fast as my feet would carry me. I imagined Jasper or Mr. Tope pursuing me. If I were caught, how would I explain what I had been doing? They would take me for a thief. And if they discovered my true identity, as they surely would, it would only confirm their suspicions about Neville. There would be whispers about 'bad blood.'

"Halt!" a man's voice shouted, and I could hear running footsteps behind me. I dodged through a hedge and across a lawn to try to evade my pursuer, but he sprinted after me. Then I had the bad luck to trip, and my pursuer tackled me. We rolled over the ground, but though I struggled, I was soon pinned down by someone stronger than myself. Out of breath, I looked up at the startled face of Mr. Crisparkle.

"Helena!" he said, so astonished that he forgot to call me Miss Landless.

My hat had fallen off and my hair had come loose.

He jumped off me and helped me to my feet.

"I didn't hurt you, did I?" he asked anxiously, trying to brush me off.

"I don't think so," I said.

"Whatever are you doing here and dressed in those clothes? I thought you were a man."

"That's what I want everyone to think."

"Why were you running like that?"

"I didn't want to be caught."

"Caught doing what?"

"Breaking into the Gate House."

He looked quickly around. The street seemed peacefully deserted. Somewhere a dog was barking.

"You did what?" he asked.

"I broke into the Gate House," I repeated calmly.

"Are you out of your mind?"

"I'm determined to prove Neville's innocence. Until the truth is known, he's under a cloud of suspicion."

"But you're placing yourself in danger," he said. "Don't you realize that? Jasper may be capable of murder for all we know."

"Sshh," I said, "someone's coming." The sound of shoes crunching on pavement came from the street nearby.

"We can't talk here," Crisparkle said. "Come with me to Minor Canon Corner. Mother's gone to bed. I can find you something to eat and we can talk."

I put on my hat and we walked to Minor Canon Corner, which was only a short distance away. Once we were in the kitchen I took my hat off again. Crisparkle went to check that his mother was sleeping. When he returned, he stopped in the doorway and stared at me.

"Your hair! What have you done to it?"

"I cut it."

"Why ever did you do that?"

"So I would look like a man."

"Why would you want to look like a man?"

"So I could ask questions without people knowing who I am."

"You shouldn't be here in Cloisterham," he said,

fetching some cheese from the cupboard. He set it on the table and sat across from me.

"And why not?"

"Because it's dangerous. Don't you realize how worried everyone's been? Mr. Grewgious sent me a message by post that you had run off. He thought you might come here and asked me to keep an eye out for you, but he didn't warn me you might show up in Neville's clothes."

"I'm sorry if I made him worry, but I couldn't tell him because he would have tried to stop me."

"Of course he would have, and so would I. We had no idea you would be so foolhardy, especially right after you and Neville were attacked. I must say I'm surprised at you. I thought you had more sense."

"I had to see what I could find out," I said.

He cut a piece of cheese and laid it in front of me. "And have you found out anything?"

"Jasper took a tour of the cathedral tower and crypt with Durdles less than a week before Edwin Drood disappeared."

He frowned. "You think there's a connection?"

"He drugged Durdles."

"You mean Durdles had too much to drink? There's nothing unusual about that. Durdles frequently has too much to drink. Everyone in Cloisterham knows that."

"This was different," I said. "I'm sure he was drugged. Just as Neville was drugged."

"Why would Jasper drug Durdles?"

"I'm not sure. Maybe to steal his keys. Durdles has keys to the crypt and the tower."

"Also to many of the tombs."

"Then Jasper could have hidden Edwin's body in a tomb?"

"Possibly."

"Couldn't someone search for it?"

"We can't just go about disturbing the dead. The whole town would be up in arms."

I took a bite of cheese half-heartedly. I was not really hungry. "I found his diary tonight. I read some of it, but there was nothing to suggest he murdered Edwin. It was all about how he doted on him."

"And how he vows to get revenge."

"You've seen it?" I asked, surprised.

"He showed that last bit to me. I think he also showed it to the Dean and to Sapsea and maybe to Mr. and Mrs. Tope."

"You think he wrote it for others to read?"

"I have no idea. I advised him to throw it away."

"He didn't."

"You shouldn't have been there," Crisparkle said. "What if he had come home? What if he had caught you reading his diary?"

"He did come home."

"What?"

"I hid. When he was asleep, I slipped out."

"Thank God he didn't see you."

I looked away. In his opium trance, would Jasper know whom he had seen? I hoped not.

"Who is Datchery?" I asked, thinking Crisparkle might know more than I did about this new face in town.

"He's just a retired man looking for a place to settle. Very friendly. Why do you ask?"

"He's watching Jasper," I said.

"Oh, I'm sure you're mistaken."

"And he's asking questions about him."

Crisparkle looked thoughtful. "Then you might be right."

"I have some questions too," I said. "You've lived here all your life?"

"Yes, I was born here," he said. "My father and my six little brothers and sisters are buried in the cathedral cemetery."

"Has Jasper also lived here all his life?"

"No, he came here about six years ago. He must have been about twenty. He was hired to be the new choirmaster. Our last one had died."

"Do you know where he lived before that?"

"No, I don't remember, a small town in the south of England I think, but I do remember his brother-in-law, Edwin's father, helped him get his position here."

"What about Edwin Drood? Did he grow up here?"

"No, his family lived in London. He just came here to visit Jasper and to court Rosa."

"What about Edwin's family?"

"His mother died when he was very young and his father when he was about fifteen. Jasper was appointed his guardian."

"Why is Edwin Drood's father buried in the cemetery?"

"The family had a house here once—Edwin's grandparents. Edwin's father was stationed in India. In fact, he met his wife there. When they came back they settled in London and the house was sold. But he specified in his will that he wanted to be buried here. I guess he thought of it as home."

We had finished the cheese. "I should go now," I said.

"Where?" he asked.

"The Travellers'."

"You can't!" he said. "It's completely inappropriate for a respectable young woman."

"You forget," I said. "I'm not a young woman. I'm Henry Poker." I put my hat back on. "Besides, I've stayed there two nights already."

"You can't stay in Cloisterham," Crisparkle said. "You must go back to London. I insist on it. How you've gotten by this long pretending to be a man, I can't imagine. Anyone can see you're not."

"I think I make a very convincing young man," I said. "And, besides, I kind of like being Poker. Neville's clothes are much more comfortable than mine, and no one makes a fuss about my going out after dark."

"Your brother told me that you used to dress up in his clothes and run about with him in the bazaar, but I assure you young women don't do that in England. Not respectable young women."

"That's unfortunate for them."

"You must go back first thing in the morning. Do you have money for the journey?" He began to search his pockets. I stopped him.

"I can't take your money," I said.

"Why not?"

"You have already given so much to Neville that I don't know how we'll ever be able to repay you."

"It was simple Christian charity, as this would be."

"Nevertheless, I can't take it."

"I had no idea you were so obstinate. Proud, yes, but obstinate?" He shook his head. "When all this is over. . . ."

Before he could finish his sentence, there was a noise in the doorway which caused both of us to turn. Old Mrs. Crisparkle stood there, looking small and frail in her sleeping cap with a shawl wrapped around her thin shoulders.

"Mother!" Crisparkle said. "What are you doing up? You'll catch cold."

She squinted at me through her spectacles. "Who's that?"

I held out my hand. "Poker," I said. "My name is Henry Poker."

Looking doubtful, she took it. Her hand felt small and fragile.

"Not much of a name," she sniffed, "but folks can't help the name they're born with." She turned as if to leave us. "For a moment I thought you were that young man Septimus was tutoring."

"No, Mrs. Crisparkle, I'm not him," I assured her.

"Good," she said, "because he drank too much. I don't approve of young men who drink too much, do I, Septimus?"

"No, indeed, Mother."

"Septimus would never come home in such a state. He's always been a good boy."

Mr. Crisparkle reddened and looked uncomfortable.

"Well, I'm glad you're not that other young man—what was his name?"

"Neville, Mother. Neville Landless."

"Although you look a good deal like him."

"I think I'll walk Mr. Poker over to the Travellers' before I turn in," said Mr. Crisparkle. "Will you be all right?"

"Of course I will," she said. "Why shouldn't I be?"

The old lady turned and tottered off toward her bedroom. Mr. Crisparkle and I went outdoors.

"Are you sure you wouldn't prefer to stay at the Crozier?" he asked. "It's much more suitable."

"That's okay," I said. "I don't mind the Travellers'."

"But you *must* go back to London tomorrow," he said. "Mr. Grewgious would never forgive me if I let you stay in Cloisterham."

He looked so determined as he stood there that I couldn't help smiling. I knew that if I stayed, he would probably be so busy hovering over me that others might become suspicious. Datchery already seemed to suspect I wasn't a man. Jasper might even have recognized me. And my money would soon run out. Perhaps it was time to return to London. I could check on Neville and tell him what I had found out so far.

"I think I'll go back to London tomorrow," I said. "I've found out enough for now."

Mr. Crisparkle looked relieved. "Thank goodness." Then he added, "And you must promise not to come back again disguised as a man."

"I won't promise that," I said.

"It's too dangerous," he insisted. "Surely you must realize that."

"I'll be careful."

"Obstinate," he said, shaking his head. He sighed. "Well, you must at least allow me to walk you back to the Travellers'."

It was dark and probably no one would notice, and so to this I agreed.

. . .

The next morning I arose early and was eating breakfast when Deputy spied me sitting at one of the small wood tables that served as dining room for the Travellers' and sauntered over, hands in pockets.

"You leavin', Mr. Poker?" he asked, eyeing my bag.

"I guess I am."

"Got your fill of ruins?"

"For now, but I may be back soon. Would you like the rest of my breakfast?"

He looked at my sausages with interest. "You don't want it?"

"I'm full," I said.

After a quick look around he bolted down the sausages.

"You hear what happened last night?" he asked when he was finished and had wiped his mouth on his sleeve.

"No, what happened?"

"A crime, that's what. Burglary."

"What was stolen?"

"It's not so much what was stolen, but where."

"Where then?"

"The Gate House."

"Mr. Jasper?"

"Nope. Tope."

"Was something stolen?"

"No, but that's because Mr. Tope scared them off."

"Then no one knows who did it?"

"Folks say it was either tramps or one of our boys, but none of our boys steal, 'cause if they did, they'd lose their job here, so it must have been tramps."

"Must have," I agreed.

I wondered what Deputy would say if he knew that the thief was sitting across from him. Without doubt I had had a close call the night before. I was relieved to know Mr. Tope hadn't seen me. Jasper, on the other hand, had but perhaps was too much under the influence of opium to remember. With luck he would think it was something he had dreamed. If he told anyone that Mr. Poker had broken into his rooms, who would believe him? Besides, Mr. Poker would be gone.

12

The cathedral bells were chiming as I left Cloisterham. I spent most of the omnibus ride and then the train ride thinking about Jasper. If he had in fact doted on Edwin as much as he claimed in his diary, then he could not possibly have harmed him. If, however, he had harmed Edwin that night, then the diary was not to be trusted. Had he set about deliberately to persuade Edwin, and the people of Cloisterham, that he was a doting uncle, when in fact he intended to murder his nephew? If so, how long had the pretense gone on? Months? Years? And for what reason? Love of Rosa? Had Jasper been so intent on preventing the marriage of Rosa and Edwin that he had resorted to killing Edwin? Was he a murderer as well as an opium user? Had he murdered Princess Puffer's daughter too? Was he some kind of monster? And did he know it was me who invaded his rooms last night? That was a question I kept coming back to. When he opened his eyes and said, "You!," whom had he seen? Poker, the young stranger about town who was interested in ruins? Helena Landless, sister of the young man whom he hated so much? Or had he seen someone else entirely? Had he mistaken me for Neville, whom everyone said I resembled? Or in his opium daze had he thought he saw someone who was supposed to be dead—Edwin Drood himself?

I was no closer to a solution when I arrived back in London. From the train station I took a cab to the Staple Inn. I would see Mr. Grewgious first and let him know all that I had learned. However, that was not to happen yet. I had just stepped out of the cab when a stranger appeared beside me. He wore loose but respectable clothes and his hat shadowed his face.

"I have been waiting for you, Miss Landless," he said.

With surprise I recognized the young Chinaman who had rescued Neville and me the night of our attack.

He tipped his hat to me. "I have a message from Princess Puffer. If you would be so kind, would you come to her? She has something important to tell you."

"Can't it wait?" I asked. After traveling for over three hours, I had been looking forward to a cup of tea and a bath. Besides, I was anxious to find out how Neville was faring.

"It's your choice," he said with a slight shrug. But he stood there watching me.

I wanted to tell Mr. Grewgious everything I had learned and hear his opinion about what we should do next. I knew he would not approve of me returning to Princess Puffer's opium den. Neither would Mr. Crisparkle. But now my curiosity was aroused. What did Princess Puffer want to tell me? Was it something about

Jasper? Would it get me closer to knowing what had happened that night?

"Where is she—at her opium den?" I asked.

A single nod, almost imperceptible. I could not read his eyes.

"I suppose you'll show me the way?" I said with a sigh.

Another nod, his face hidden by his hat as he leaned down to pick up my bag.

We found a cab in the next street and were soon on our way. Sitting across from Jack as the cab bounced through the streets, I wondered who he was.

"Where do you live?" I asked.

"By the docks," he said, looking out the window.

"Do you work there?"

"When I can."

"Do you have a family?"

"I have a father."

"You're fortunate."

"Am I?" There was bitterness in his voice. "I'm the son of Jack the Chinaman, who runs an opium den in Shadwell across from Princess Puffer. My father's an opium addict who barely knows when I come and go. He only cares about making enough money to pay for his next pipe."

"I'm sorry," I said.

"Princess Puffer is my family."

"Do you smoke opium?"

He shook his head. "Never. I've grown up seeing what it does to people."

"At least you have a father," I said. "I never knew mine."

"Mine would let me starve. Probably I would have starved if it hadn't been for Princess Puffer. She's never had much but when I was hungry she always gave me food. She's the only mother I've ever known."

"What happened to your real mother?" I asked.

"She died when I was little. Somewhere back in China."

"Our mother died when we were little too. But I remember her. I have a picture of her."

"Then you are more fortunate than I," he said. "I have no picture and I remember nothing."

I didn't know what to say. I had always considered it a tragedy that my mother had died. Losing her had seemed much worse than losing my father because I had no memory of him at all. But compared to Jack I did seem fortunate. I couldn't imagine what it would be like to live in a place like Shadwell and to go hungry because there was not enough food. Compared to Jack, I was fortunate indeed. I resolved then and there that if there was any way I could help him I would. After all, he had helped Neville and me the night we were attacked and it was only right that I should repay him somehow.

The buildings grew shabbier and the streets narrower as we neared the docks. The cab stopped between a row of rundown shanties, and Jack and I got out. He paid the cab driver and then led the way to Princess Puffer's.

We climbed the narrow stair that led to her room. This time a scrawny man with a patch over one eye stood guard by it.

"Wait here," Jack said and disappeared inside. In a few minutes he was back. "She has a customer, but you can come in."

I noticed right away the insidious smell of opium. It took a few minutes for my eyes to adjust to the dim room. A tall thin dark-skinned seaman was sprawled sideways across the bed sleeping. Princess Puffer sat nearby in a chair, rocking. Jack pulled up a second chair so rickety I wondered if it would break when I sat on it. Then he squatted on the floor beside us.

The seaman mumbled something in his sleep.

"Don't pay him no mind," Princess Puffer said. "He's on a journey and won't wake up for a while."

"Why did you want to see me?" I asked.

"Want to ask you a favor," Princess Puffer said. "I helped you when you needed it, didn't I, dearie? Well, now, I'd like you to help me." She started coughing and couldn't continue until the fit had passed. "My lungs are bad," she croaked. "Awful bad."

Jack handed her a small dark bottle and she sipped. I wondered if it was laudanum.

"Thankee, Jack," she said. "You're a good boy."

"What favor?" I asked.

"All in good time," Princess Puffer said. "First I have to tell you a story." She closed her eyes and rocked. Jack's hat was off and the candlelight flickered on his face as he watched her. I wondered if he had looked at her like that as a child at her knee.

"I had a daughter," she said. "Her name was Jenny. She was a little younger than Jack. From the time she was a wee little thing she could sing like an angel. She deserved a mother better than me, but I was what she got, and she never complained, good girl that she was. Jack can tell you. They were that close—like brother and sister." She crossed her fingers. "Back when she was growing up, I wasn't smoking. That came later. No, then it was drink. I couldn't help myself. No, it wasn't much of a life for a child. I admit it. But I was that fond of her. She was all I had. I

186

took care of her when I weren't too drunk to, and when I was, she took care of me." The old woman's eyes were bright with tears. "She used to stand on a corner and sing and people would give her money. That's how she met him."

"Who?"

"I didn't know his name."

"Jasper?"

"You can call him that if you want. A gentleman, she said, young, dark, handsome, mysterious. He started showing up regular. Sometimes he would follow her through the streets at night. I tried to warn her. She was only fifteen. He told her he could make her a famous singer. He filled her head with grand ideas. But she was afraid of him too. She said there was something about him which made her blood run cold, something about his eyes and the way he looked at her. She said it was like he was trying to reach into her mind and get ahold of her." Princess Puffer reached out claw-like fingers to grasp at the air.

"What happened to her?"

"She disappeared. One night she didn't come home. That was in November almost two years ago. I never saw her again."

"Did you tell the police?"

"What do they care about girls like my Jenny? Girls who sing on street corners in the East End and disappear aren't no concern of theirs."

"You think Jasper killed her?"

The old woman leaned closer. "I know he killed her."

"You have proof?"

"All the proof I need," she said, rocking.

"Then you should go to the police."

"They wouldn't listen to an old opium smoker like me," she said. "But they would listen to a respectable lawyer."

"Mr. Grewgious? But he's not a criminal lawyer."

"He's a lawyer, ain't he?"

"He handles the legal business for a few estates."

"It don't matter. Tell him the story I told you. Tell him about my Jenny. I only want justice."

"But you don't know that it was Jasper," I protested. "There must be many men in London who fit that description."

"Ah," she said, holding up a bony finger, "but do they all know a Ned who has a sweetheart?"

"What do you mean?"

"I mean the gentleman who frightened my Jenny told her about a boy named Ned, who weren't but a child but he was betrothed to another child. He told her she reminded him of the little girl, Ned's sweetheart."

"Rosa!" I said.

"I don't know any names but Ned," she said. "And it's a common enough name. England is full of Ned's. But then time passed and a certain gentleman comes to me. I've seen him before. He don't come often, but I remember him. There's two things about him that made me wonder if he could be the one—his eyes—yes, he had dark, staring eyes that gave you the shivers. And then there was his voice. Sometimes he sang. He had a lovely voice. The opium didn't take it away. But I told myself there were lots of gentlemen with dark eyes who could sing. Still, I listened whenever he came. I listened closely. They talk when they dream, you know. It can be hard to hear, but

I've had a lot of practice. So when he came, I kept my wits about me, and I listened. There was always a fellow traveler, and always it ended up the same. The fellow traveler died. Sometimes he fell from a high place, sometimes he fell on a spike, and sometimes he was strangled." The old woman nodded. "The details changed, but it was always the same dream, like he was practicing it in his mind. Over and over the fellow traveler died."

"But I still don't see—"

She held up her hand to silence me. "It was that night last December just before Christmas when I heard the fellow traveler's name. It was Ned, and Ned had a sweetheart."

The man lying across the bed moaned softly, startling me. I had forgotten about him. I imagined Jasper lying across her bed in just such a fashion. How could he have fallen so low?

"I wasn't going to let him get away, was I?" Princess Puffer continued. "I followed him. He went to the train station and got on a train and I did too. He got off the train and got in an omnibus and I did too. He got off in Cloisterham, and I did too. But then I lost him. I wandered around all day hoping I might see him again, but no such luck. I'd used up all my money, and I badly needed a smoke—I was getting the all-overs—and then I met a nice young man who gave me three and sixpence. . . ."

At that moment the man on the bed sat bolt upright, his eyes staring into space, clutching at his belt for a weapon that wasn't there. He was a fierce-looking Lascar.

"It's all right," Princess Puffer told him. "You go back to sleep and dream some more."

The man lay down again and flung one arm over his eyes.

"Has Jasper been here again?" I asked.

"The gentleman what I described has been here again. Just three days ago. He stayed away a long time, but I knew he'd be back. Once they get the taste, they have to have more. My mix is good. They won't find better. This time I was ready. When he left in the morning, I followed him again. And this time I found him. I know who he is, respectable choirmaster of Cloisterham. And I'm going to make him pay for what he did."

"Even if he is the same man, you have no proof that he murdered your daughter."

"I want to see him punished before I die," she said stubbornly.

I saw it was useless to argue with her. "All right I'll talk to Mr. Grewgious," I said. "I'll tell him about your daughter. But he may not be able to do anything."

"You just tell him," she said. "Tell it the way I told you."

"Is there anything else I can do for you?" I asked, looking around the dark and dingy room. I was beginning to feel the darkness pressing in on me. I wanted to go back out in the sunlight.

"Just do this one thing, dearie, so I can die peaceful."

"We should go now," Jack said in a low voice. "He's waking up." He nodded toward the man on the bed, whose eyes had just fluttered open.

Once we were out in the air again, I noticed a Chinaman sitting across the way in the doorway of another shanty as rundown as the one we had just left. His chair leaned against the wall behind him and his eyes were closed. He seemed to be sleeping. "Is that your father?" I asked.

"That's him," Jack said.

"Do you live there?"

He shrugged. "I sleep there sometimes."

I couldn't imagine it. "Don't you want to leave this?" I asked, looking about at the squalid street that stank of garbage and sewage.

"I suppose I will one day."

"If you stay too long, you'll end up like Princess Puffer and your father."

"It's not easy to leave. I have nowhere to go. Come on. We have to find a cab."

"You could get a job," I said as we started walking.

"I get work at the docks when I can. It doesn't pay much, but what else can I do? I could sign aboard a ship, but then who'd take care of Princess Puffer? With Jenny gone, I'm all she has."

"Can you read and write?" I asked.

"Some. Jenny taught me what she knew. I taught myself some. It's not much."

"Neville could teach you. He's studying to be a teacher."

He glanced sideways at me. "Why do you want to help me?"

"I don't like to think of you ending up like Princess Puffer."

"Most people don't care. Most people stay clear of this part of London."

"No one should have to live like this," I said, glancing around at the dilapidated shanties crowding the narrow and filthy lane.

"But they do. And not just in London."

I knew he was right. I remembered the beggars in the streets of Colombo.

He looked at me quizzically. "You aren't afraid to come here?"

"No. Well, yes, maybe, a little."

"Can I ask you a question? Do you always dress like a man?"

"No, but there are places where it's unsafe to go as a woman. If I dress as a man, no one questions my right to go there. It's a nuisance always being left behind because I'm a woman."

"And so that's why you were dressed like a man that night with your brother?"

"Yes, it was."

"It didn't keep you from being attacked," he observed.

"No, it didn't. But at least I got to see the backstreets of London by night. Dressed in skirts I never would have been allowed."

We walked for a few minutes in silence. I wondered how far we would have to walk in order to find a cab.

"How's your brother?" he asked.

"I don't know. I was on my way to find out when you asked me to come here."

"You and your brother are close?"

"Yes, very. We're twins, you know."

"I didn't know."

"We're different of course in some ways, but in others we're almost like two halves of the same person. Sometimes I know what he's thinking, and sometimes he knows what I'm thinking. Do you have any brothers or sisters?"

"No, but Jenny was like a sister to me."

"Do you believe Jasper killed her?"

"As you said, there's no proof. If there were proof, he'd be dead. Opium dens are dangerous places. Accidents happen. Princess Puffer always tries to disarm her clients before they smoke, but you never know—the men who go there are a vicious lot. Anything can happen. A knife in the back. . . . a throat slit."

"Why didn't she kill him?"

"She wants to see him hang."

We spotted a cab just then stopped in front of a warehouse. Jack showed the driver we had the fare and he agreed to take us back to Holborn.

"Where were you these last three days?" Jack asked as we sat across from each other in the cab.

"Were you watching for me all that time?"

"I was," he said. "Where were you?"

"Cloisterham."

"That's where he is, isn't it? This man Jasper."

"Yes," I said.

"And in that place you also dress like a man?"

"It was a disguise."

"Why did you need a disguise?"

"So Jasper wouldn't recognize me. So I could move about freely."

"And in this disguise he didn't know you?"

"No, he didn't. At least I don't think he did."

"You don't seem certain."

"I can't be sure."

"You should be careful. He may be dangerous."

"Everyone keeps telling me that."

"Will you go back again?"

"Maybe."

He thought a minute. "Maybe I will also go to Cloisterham."

"Why?" I asked.

"Because of Jenny," he said. "I loved her. We played together. We said we'd get married when we grew up. I'd like to know what happened to her."

13

After the cab had rolled away, I was again standing in front of the Staple Inn with my bag. I entered and climbed the stairs to Mr. Grewgious's chambers. Mr. Bazzard answered the door in response to my knock. He looked astonished when he saw me. Behind him, Mr. Grewgious sprang up from his chair.

"Miss Landless, where have you been?" Mr. Grewgious demanded. "We've all been worried, haven't we, Bazzard?"

"We have indeed," said Bazzard.

"I've been in Cloisterham," I said.

Mr. Grewgious looked at me sternly. "What the devil were you doing in Cloisterham and why are you wearing your brother's clothes?"

"First tell me how Neville is doing," I begged.

"Neville is mending most admirably. He has Rosa and Miss Twinkleton fussing over him like an invalid. In fact, with so much attention lavished on him, he may never want to get well."

Relieved to hear Neville was improving, I spent the

next half hour relating all that I had learned. I told them about the mysterious Mr. Datchery, who was watching Jasper, about Jasper's late night tour of the cathedral crypt and tower with Durdles and how Durdles had been drugged, and about my search of Jasper's room and how I found his diary and what was written in it.

"You ought not to have gone there," said Mr. Grewgious. "It was far too dangerous."

"Far too dangerous," agreed Mr. Bazzard.

"As for Datchery, I hired him to find out what happened to young Edwin Drood."

"You hired him?" I said.

"That's right. Mr. Datchery is a private detective. He comes highly recommended."

So that explained why Mr. Datchery had been watching Jasper so closely. I had not been the only one in disguise. "And has he found out anything?" I asked.

"He has barely had time to begin his investigation," Mr. Grewgious said. "You must have a little patience. Now look here, if Jasper killed Edwin Drood, he's a dangerous man. He has threatened both you and your brother, and may be responsible for the attack on Neville. Rosa could be in danger as well. The poor thing was left in my protection when her parents died, and by God I will protect her." He stood up and paced the room. "As for Jasper's tour that night with Durdles, I already knew about that. Durdles told me himself. I too reached the conclusion that you have reached—that Edwin Drood did not fall into the river or the weir that night but was pushed or thrown from the cathedral tower." He paced back and forth again. "In fact, I have proof."

"Proof?" I could hardly believe it. What proof could there be?

"Shall I show her?" he asked Bazzard.

"I think you should," Bazzard said.

Mr. Grewgious took a ring of keys from his pocket, scowled at them until he found the one he wanted, and used it to open a bureau against the wall. He next opened a little drawer from which he took a very small box and a folded square of black cloth. His hands trembled slightly as he handed me the box.

"Open it," he told me.

I did. Inside was a beautiful ring of diamonds and rubies set in gold and shaped like a rose. "What is it?" I asked, still not understanding.

"That ring belonged to Rosa's mother. It was given to her by Rosa's father when they became engaged. He had it made specially for her. I was there when he removed it from her finger after she had drowned." He stopped and looked out the window for a minute as if the memory still had the power to overwhelm him. "Her father, when he was dying, entrusted it to me, to give to Edwin to put on Rosa's finger at such time as they finalized their marriage plans. The last time I saw Edwin Drood was here in this room. I gave the ring to him—Bazzard was my witness—" (here Bazzard nodded solemnly) "to put on Rosa's finger, if indeed both were agreed to the marriage, and if not, he was to return it to me and it would go back into its drawer. I had some reason to believe the two young people had their doubts about the step that they were taking, and I wanted them to think about the seriousness of what they were doing before it was too late. Marriage is a bond that should not be entered into lightly. Their fathers may have thought their marriage was a good idea, but what did the two young people think?"

"Precisely," Bazzard said. "What did the two young people think?"

"Rosa never mentioned a ring," I said.

"She hasn't seen the ring since her mother died. Edwin didn't give it to her because they mutually agreed not to proceed with the wedding. I'm sure he fully expected to return it to me two days later when I was to arrive in Cloisterham, only by then Edwin himself was nowhere to be found."

"Then how did you get it back?" I asked.

"Just the question to ask," said Bazzard. "Most astute of you, Miss Helena."

"It was found near the cathedral wall, in the graveyard," Mr. Grewgious explained. "I think that's where Edwin fell. Look at the outside of the box."

I closed the box and saw a dirty stain. "Blood?"

"I think so. If I'm right, that's Edwin's blood."

He spread out the black cloth and waited as if he wanted me to notice it. Unfolded, it wasn't a square but a long neck scarf.

"What's that?" I asked.

"Exactly," Bazzard said.

"What would you say if I told you John Jasper was wearing that around his neck the day Edwin Drood disappeared?" Mr. Grewgious said. "What would you say if I told you it was found caught on one of the broken hands of the clock?"

"Then you can prove that Jasper was on the tower that night," I said, excited.

He nodded and sighed. "But unfortunately there's no

proof young Edwin Drood was murdered unless we can find his body. A blood stain on a ring box is not enough."

"What I don't understand is how Edwin's watch and shirt-pin got into the weir," I said.

"No doubt Jasper took them from the body so no one could identify it. He knew Edwin had two pieces of jewelry. He didn't know about the ring. It must have fallen out of Edwin's pocket when he fell."

"The body must be in the graveyard or the crypt," I said.

"Along with many other bodies," Mr. Grewgious said. "Unfortunately it might never be found."

"It may not be the first time Jasper has killed," I told him. "Princess Puffer thinks he killed her daughter."

Mr. Grewgious blinked. "Does she indeed? Why didn't you tell me this before?"

"I only found out about it today."

I told him how Jack had met me upon my arrival, and I had gone to Shadwell again. Mr. Grewgious let out a groan but did not interrupt me until I had told him the whole story I had heard from Princess Puffer about her daughter Jenny.

"How long ago did this happen?"

"Two years ago."

"Another disappearance," he said. "And no more proof that the girl is dead than Edwin."

He carefully folded the scarf and put it and the ring box back in the little drawer and locked the bureau again.

"You are probably wondering how these things came to be in my possession." He cleared his throat. "They were found by Durdles on the morning after the storm. It was Durdles who had to go up on the roof, Durdles who found the black scarf caught on the face of the clock. Others thought the storm had broken the hands, but I think Edwin Drood, struggling for his life, broke them. Durdles recognized the scarf right away. He knew if he gave it to Sapsea it would be handed back to Jasper. So he slipped it in his pocket. When Drood turned up missing, Durdles searched the ground at the base of the cathedral, directly beneath the clock. That's when he found the box with the ring inside.

"Rosa was the one who wrote to me about Edwin's disappearance and begged me to come to Cloisterham as soon possible. She told me in her letter how the engagement had been broken off the night Edwin disappeared. As you know, he had wanted me to break the news to Jasper to lessen the shock. When I went to find him, Jasper was out with the volunteers who were searching for the body, so I used my time to find out what I could. Mr. Sapsea told me it was almost a certainty that your brother had done away with Edwin Drood. The whole town believed it. Mr. Crisparkle thought Edwin might have gone back to the river and fallen in by accident.

"I was leaving Minor Canon Corner when a particularly dusty-looking man stopped me on the street and asked if he might have a word with me. He said he had found something valuable but he didn't know who had lost it and wanted my advice on how to locate its owner. I thought it a peculiar request and would have turned away except for something urgent in his manner. He then showed me the box. Of course I recognized it at once. I lost no time opening it to see if the ring was inside and found it was. I told him I knew its owner and asked how it had come to be in his possession. He explained how he had found it at the base of the cathedral after the storm. Then he said he had found something else that day and showed me the scarf. He had seen Jasper wearing just such a black scarf around his neck the day before Edwin disappeared. It seemed to me only too clear what had happened to Edwin Drood. But no one in Cloisterham would believe us when they all thought Jasper doted on his nephew. I knew better. I knew there was some reason Rosa feared him, and I had thought his reactions odd that evening I informed him of Edwin and Rosa's arrangements for formalizing their engagement. Mr. Durdles, it seemed, also had reason to suspect Jasper. We agreed that I would keep the ring and the scarf until such time as they might be needed. In the meantime I promised to do all I could to find out what had happened. To those ends I hired Mr. Datchery, who was recommended to me by Scotland Yard.

"Before leaving Cloisterham, I went to Jasper as promised to inform him that the engagement had been broken. I could not help thinking that here was a man who had, in all likelihood, murdered his nephew three days before in order to be rid of a rival. He might fool all of Cloisterham with his frenzied efforts to find Edwin, but he did not fool me. Mr. Tope let me into Jasper's rooms, where I sat looking at a rather impertinent portrait of my ward mounted over the chimneypiece while I waited for him to return. When at last he entered and collapsed into his easy chair, exhausted and covered with mud, I felt no sympathy. When he learned that the engagement had been broken that night, that Edwin and Rosa had agreed to part, that in fact there would have been no marriage after all, he fell to the floor in a sort of fit. I summoned Mr. and Mrs. Tope, but I felt no sympathy."

"You think he murdered Edwin to prevent his marriage to Rosa?" I asked.

"I do. Everything points to it. And if Edwin had just told him that on Christmas Eve over dinner, he might still be alive today. I'm afraid Edwin's reluctance to break the news to his uncle led to his own tragic death. And as Jasper has since discovered, even with his rival gone, he has no hope of persuading Rosa to marry him. To commit murder!—and all for naught." He shook his head at the senselessness of it.

"Surely there is some way to bring him to justice," I said.

"Perhaps, but you must leave that for us," Mr. Grewgious said. "It is much too dangerous for you."

"Are there still watchers?" I asked, looking across the street at the second-floor window where I had once seen Jasper lurking.

"They may be there even if we don't see them. So long as Jasper is about, neither you, nor Neville, nor Rosa are safe."

Bazzard cleared his throat. "Sir, you haven't mentioned the Indian."

Mr. Grewgious sighed. "Ah, yes, I mustn't forget the Indian."

"What Indian?" I asked.

"A mysterious man, clearly foreign, dressed all in white with a turban wrapped around his head who came here yesterday looking for you and your brother. I told him I was acting as your guardian until you come of age and until then he must deal with me. He said he had something for you but was instructed to deliver it only into your hands.

As you were not here, whatever it was went away with him again."

"What do you think it was?"

"I have no idea," Mr. Grewgious said wearily. "But we must be careful. It could be a trick. Jasper could have hired him to find out where you are. Or even to kill you."

I looked at Bazzard. "Oh, yes," he said, looking very serious.

"And now, my dear, I'm sure you're anxious to see your brother. However, perhaps you would like to freshen up first? Your trunk is still upstairs where you left it, although we took the liberty of sending Neville's clothes to him."

"A dress perhaps?" Bazzard suggested.

"Oh, yes, a dress. Excellent suggestion," said Mr. Grewgious.

"But won't the watchers recognize me if I wear a dress?" I asked.

"Yes, they might," agreed Mr. Grewgious. "However, I doubt your present attire would meet with Miss Twinkleton's approval, and since we want to keep her good opinion, it would be wise for you to wear a dress."

"I quite agree," Bazzard said.

And so thirty minutes later, I reappeared in Mr. Grewgious's office in one of my dresses and wearing a hat. There was not much I could do about my hair now that it had been cut except cover it up, but Mr. Grewgious seemed satisfied. I told him I could go alone to Mrs. Billickin's, or Bazzard could take me, but he insisted on escorting me and Bazzard was sent to find a cab. Once it pulled up to the door, Mr. Grewgious and I rushed out, climbed in, and were swept away, whirling around several corners in an attempt to foil any watchers who might try to give chase.

Rosa was overjoyed to see me again when I showed up at Bloomsbury Square. "You naughty thing to run off like that and tell no one where you were going," she said after hugging me tightly. "Where have you been? We thought you'd been abducted and shipped off to a slave harem."

Before I could answer, Miss Twinkleton emerged from her sitting room. "Oh, thank heaven, you're safe," she said and then clapped her hand to her mouth to stifle a small cry. "My dear, what has happened to your hair?"

"I cut it," I said, removing my hat so she could get the full effect.

"Your beautiful hair," Miss Twinkleton said and looked as if she might cry.

"Never mind," Rosa said. "It's not as bad as that. If the other girls at school see it, they'll all be wanting to cut theirs too. In fact, I've half a mind to cut mine too."

"You shall do no such thing," said Miss Twinkleton, aghast.

Mr. Grewgious cleared his throat. "We've come to see the young invalid. How is he doing?"

"It's a wonder he isn't dead, considering what poor fare *she* feeds him," said Mrs. Billickin, who had just emerged from her back parlor to see what all the commotion was.

Miss Twinkleton, looking offended, turned to Rosa. "Kindly tell *a certain person* that I do the best I can considering what poor pickings London offers."

"They bicker constantly," Rosa told me in a low voice. "They haven't been speaking to each other for days now, and I'm caught in the middle. It's so ridiculous." She linked arms with me as we climbed the stairs. "Neville's coming along fine, the doctor says. I'm so glad he's here. Otherwise, there'd only be Mrs. Billickin and Miss Twinkleton firing shots at each other over my head. Neville gives me someone nearer my own age to talk to. You're ever so lucky, Helena, to have a brother. I'm terribly envious of you. Every girl ought to have a brother, I think. But since I don't, I've decided you must share Neville with me. You don't mind, do you?"

"Not a bit," I said. And I was sure Neville had no objections either.

He met us at the top of the stairs, his arm still in a sling and a bandage wrapped around his temple. "Here you are at last," he said. "Where have you been? I've been worried to death. You didn't go back there, did you?"

"Where?"

"To the opium den. Mr. Grewgious said he fetched us from an opium den in the East End. When you disappeared, I thought maybe you had gone back there. It would be just like you, rushing back to see if you could get into some more trouble."

"That isn't like me at all," I said. "I've been to Cloisterham to try to clear you."

"Even worse," said Neville. "Don't you know there may be a murderer loose in Cloisterham?"

"I don't think you missed me at all," I said.

"He did," Rosa insisted. "He asked every hour of every day where you were, and I had to keep making excuses for you."

"Like a true friend," I said, smiling.

"Well, I should hope so," Rosa said. "Now tell us, did you find out anything?"

"Nothing definite," I said.

"You shouldn't take such chances," Neville said. "Did Jasper give you any trouble?"

"I disguised myself."

"You wore my clothes?"

"Well, how else was I going to find out anything?"

"You're so much braver than I," Rosa said. "I could never go back, not so long as *he* is there." She shuddered.

"I'm glad to see you're better now," I told Neville.

"The doctor says it will take a few weeks for my arm to mend, and I'm to take it easy until then. He said I'm lucky I have such a thick head."

"Indeed you are," I agreed. He smiled then.

"Neville's trying to teach me Greek," Rosa said, "but I don't think I'll ever make sense of it. I'm quite hopeless."

"Nonsense," said Neville. "It just takes a while to catch on. Ask Helena. She knows almost as much Greek as I do, more probably because it comes so easy to her."

"It doesn't come easy," I protested.

"And Rosa is teaching me to play the piano," said Neville. "One-handed of course."

I could see he was happy to be so near Rosa. Gone was the gloom that had enveloped him at Staple Inn. Perhaps a broken arm and a blow to the head were a small price to pay to be so near her. Rosa hovered about him like a little bird.

Miss Twinkleton put her head into the room to tell us we were wanted in the parlor. Mr. Grewgious had something to tell us. We followed Miss Twinkleton down and found Bazzard and Mrs. Billickin seated in the wing chairs waiting. We found chairs of our own and gave Mr. Grewgious, who was standing, our full attention.

"Now that everyone's here," Mr. Grewgious said, "I want to make a suggestion. There might be a way to find out what happened the night Edwin Drood died, at least the part of it that Neville witnessed." He exchanged conspiratorial glances with Bazzard. "Actually it was Bazzard's idea. Bazzard is a man of many talents whom I am very fortunate to have in my employ."

"Very kind of you, sir," said Bazzard.

"My cousin is much undervalued, I fear," Mrs. Billickin said to no one in particular. "He has a remarkable mind."

"Indeed," Mr. Grewgious said. "I have always known Bazzard was intended for higher things. It is a mere quirk of fate that he toils as my clerk."

"What is your idea?" Neville asked politely to bring him back to the point.

"Mr. Bazzard's idea," Mr. Grewgious corrected him.

"What is Mr. Bazzard's idea?" Neville asked.

"Animal magnetism," Mr. Grewgious said.

Bazzard grinned and nodded his head enthusiastically.

"Perhaps you've heard of Dr. Molesworth?" Mr. Grewgious looked around at us hopefully. We had not. "Dr. Molesworth is a practitioner of animal magnetism. He has used it on several of his patients to help relieve headaches and difficulties sleeping. Dr. Molesworth recently delivered a lecture which Bazzard had the good fortune to hear. In his lecture he explained that he has observed in his patients that there seem to be two states of consciousness, one while magnetized and the other when not. It seems a person can do things under the influence of magnetism that he cannot remember when awakened, but if he is magnetized again, he will remember them. The same principle applies sometimes in cases of drunkenness. A person may lose his hat or his key while drunk and not remember where he put it until he is drunk again. It then occurred to Bazzard that we might try such a method to find out what Neville has forgotten about that night he dined with Drood and Jasper. We have asked Dr. Molesworth, and he said he would be willing to try. It is of course up to you, Neville. What do you think? Would you be willing to try such an experiment?"

We all looked at Neville. "But I wasn't magnetized that night," he objected.

"Are you sure you weren't?" asked Mr. Grewgious.

"Surely I would know if I had been."

"Would you?" Mr. Grewgious turned to me. "Helena, what do you think?"

"I think the wine was drugged," I said without hesitation.

Miss Twinkleton gasped and looked as if she might faint. She began to fan herself with her hand.

"My apologies, Madam," Mr. Grewgious said. "I did not mean to distress you."

Rosa ran for the smelling salts, and soon Miss Twinkleton was restored to herself.

"Miss Landless is right," Mr. Grewgious said. "We have reason to believe there was laudanum in the wine."

"Laudanum!" said Rosa.

"Oh, my," said Miss Twinkleton.

"I suspected it all along," declared Mrs. Billickin.

"Then isn't that what I should drink again to recall the events of that night?" said Neville.

"An excellent suggestion," Mr. Grewgious said. "Just

what Dr. Molesworth recommended. However, I think Jasper also practices magnetism. I think he attempted to practice it on Rosa."

Miss Twinkleton again let out a gasp and looked dangerously pale.

"Would you prefer not to hear more, Madam?" Mr. Grewgious asked, turning to her with concern.

"Please continue," Miss Twinkleton said. "Rosa has been like a daughter to me since she was seven years old. I wish to know everything that concerns her. I feel responsible. I allowed that man into the seminary to give singing lessons to the girls. I allowed him to give singing lessons to Rosa."

"You had no way of knowing," Mr. Grewgious said. "Don't blame yourself. He has managed to deceive all of Cloisterham as to his true nature."

"So you think he magnetized me as well as drugged me?" Neville asked.

"I do," Mr. Grewgious said.

"As do I," said Bazzard.

"Do you think he also magnetized and drugged Edwin Drood?" Neville asked.

Mr. Grewgious looked at Rosa, who stopped ministering to Miss Twinkleton to hear his answer. "I do," he said again.

"What if Mr. Neville killed Mr. Drood and doesn't remember it?" Mrs. Billickin asked.

"He didn't," I said quickly, rushing to Neville's defense. I knew the same thought was going through Neville's mind. It had nagged him since Edwin's disappearance. It was his secret fear. He believed he had not killed Edwin Drood. He did not remember killing him. But suppose he had done it, as Mr. Grewgious explained, in an alternate state of consciousness and did not remember? To be magnetized meant running the risk of finding out that he himself might be the murderer.

"Of course he didn't kill Edwin," Rosa said. "How could you think it for a minute?"

Neville threw her a look of gratitude and took a deep breath. "I'll do it," he said. "I'll let your Dr. Molesworth magnetize me. I want to know the truth about what happened that night."

I was proud of Neville. I knew it had taken courage for him to say that.

Just then someone rapped sharply on the door. Mrs. Billickin hoisted herself up from her chair and laboriously made her way from the room, so laboriously in fact that the caller rapped again before she got there. We listened intently while she answered the door, but not until another minute had passed did we learn who had arrived. She returned at her usual limping gait, brought on by an assortment of aches and pains, followed by Mr. Tartar.

"Tartar! How good to see you!" said Neville, springing up to shake hands with his one good hand.

"Mr. Grewgious told me where you are and so I came to see how you are doing." Tartar stood in the doorway holding his hat in his hand.

"Mending very well, thank you," Neville said.

Tartar looked around the room at the rest of us, beaming with delight. "And I see you found Miss Landless."

"She found us," said Mr. Grewgious.

"I've been keeping your bean plants watered for when you come back," he told Neville.

"I don't know when that will be," Neville said.

"It isn't safe so long as Jasper is about," Mr. Grewgious said, "and in fact I must find a safer place for your sister."

"Oh, have her stay here," Rosa urged. "It'd be ever so much fun, all three of us under the same roof."

"I'm afraid that might be a bit crowded for Mrs. Billickin." He looked at that good lady, who had just managed to lower herself into her chair again.

"It would," Mrs. Billickin agreed.

"There you are," Mr. Grewgious said, slapping his hand on his knee. "We'll have to find someplace else."

"Nearby I hope," Rosa said, "so we can see each other frequently. Oh, it would be perfect. Two companions of my own age." She glanced shyly at Mr. Tartar. "Then perhaps we could all go up the river together sometime."

"Yes," said Mr. Tartar. "When Neville's arm is mended, I can teach him to row."

Neville looked from Tartar to Rosa, from Rosa to Tartar. I felt a sinking feeling inside of me.

"Mr. Tartar keeps a boat at the Temple Stairs," Rosa said, blushing. "It's ever so pleasant to go up the river where everything is green and pleasant and flowers are blooming."

"Ah, yes," said Mr. Grewgious. "Bazzard, have you been up the river lately?"

"No, indeed," said Bazzard. "I fear I'm not nautical."

"Nor I," said Mrs. Billickin. "Dry land for me."

"And you, Miss Twinkleton?" asked Mr. Grewgious. "Are you nautical?"

"When I was young perhaps, yes, I believe I was, but that was quite a long time ago. I barely remember."

"And were you ever up the river?" Neville asked Rosa.

She blushed even more deeply and kept her eyes on a design in the carpet. "Mr. Tartar and his man Mr. Lobley kindly took Mr. Grewgious and me on my first day in London."

I could see Neville turning this over in his mind. He had not seen Tartar and Rosa together before. Tartar's eyes would circle the room, but it was always on Rosa that they came to rest. Rosa had never before blushed so frequently. She stole glances at Tartar and almost knocked a small ornamental shepherdess off a table beside her.

Poor Neville. He was so enamored of Rosa, and he had thought perhaps she was enamored of him, but he never made Rosa blush like that. She never grew so confused when he was near. She didn't look at him the way she looked at Tartar. It was a blow for him.

I looked out the lace curtained window to distract myself from the hurt in Neville's eyes. The windowpane was begrimed, making the street outside look begrimed as well. The houses across the way looked begrimed, as did the people walking by, and the passing carriages. The only thing that didn't look begrimed was the Indian man across the way, dressed in immaculate white from his turban to his sandaled feet as he stood there like a vision, patiently watching Mrs. Billickin's house.

I wondered if I should say something to the people around me and call their attention to him. I was sure he must be the Indian man who had inquired of Mr. Grewgious about us. But how had he found us at Mrs. Billickin's, where we thought we were safely hidden? And what did he want?

Mr. Grewgious cleared his throat and I realized I was not paying attention. I glanced over at Neville to see if I could catch his eye, but he had sunk back in his chair gloomily focused on his own thoughts. Mr. Grewgious rubbed his hands together in anticipation. "And now I have an announcement to make," he declared. "Don't I, Bazzard?"

"I suppose you do, sir," Bazzard said.

Mr. Grewgious rocked back and forth on his heels, as if he could not decide how to begin.

"Well, what is it?" Rosa said.

"Bazzard has some good news," Mr. Grewgious said. "Some very good news."

We all looked at Bazzard, who said nothing but sat straighter in his chair.

When Bazzard did not speak, Mr. Grewgious took a deep breath and spoke for him. "Bazzard has written a play."

He waited expectantly until Miss Twinkleton murmured, "Oh, my."

Apparently satisfied with this reaction, he continued. "In fact, Bazzard has written a tragedy." He looked around at all of us triumphantly, as if he had written it himself. "And what is the title of this play?"

We had no idea.

"The Thorn of Anxiety," Mr. Grewgious said, drawing it out as if that were the most astonishing thing of all.

Bazzard nodded solemnly to confirm this was indeed the title.

"Until now no one has been willing to bring it out," Mr. Grewgious informed us, "a source of much disappointment to the author."

"Until now," echoed Bazzard, looking around at us significantly.

"Oh, you've found someone!" said Rosa, clapping her hands together.

"I have," said Bazzard.

"Someone who could never write a play himself," said Mr. Grewgious, "but who could be of small service to another more gifted." He bowed to Bazzard and Bazzard bowed back.

"I thank you," said Bazzard. "You won't regret it, sir."

"Oh, that is good of you, Mr. Grewgious," said Miss Twinkleton.

"We have a theatre," said Mr. Grewgious. "We have a contract with the theatre owner. We have an arrangement. We have, in short, everything except the actors."

"And where do you get those?" Rosa asked innocently.

Mr. Grewgious looked slowly around the room at us.

"Us?" said Neville. "Are you serious?" He apparently forgot for a moment that his heart had just been broken.

"Oh, it would be such fun," said Rosa.

"But what of Jasper?" asked Miss Twinkleton. "Is it safe to act in a play when he's prowling about?"

Mr. Grewgious held up a hand. "Just what I asked myself. What of Jasper?"

"I'm not afraid of him," Neville said. "I don't want to live my life hiding from him."

"I won't lie to you," Mr. Grewgious said. "There would be some risk. But if we are careful, he need not find out, and I think a play might be just the thing to pick you all up. It's time we brushed the cobwebs off and let some fresh air in. Bazzard will get his play performed and you will have something else to think about besides murder and missing persons."

"What is the play about?" asked Rosa.

"Will there be a part for everybody?" asked Neville, sitting straighter. Evidently he did not think his bandaged head or broken arm should be an impediment.

"Yes, there will be a part for everybody," Mr. Grewgious assured him.

Everyone began to talk excitedly.

Now that we were interested, Mr. Grewgious sat back in his chair and let Bazzard answer all our questions. Looking around the room, I was glad to be back with friends again. How clever Mr. Grewgious was! Just when Neville and Rosa were beginning to tire of their confinement, he came up with this idea of putting on a play. Of course it would help Bazzard too. That was so like Mr. Grewgious, who underneath his awkwardness and dryness was one of the most generous people I had ever encountered. He was right. A play would be just the thing to take our minds off our troubles. I would forget Jasper and Cloisterham for a while. I would have some fun. Wasn't that exactly what Edwin would have recommended if he were there with us? I was sure he would have loved putting on a play.

I forgot all about the Indian man until some thirty minutes later when I was leaving with Mr. Grewgious and Bazzard, and by then he had disappeared as completely as if he had only been a figment of my imagination after all. I looked up and down the street, but since he was nowhere to be seen, I didn't tell anyone about him.

14

That night I slept again in the attic rooms at Staple Inn that I had shared with Neville. At nine o'clock in the morning Mr. Grewgious and I fetched Neville from Mrs. Billickin's and made our way by cab to Dr. Molesworth's brick house in Kensington.

A dour-faced maid admitted us and led us to the doctor's study, a gloomy room lined with shelves of books. I noticed a skull sitting on his desk and tried not to stare at it. Dr. Molesworth was a short, beady-eyed man with a shiny dome of a head and a monocle. He directed Neville to an armchair in the center of the room while Mr. Grewgious and I were seated in chairs against the wall, where we would not distract Neville.

I had heard about animal magnetism, but I had not previously seen a demonstration of it, nor had Neville. I sensed his nervousness as he sat waiting for Dr. Molesworth to begin.

"Will I remember what I said afterward?" he asked.

"Only if I tell you to," said the doctor.

"Then please tell me to. I would like to know what I said."

"Very well."

Neville looked at me. I gave him what I hoped was an encouraging smile.

The dour-faced maid brought in a glass of wine on a silver tray. We watched as Dr. Molesworth carefully measured a few drops of laudanum into the wine. He then handed the glass to Neville.

"We must try to re-create your state of mind that night as nearly as possible if we are to be successful in our experiment," he explained. "Since Mr. Grewgious tells me you may have been given laudanum, it's necessary to give it to you again. Otherwise you may not remember the night exactly as it was."

As Neville drank the wine, a grandfather clock in the corner of the room began to chime. "Now what?" he said as he handed back the glass.

The doctor placed a low stool in front of him and sat down on it. "I want you to give me your full attention," he told Neville. "I want you to look into my eyes. Under no circumstances are you to look away. Do you understand?"

Neville nodded. Dr. Molesworth leaned forward and began to make passes with his hands in the air in front of Neville's face. Mr. Grewgious and I watched silently as the doctor and Neville stared into each other's eyes and the doctor's hands darted smoothly in and out, never quite touching Neville. He kept this up for perhaps ten minutes, then abruptly stopped. Neville stared straight ahead. Dr. Molesworth waved a hand in front of his eyes, but Neville didn't blink.

"Is he mesmerized?" Mr. Grewgious asked.

"He is," said Dr. Molesworth. "What do you wish me to ask him?"

"Ask him to tell us about last Christmas Eve when he dined with John Jasper and Edwin Drood."

The doctor nodded. "Neville, I'm going to ask you to go back in your mind to last Christmas Eve. Tell us what you remember of that night."

Neville's face took on a troubled look.

"I don't . . . ."

"Don't what?"

"I don't want to go."

"You must," said the doctor. "You must go back."

"I . . . I don't want to go to Jasper's."

I held my breath. My chest felt tight with anxiety. I was tempted to jump up and put a stop to the experiment, but I forced myself to stay seated.

"Why not?" the doctor asked.

"I'm afraid . . . ."

"Afraid of what?"

"Afraid of what might happen."

"What might happen?"

"I don't know. Something bad."

"Look around you," Dr. Molesworth said. "Tell me what you see."

Neville frowned in concentration. "I see the archway of the Gate House. I see the postern stair that leads to Jasper's rooms."

"Very good. What else?"

"There's a storm coming. There are dark clouds over the river. The air feels strange."

"Go on."

"I hear the cathedral clock chime. I don't want to go in,

but I suppose I must. Helena wants me to. Mr. Crisparkle will be disappointed if I don't. It's all been arranged."

If only I hadn't pushed him to go that night! If only we could turn back time and do it differently! Edwin would still be alive and Neville would not be suffering as he was.

"What happens next?"

"I climb the stair. No one answers my knock, but the door is unlocked so I let myself in."

"What do you see?"

"Jasper's sitting room. No one else is there. I'm alone."

"What do you do?"

"I leave my walking stick by the door. I look at the portrait of Rosebud over the chimneypiece. I push a few piano keys. I look at the portrait of Rosebud again."

Dr. Molesworth threw a glance at us to see if we understood and Mr. Grewgious nodded.

"Can you describe this portrait of Rosebud?"

He sighed. "She's beautiful. She's an angel."

"What happens next?"

"Edwin Drood arrives."

"How does he seem? Is there anything unusual about him?"

"No. Yes. He seems quieter, more thoughtful."

"What do you talk about?"

"He asks me about my walking stick. I tell him I'm leaving on a walking tour in the morning. He asks if my sister is going too. 'No, I'm going alone,' I tell him. He picks up my walking stick—my staff—and swings it about. 'It's too heavy,' he says. 'Ironwood, isn't it? You'll get tired of carrying it.'"

"Do you talk about anything else?"

219

"He tells me he had a strange experience on the way. He asks if I believe in omens. I say, 'I do.'"

"What happens next?"

"Jasper arrives."

"How does he seem? Is there anything unusual about him?"

"No. He seems in very good spirits. We hear him singing as he comes up the stairs."

"Tell everything you remember."

"He takes off his hat and coat and scarf. He tells his nephew how much he missed him and how happy he is to see him, how good it is of him to come. He asks if Edwin—he calls him Ned—has anything to tell him. Edwin says he almost got run down by a cab one week ago, but I don't think that's what Jasper meant. Jasper offers us drinks. I remember that his wine led to near blows the last time and try to decline.

"'You must! I insist. It would be inhospitable,' Jasper says. 'Ned is not afraid to drink my wine, are you, Ned?'

"'Indeed not, Jack.'

"'Then neither am I,' I say.

"Jasper notices my walking stick. 'What's this?'

"'I'm off on a walking tour tomorrow.'

"'Rather heavy, isn't it?'

"'So everybody tells me.'

"'Well, never mind. I'm sure it will come in quite handy. And now let's see what Mrs. Tope has cooked for us.' He steps to the table and lifts the covers off two platters. 'Look, here's lamb and potatoes. Ned, you must eat up. How many more meals will we share before you're off to Cairo? Ah, how I envy you, with your whole life ahead of you, an adventure, and little Rosebud by your side. A toast!

To Rosebud! To the bride-to-be.' We toast. Although I don't like the idea that she'll be his bride. I still think he doesn't deserve her. But I try to hide my feelings.

"'Another toast,' says Edwin Drood. 'To your sister, Mr. Neville, Helena of Troy.'

"I ask him what he means. I suspect he is being impertinent.

"'I only meant that she is beautiful,' he says.

"I decide to let it pass. We toast again.

"Then Jasper draws our attention to the food. 'Mrs. Tope has quite outdone herself. Have some more gravy? You don't know how it warms my heart to see you two young men overcoming your differences. We should sing a song now. Let's move to the piano. But first another toast. To the future. Ah, how I envy both of you, your lives ahead of you.'

"'You're not old, Uncle Jack,' says Edwin.

"'But it's too late for me. The die is cast. Here I am and here I will remain. A choirmaster. Never anything more. No grand adventures.'

"'Don't get gloomy, Jack.'

"'You're right. Tonight's a cause of celebration. Let's see, we toasted the future. Let's toast the past.'

"'The past, Jack?'

"'Yes, the past. I remember when you were just a little thing. I taught you to play cricket.'

"'You're getting sentimental now,' Edwin says.

"'Not at all.'

"'All right we'll toast the past.'

"'The past is important. When you're young, you don't realize that. The past is where we've been, what we are. So many people have no idea who they are.'"

Neville stopped. In the silence I could hear the ticking of the grandfather clock.

"What's the matter?" Dr. Molesworth asked.

"I don't feel well," Neville said.

"You feel sick?"

"The room is going 'round. I thought I saw . . . ."

"What do you think you saw?"

"I thought I saw a bird sitting on the music stand. A large beautiful bird with red and green feathers. He was looking straight at me."

"Perhaps you had too much to drink."

Neville scowled. "Need some air," he said thickly. "That's thunder, isn't it? The storm is getting closer. We'll watch it roll in, down by the river. Just Drood and I. Jasper too tired. 'You young men go on and get some exercise. Don't forget your walking stick.'"

"Go on," said Dr. Molesworth.

"We go down the stairs. It seems much harder going down than coming up. The stairs are steeper. My feet feel heavier. It seems to take forever to get to the bottom. Now we're outside. The wind is blowing. It takes my hat and Edwin and I have to chase after it. I feel drops of rain on my face. I can feel each separate drop as it falls. I think I have never really noticed how a raindrop feels before. A fork of lightning rips across the night sky. 'Blow winds and crack your cheeks! Rage! Blow!' I shout into the night. Edwin laughs. He says all evening he has felt oppressed, like something bad was going to happen, but now he feels as if a weight has been lifted. 'I don't know what the future holds,' he says. 'Always before I knew, and now I don't.'

"I think I know what he means. Everything seems different somehow. The houses are different, the bricks in the street are different. It's like the whole world has been stretched or tilted. The very horizon seems farther off. When we get to the river, the waves loom high like ocean waves. I feel as if I might see all the way to India if I look hard enough. And the water seems closer—like a road you can step out on. The lightning flashes brighter than I've ever seen it before, and the thunder is deafening. 'Blow, winds, and crack your cheeks!'"

"What happens next?" Dr. Molesworth asked.

"It starts to rain."

"And then?"

"We turn around and come back."

Mr. Grewgious leaned forward. "Both of you? Are you sure?"

Dr. Molesworth threw a disapproving look at Mr. Grewgious for interrupting. "Both of you returned?" he asked.

"Yes, he walked me back to Minor Canon Corner. We said good-bye there. He said he had half a mind to join me on my walking tour in the morning. I had the feeling he didn't want to leave, but then it began to rain harder, and so we said goodnight."

"You parted amicably?"

"Yes."

Dr. Molesworth turned to Mr. Grewgious. "Is there anything else you would like me to ask?"

Mr. Grewgious shook his head. "I think we've heard all he knows."

"Miss Landless?"

I shook my head. I was trembling. It was as if I had seen Edwin Drood in front of me, saying goodnight to Neville. He had walked off into the rain. It was only a short distance from there to the Gate House. Somewhere Jasper was waiting for him.

"When you awake, you will remember all that you have told me," Dr. Molesworth said. "And now awake!"

Neville blinked. He reached one hand to his head as if he felt dizzy or had a headache. "Now I remember," he said. "Why didn't I remember before? How could I have forgotten so much?"

"If your Mr. Jasper magnetized you that night, he may have suggested that you forget everything that happened," explained Dr. Molesworth.

"But I don't remember him magnetizing me," Neville said.

"He might have done it without your being aware. Some magnetizers can do it with just their eyes or by projecting their thoughts. I have even heard of magnetizers who can project their thoughts to someone in a different room."

This was a frightening piece of information. I thought of Jasper's eyes, so dark, so smoldering. I remembered how he had looked at Rosa that night at Minor Canon Corner, as if he could control her with his gaze. Had he magnetized Rosa? No, I didn't think so. If she had truly been under his control, she would not have broken down. Something protected Rosa from him, maybe her innocence or sweetness. But perhaps he had been more successful with the two young men, especially when they were under the influence of his wine.

"But we still don't know who killed Edwin Drood," said Neville.

"We know *you* didn't," said Mr. Grewgious.

"That's right, I didn't, did I?" Neville looked relieved.

We accompanied him back to Bloomsbury Square then, after which Mr. Grewgious and I returned to the Staple Inn. There Bazzard was waiting with a letter marked URGENT that had arrived by post. Mr. Grewgious read it with an impassive expression. "It's from Crisparkle," he announced when he had finished. "A body has been found."

15

Mr. Grewgious scowled at his watch. "I suppose I should leave at once."

"I suppose you should," Bazzard said.

"If you please, sir, I'd like to go too," I said.

"I don't think that would be a good idea," Mr. Grewgious said. "I quite understand your concern, but we must think of your safety. Cloisterham might not be safe for you."

"No, it might not be," Bazzard agreed.

"If you don't let me go with you," I said, "I'll go on my own."

"What?" said Mr. Grewgious. "You would run off again? Don't you understand how dangerous that could be?"

"Well, then I'll go as Poker."

"Who's Poker?"

"He's a young man interested in Cloisterham's ruins. In fact, they say he's writing a book."

Mr. Grewgious tried to hide a smile. "Is he now?" Then

he turned serious again. "You mean you intend to dress up in your brother's clothes again? Do you really think you can pass yourself off as a man as easily as that? Because I very much doubt it."

"I can," I said. "I have."

"What would Miss Twinkleton say if I let you do such a thing?"

"She doesn't have to know."

"Bazzard, what do you say?"

"Miss Helena seems determined to go," said Bazzard. "Maybe it would be safer for her to go as Poker."

Mr. Grewgious looked from him to me and sighed. "Oh, very well. You're probably right. If I say no, she'll go anyway. I might as well take her with me. At least I can keep an eye on her."

And so it was that I returned to Cloisterham once more as Henry Poker.

It was midafternoon when the omnibus rolled into Cloisterham. After disembarking, Mr. Grewgious and I walked to Minor Canon Corner. Mr. Crisparkle opened the door for us and his eyes widened when he saw me.

"Miss Landless," he said, "I really didn't expect to see you back so soon."

"It would be better for you to address me as Mr. Poker," I suggested.

"I tried to reason with her," Mr. Grewgious said, sighing. "It didn't do any good. And so here we are."

"Well, come in," said Mr. Crisparkle. "I had a feeling I hadn't seen the last of Henry Poker."

He motioned for us to follow him into his study, then softly closed the door.

"Mother is taking a nap," he explained in a low voice.

"So what's this about a body?" Mr. Grewgious asked as soon as he was seated in a chair. "Have they found Edwin Drood?"

"We're not sure," Mr. Crisparkle said. "It's a man's body, but it's in such bad condition that we can't identify it. Durdles says quick-lime must have been thrown on it."

I shuddered. Poor Edwin!

"Where was it found?" asked Mr. Grewgious.

"In the crypt. Durdles found it. In a sepulchre—along with the remains which belonged there. He said he could tell by the sound that something was there which didn't belong."

"So we may never know if this is Edwin Drood?" I asked.

"They're sending for Scotland Yard," Mr. Crisparkle said. "Whoever it is, there's most likely been foul play. Otherwise it wouldn't have been disposed of like that."

"Why don't we find Durdles and see what he has to say," suggested Mr. Grewgious.

"Let me just check on Mother first," Mr. Crisparkle said.

Once he had assured himself that old Mrs. Crisparkle was still sleeping, we walked across the Monks' Vineyard, past the Travellers' Twopenny, and soon found ourselves at the stonemason's house with its assortment of half-finished stones and statuary, all covered with a fine dust. Two journeymen at work in the yard barely glanced up at us. Deputy was sitting on the front steps scratching a scab on his knee. He jumped up when he saw us and grinned.

"Poker! You're back!" he said.

"Is Mr. Durdles at home?" Mr. Crisparkle asked.

"Maybe he is. Why do you want to know?"

"We want to talk to him," Crisparkle said.

Mr. Grewgious fished in his pocket and found a half-penny, which he placed in Deputy's grimy palm.

"All right then," Deputy said, after biting the coin. "You can go in." He stepped aside, and we entered the dark interior of Durdles' house. As I passed Deputy, he tugged on my coat.

"There's a message for you over at the Travellers'," he whispered.

"A message for me?" This was strange since no one knew I would be returning, not even me.

"I told 'em you were gone, they might just as well throw it away."

"Who's it from?"

He shrugged. "Don't know."

I wondered if Sapsea had written another poem that he wished to favor me with. I decided if the message was from him, I would ignore it. I was not going to spend any more time listening to his inanities or reading his poetry.

We all crowded into Durdles' little kitchen, where Durdles sat with a bottle of murky liquid on the table in front of him and Mr. Datchery across from him. They looked up when we entered, but neither of them seemed surprised to see me with Mr. Grewgious and Mr. Crisparkle.

"What do you think about this body that you found?" Mr. Grewgious asked Durdles after everyone had shaken hands. "Could it be Edwin Drood?"

"Might be," said Durdles. "Whoever he is, looks like he

broke his neck. One thing's for sure—he didn't put himself in there."

"Mr. Datchery?"

"Too badly decomposed to tell. Unfortunately there's nothing by which to identify him—no jewelry. However, we do have these." He pulled a number of small nails out of his pocket and laid them on the table.

"What are they?" asked Mr. Grewgious, picking one up and examining it more closely.

"All that's left of his boots," said Durdles.

Mr. Grewgious sighed and laid the nail back down. "Well, we'll see what Scotland Yard can make of this."

When we emerged from Durdles' house, Mr. Grewgious pulled out his watch. "I'm afraid the trip has been a bit of a disappointment. Don't you agree, Mr. Poker?"

"I suppose it has," I said.

"I think I'll rent a chaise to go back to London instead of waiting for the omnibus. What do you think of that, Mr. Poker?"

"It sounds like a fine idea," I said.

"Well, I'd better get back to Minor Canon Corner," Mr. Crisparkle said. "Mother will be waking up and she'll wonder where I am."

"And I'd better get back to the Gate House, where I can keep an eye on a certain person," said Datchery. "Nice to see you again, Mr. Poker." He tipped his hat to me.

"Mr. Grewgious," I said when we were alone again, "it's such a pleasant afternoon here in Cloisterham that I'd really like to walk around a bit before going back to dusty London. If you don't mind, I'll catch the omnibus later."

He looked about to protest, then merely shook his head and sighed. "Oh, very well. But try to be back before dark."

"Of course," I said.

"And try not to get into trouble."

Left to my own devices, I lost no time circling back to the Travellers' Twopenny. I made straight for the gaunt-looking proprietor, whom I knew from my previous stay could usually be found dozing behind his desk, and after waking him, asked about the message that had been left for me. After much fumbling in several drawers, he found an envelope addressed to Mr. Poker.

I thanked him and went out on the porch to read it where there were no prying eyes. Inside the envelope was the following message:

Dear Mr. Poker,
Please join me Friday evening for dinner if you can. I understand you are interested in seeing my lodgings. I eat around six.
Respectfully, John Jasper

Of course I would not accept his invitation, I told myself. Even if he had not guessed my true identity, he was still a dangerous man who may have murdered at least two people, as everyone kept reminding me. For all I knew he might have no qualms about murdering Henry Poker too. Also, Mr. Grewgious expected me to be back in London before nightfall. If I stayed to dine with Jasper, I would not arrive until after dark. On the other hand, this might be a rare opportunity to observe the choirmaster at first hand and to draw him out. What incriminating crumbs of information might he drop if he thought he were only conversing over dinner with a young man from London interested in old architecture and ruins? The more I thought about it, the more I was tempted to keep the appointment. How could I pass up an opportunity like this? I told myself I would think of some excuse to tell Mr. Grewgious to explain why I was late returning to London.

To kill time until the appointed hour, I strolled the familiar route through the Monks' Vineyard to the cathedral and again wandered among the old tombstones, sepulchres, and monuments. I could not help thinking about the people buried there. They had once been like us—their lives full of grief and joy, love and hate, tears and laughter, struggle, unhappiness. We none of us knew when our little time upon the earth would draw to an end. I found myself again in front of the sepulchre engraved with the name of Edwin Drood. I knew the remains within were those of the father and not the son, but still I could not resist tracing the worn letters with my fingers. How soon young Edwin Drood's life had come to an end! So young, so handsome, with so much to look forward to, his life had been cut short.

I told myself it was for his sake that I must dine with Jasper. And for Neville's too, whose life might well be in danger so long as Jasper lived and hated. There was danger I knew, but I would take that risk. I didn't know if Jasper had recognized me on any of our previous encounters. I hoped not. The invitation was addressed to Poker, and as Poker I would go. I would be careful. Jasper might be a murderer luring me to his rooms to kill me, but I would keep my eyes open. I would be wary. And I would find out all I could.

. . .

It was dusk as I made my way up the postern stair of the Gate House. I couldn't help but think of how Neville and Edwin had climbed these stairs last Christmas Eve. The cathedral clock was chiming the hour. It was six o'clock. There had been no sign of Datchery across the way. His door was closed and the window dark. I felt very alone, but I raised my hand and knocked.

Jasper looked surprised to see me when he opened the door. "Hallo, there," he said, blinking. I wondered if he had been dozing. He looked a little glassy-eyed.

"You invited me to dinner," I reminded him, holding up his message for him to see.

"So I did," he said, as if suddenly remembering. "So good of you to come." He led me into his sitting room. "I thought you might have left Cloisterham."

"I did," I said. "But I came back again."

"And where did you go?" he asked politely, sitting down in a chair across from me and regarding me curiously over the steeple formed by his fingers as they pressed together.

"To London."

"Ah, London. . . ." His eyes narrowed. Was he remembering opium dens and narrow winding streets through which he had pursued Neville on foggy nights? "You said you live there, didn't you?"

"Yes, I did. I mean, I do." I wished he would not stare at me so intently. I would have to be careful he didn't use animal magnetism on me.

"And do you have family there?" he asked.

I knew I must not hesitate. He might be testing me. If

he had any suspicions, I must put them to rest. "Yes," I said, ticking them off on my fingers, "three sisters, three brothers, my parents, an aged grandfather, and of course aunts, uncles, and dozens of cousins." I thought if I was going to give myself a family, I might as well be generous. I was proud of how promptly I had come up with my answer.

"You're very fortunate," said Jasper. "I had only my dear nephew, and now that he's gone, I have no one at all. I am alone in the world. I must confess sometimes it makes me quite melancholy to think about it."

"I'm very sorry for your loss," I said.

"He was murdered, you know."

"I did hear that."

"Did you know him?" He said it so swiftly and looked at me so closely, I was startled.

"No."

"Perhaps in London? He was studying engineering in London." His eyes bored into me as if he would see into my soul.

"No, I'm afraid not," I said. "It's a very large city."

"A pity. You would have liked him. Everybody liked Ned."

For a minute I thought I saw tears well up in his eyes. Embarrassed, I looked away. I studied Rosa's portrait over the chimneypiece to give him time to recover. She looked as if she were just about to make a saucy remark. I struggled not to smile.

"Ned painted that," he said.

"It's . . . very striking."

"Oh, it's just something he dashed off. I doubt the young lady would be pleased if she saw it. It was a joke, you might say. But I have to admit he did catch her. Pretty, isn't she?"

"Very."

"You don't know her by any chance, do you?" He said it so casually, but again I felt he was watching me for a misstep.

"I'm afraid I don't," I said, trying to match his casual tone.

"She was his fiancée."

"I'm sure she was very distressed by his murder."

"Yes, she was. Did you know they just found a body?"

I tried to look surprised. "A body?"

"I thought you might know about it since you're studying the cathedral. You are studying the cathedral, aren't you?"

"And other ruins."

"Of course. Cloisterham is full of ruins." He looked at the portrait again. "I thought you might have heard about the body. I thought you might know if it's . . . my dear boy."

In spite of myself I felt moved by pity. "I'm sorry. I know nothing."

He looked back at me. "Well, never mind. You must forgive me. I'm sure you're hungry and the food is getting cold." He opened the door to his little dining room and I saw that the table had been set for two. Then had he been expecting me after all? Had he just pretended at the door to be surprised? I didn't dare ask. Everything was neatly arranged. Silver covers were keeping the food warm. Jasper turned his back to me as he poured the wine at the sideboard.

"Please, none for me," I said, determined not to make the same mistake as Neville.

"What?" he said, turning. "But you must. I assure you it's excellent wine."

"I don't drink," I said.

"Why ever not?"

"I choose to abstain," I said. "I had an uncle who had an unfortunate attachment to drink. I resolved not to follow his example." In a way my statement was true. Not an uncle, but my stepfather.

"You could have wine with dinner and yet not become a drunkard. I think you're being very narrow for one so young."

"I don't wish to drink," I said firmly.

"Ah, well," Jasper said, sitting a glass of wine in front of me anyway, "perhaps you will change your mind. In the meantime, you will allow me to drink, won't you? I'm older, and I fear entrenched in my vices, although drunkenness is not one of them. Sometimes I think it would be preferable if that were my worst vice."

"What worse vices are there than drunkenness?" I asked innocently.

He paused, wineglass in hand, considering. "Boredom."

It was not the answer I had expected. "That may be a vice but surely not worse than drunkenness," I protested.

"The alcoholic cannot help himself. He drinks because he has to drink. You might say, it's not his fault. But the man who succumbs to boredom could change his situation, couldn't he, if only he had the will!"

"Do you find life in Cloisterham so boring?" I asked. "To me it seems a pleasant enough place, far pleasanter than London."

"What is there to do in such a town?" he said. "Look at the people who surround you. Fools and pompous asses. And all your daily round predictable from the moment you rise until the moment you retire. And ahead of you no hope of change until the day you die."

"Why don't you go to London then?"

"London would be no better for someone like me. I would be as bored there as here. This great cloud that hangs over me is like a curse that was put on me the day I was born." He stared at his plate moodily, then raised his dark tortured eyes to me. "Have you never felt boredom, Mr. Poker? Felt it suck out your soul and leave you a husk?"

"No," I said softly.

"Have you never felt darkness creep into you and extinguish all the light? Have you never felt everything is hopeless? Have you never thought it would be better to die than to suffer another day?"

"No," I said again.

"I have," he said, staring.

I looked down at the wineglass in my hand, halfway to my mouth. I set it down again.

"I apologize," he said, pressing the tips of his fingers to his forehead as if he had a headache. "You must overlook my low spirits. I'm afraid I'm a poor host. I haven't been myself since my dear boy died."

"It's understandable," I murmured.

"You are fortunate to have such a large family," he said. "Having none makes me quite melancholy. I am so very alone."

"Perhaps you need a wife," I suggested.

He was looking at me again in that peculiarly intense

way. I looked away, at the gravy bowl. It had shaken me a little to find myself holding the wineglass a few minutes before. Had that been an accident, or had he been exerting his power of magnetism? I reminded myself I must be careful not to look too long or hard into his eyes.

"Would you like more gravy?" he asked, his eyes never wavering.

"I think I've had enough."

"You have a brother?"

This startled me. "Three," I corrected him, determined not to be tripped up in my story of a large family.

"Younger or older?"

"Two younger and one older," I said as confidently as I could.

He sighed. "I always wished I had a brother. Are you close? You don't mind my asking, do you?"

"No, not at all. Yes, we're close."

"And I suppose you never quarrel?"

"Well, of course sometimes we quarrel." I assumed three brothers would not be so different from one.

"Have you ever been to the East?" he asked abruptly.

I had just taken a bite of roast beef so I could not answer at once. I felt as if we were engaged in a fencing match and he kept surprising me with thrusts I did not expect. "No," I said carefully after I had chewed and swallowed, "I never have. Have you?"

"I have," he said. "In fact, I was born in India." His eyes were two black pools that I could drown in.

"Did you grow up there?" I asked, hoping for more information about his past.

"I was sent back here for schooling when I was ten."

"Do you remember India?"

"Yes, it's not the sort of place you forget. Once you've been there, you carry it with you for the rest of your life. The sights, the smells, the sounds, the people. There's something magical about it."

I suddenly felt a rush of homesickness for Ceylon. Yes, there had been something magical about it. The bazaars, the women in their colorful saris, the men in turbans, the smell of spices, the snake charmers and the holy men, the temples and mosques, the dust, the heat, the monsoons. It sprang up before me like a vision. "Have you ever thought of going back?" I asked.

He laughed. Then his dark magnetic eyes held me again. "I did go back."

This surprised me. "What happened?"

"I was seventeen years old. India had not changed but I had. England had spoiled me. I couldn't fit in. I didn't belong there anymore. I got sick almost at once. I had to come back."

"Perhaps it was not your destiny," I suggested.

"Destiny? Did you say destiny?" Suddenly he seemed angry. His fist hit the table. "It is my destiny to be caught between two worlds and belong to neither." His eyes flashed. "Do you know what my childhood was like?" he demanded. "Do you know who my playmates were? Not proper little English boys, but street beggars. They took me in. They taught me their games. When I ran away from home, it was to them I ran."

He stood up so fast he almost overturned his chair and rushed from the room. Wondering at his strange behavior, I used the opportunity to push my wineglass farther away, where I would be less tempted to reach for it. In a minute he was back and what I saw in his hand almost made me cry out. He held my mother's red sari.

Sitting down at the table again, he held the sari stretched taut between his hands and stared at me. "A scarf like this," he said. "They taught me how to wrap it around a person's neck and pull it tight. It was a game we played. I thought it was just a game. Until one day I saw my friend kill another boy."

"Thuggees," I said, my hand flying involuntarily to my throat. I had heard of them. What English person in India had not? Our Indian nurse had frightened us with stories about them. They were thieves and murderers who preyed on travelers. They were said to be everywhere in India, a vast network of ruffians who looked no different from other Indians but would strangle their victims, rob them, and bury them by the side of the road. People who set off on a journey might never be seen again.

"So you know of them?" he said.

"I've heard of them," I admitted, unable to take my eyes from the red sari in his hands. How had he gotten it? Had he stolen it from my room at the Staple Inn? Why? Why?

Suddenly he dropped the sari on the table and again pressed his fingers to his head as if he were in pain.

"Are you all right?" Without thinking I reached out my hand to touch him. In a flash he grabbed my wrist and held it so tightly it hurt.

"Why are you here?" he asked, staring at me again, as if his eyes could bore so deeply he would find his answer. "Don't you think I know who you are? Do you know where *she* is? I could make you tell! You should be afraid of me!"

Just as suddenly he let go of my hand and bowed his head till it touched the table. He let out a terrible moan.

I jumped up, ready to flee, but he looked so unwell I hesitated to leave. "What is it?" I asked.

He raised his head and stared blindly. A film passed over his eyes. His face was deathly white and drops of sweat beaded his forehead. His breath came in short gasps.

"Are you ill?" I asked. "Should I get help?"

He clung to the edge of the table with clenched hands. "I take opium for a pain. This is what it does to me. It will pass in a moment."

In the distance the cathedral clock chimed. It was seven o'clock. He began to tremble all over.

"Go away," he said with a sob. "You shouldn't be here."

"I can't leave you like this," I said.

The door behind me opened at that moment, and Mrs. Tope appeared. She had come to clear away the dishes. She took one look at Jasper and let out a cry. Turning to the sideboard, she picked up a pitcher and hurriedly poured him a glass of water. "Drink," she said, lifting his head and holding the glass to his lips. "It'll make you feel better."

With effort he sipped the water. "Thank you, Mrs. Tope," he said weakly. "You're very good to me."

She went into the next room and returned in a few minutes with a wet cloth, which she placed on his forehead. Jasper's eyes were closed now.

"You'd better go," she said to me. "He ought to rest now. These attacks take a lot out of him."

He looked like a broken man. I wasn't sure he even knew I was still there.

Mrs. Tope began to unbutton his collar.

"Can I help?" I asked.

"No, there's nothing you can do, sir. You should leave. He doesn't like to be seen like this."

My eye fell on the red sari where it still lay on the table. I snatched it up and stuffed it into my pocket. Then, leaving Jasper to the practiced hands of Mrs. Tope, I let myself out the door.

16

It is a strange fact that if you see your enemy afflicted in some terrible way of which you were previously unaware, you may cease to hate and fear him and instead pity him. So it was that after witnessing Jasper's fit that night, I no longer hated or feared him. I pitied him. I told no one that I had dined with him, not even Neville. I told no one of what I had seen. To do so would have seemed a kind of betrayal.

From dinner at Jasper's I had gone straight to the omnibus and managed to catch it before its last departure. It was dark when I arrived in London, but as I was dressed as Poker, no one paid any attention to me. I let myself into our attic rooms without encountering anyone on the stair, and when Mr. Grewgious knocked on my door later, I was in my nightgown.

"Just wanted to be sure you got back safely before I turn in," he said.

"I'm sorry," I said. "I should have stopped by and let you know."

"No matter," he said. "Did you enjoy yourself?"

"Yes, I did. Thank you."

"You didn't run into any trouble?"

"No, no trouble."

He hesitated. "You might not want to tell Miss Twinkleton about this little outing. It might disturb her, you know."

"I won't tell her," I assured him.

In the days that followed, we no longer saw watchers in the building across the street. Mr. Grewgious stopped looking for another place to move me. He decided I might be safe where I was, and it had the added advantage of allowing him to keep an eye on me.

A week later word came from Mr. Datchery that Scotland Yard had determined the body found at the cathedral was not that of Edwin Drood. I wasn't sure how I felt about the news. On the one hand, I was disappointed because the mystery of Edwin's disappearance was still not solved. On the other, I was relieved. A part of me dreaded knowing what grisly fate had befallen him.

As the days passed, contrary to Mr. Grewgious's fears, I had no desire to return to Cloisterham. I had had my fill of it. I wanted to push it from my mind. So when Bazzard announced it was time to start rehearsals for The Thorn of Anxiety, I welcomed the chance to turn my attention to something new.

We all met together in Mrs. Billickin's front parlor one evening and Bazzard solemnly passed out copies of his play.

"It is the story of a young woman who is loved by two men," he explained.

"Do I get to be the young woman?" asked Rosa.

"You do," said Bazzard.

Rosa clapped her hands in delight.

"Are you sure Jasper's not going to find out about this?" Neville asked.

"Jasper appears to have given up his trips to London," said Mr. Grewgious. "Besides, our audience will probably be small, made up mainly of friends and well-wishers. It is unlikely that Jasper will hear about it."

"And who are the two young men who love me?" Rosa asked as if she had already banished Jasper from her thoughts.

"That would be Mr. Neville and Mr. Tartar, of course," said Bazzard.

"Which one do I end up with?"

Bazzard cleared his throat, no doubt aware that the attention of the two young men in question was riveted upon him. "Mr. Tartar," he said.

"Why not me?" demanded Neville.

"Because you are more suited to play the angry young man who vows revenge against his rival," said Mr. Bazzard.

Neville looked as if he were about to argue, so Bazzard hurried on.

"There will be a duel in which Mr. Neville is fatally shot. Miss Rosa will cry over him as he bleeds to death. It will be a most tragic ending which will leave the audience in tears."

Neville looked mollified at this. No doubt the idea of Rosa weeping over him was appealing.

"Miss Helena will play the role of her older sister," said Bazzard, "and Mr. Crisparkle will be a good friend caught between his loyalty to both the rivals. Mr. Grewgious will play Rosa's father and Miss Twinkleton her mother. Mrs. Billickin will be an aunt who doesn't approve of either young men. There are a number of other small parts, such as a butler who answers the door, a stranger in a black cape, Rosa's rich uncle, and a surgeon who attends Mr. Neville as he lies dying. We will need to find other actors to play those parts."

"I've always wanted to be in a play," Rosa said.

"I've only agreed to this," said Miss Twinkleton, "because Mr. Grewgious assures me it will be safe."

"I've never seen a play before," Neville said, "not a real one at any rate, on a stage in a theatre."

"What?" said Mr. Grewgious. "Never seen a play?"

"There aren't any theatres in Ceylon," I explained.

"Oh, you must see one then," said Mr. Grewgious. "You can't very well act on a stage without ever having seen a play. Isn't that right, Bazzard?"

"I would think it would be a disadvantage," Bazzard agreed.

"If you're going to a play, can I come too?" asked Rosa. "Sitting around here is ever so dull. I'd love to go to a play."

"Of course, dear, you shall come too, and Miss Twinkleton as well," Mr. Grewgious said.

"That's very kind of you," said Miss Twinkleton.

"I confess I haven't seen many plays either," Tartar said, "due to the fact that I spent much of my youth at sea. If you don't mind, I'd like to tag along."

"I think I should like to come as well," said Mr. Crisparkle. "I haven't been to a play in quite some time."

"Let's all go then," said Mr. Grewgious. "Mrs. Billickin, you must come too."

"If my health permits, I might join you," that lady said. "Depending of course on what you are going to see."

"Oh, yes," said Miss Twinkleton. "We should choose something uplifting and classical, not one of the vulgar pantomimes which are so popular among London theatergoers these days."

"Would *Macbeth* do?" asked Mr. Grewgious. "There's a fine performance with Macready playing Macbeth."

Miss Twinkleton hesitated. "It's a violent sort of play."

"Oh, please say yes," Rosa urged.

"Well, it *is* Shakespeare, and so I suppose it will do," conceded Miss Twinkleton.

At that Rosa leaped up, threw her arms around Miss Twinkleton's neck, and kissed her on the cheek.

So one night we all went to Covent Garden to see *Macbeth*. The men looked stiff and self-conscious in their best waistcoats. The women scarcely dared breathe with their waists cinched so tightly. We were all flounces and ruffles and hoopskirts. Rosa had insisted we curl our hair and decorate it with ribbons. Getting prepared for the evening took most of the afternoon, but I had to admit the results were impressive. I hardly recognized myself in the looking glass. In my new blue silk dress, bought specially for the occasion, I looked as if I had been going to plays all my life. And Rosa in her new pink dress with her cheeks pink with excitement looked even more like a rose than usual.

There was a festive atmosphere about the crowd, an air of anticipation that was infectious. Neville and Tartar were both determined to sit by Rosa, and so one sat on her right and the other on her left. Mr. Grewgious sat next to Miss

Twinkleton, who wore a neckline that plunged deeper than any I had seen her wear before. I was flanked by Crisparkle and Bazzard. On the other side of Bazzard was his cousin, Mrs. Billickin, dressed as usual in black. She had been uncertain she was well enough to come, until the last moment, when she had decided she was.

When the curtains opened, I forgot everything else and lost myself in the play. I had read *Macbeth* of course, but to see the three witches stirring their evil brew on the stage was a thing of wonder. Such terrible looking old crones— where had they found them? Then Macbeth strode on stage and people cheered. He had a magnificent moustache and beard and wore a bright red hat. Throughout the play the audience shouted encouragement to him. In contrast, they did not much like Lady Macbeth and booed whenever she appeared. When she urged Macbeth to kill Duncan, someone shouted, "Don't listen to her," and when the knock at the gate came, someone warned, "Don't open it." The audience kept up this noisy participation until the ghost of Banquo appeared. Shivers ran down my spine. I was sure it was exactly how a ghost would look. For once the whole theatre was quiet. However, they were not an audience to stay quiet for long. Gradually they stirred to life again. When Lady Macbeth could not get the blood off her hands, someone suggested she try soap, and a titter ran through the audience. When the trees of Birnam wood moved, it was impressive to see, at least until one tree fell down, which caused the audience in the front rows to chuck nuts at the unfortunate actor who had lost hold of his tree. During the sword fight between Macbeth and Macduff the audience seemed divided between those who wanted Macduff to win and those who favored Macbeth.

When Macbeth delivered his famous lines—"Out, out, brief candle"—tears sprang to my eyes. I almost cried when he was killed, but then a soldier must have stepped on his hand, for he sat up and swore at the man before lying down again. The audience clapped, whistled, and shouted as the curtain came down.

"Did you like it?" asked Crisparkle as we stood to leave.

"I did indeed," I said. "I wonder everyone in London doesn't attend the theatre every night."

"I've seen *Macbeth* done better," said Bazzard. "It was a middling sort of performance."

"It can't compare to The Thorn of Anxiety," declared Mrs. Billickin and received a grateful look from Bazzard.

"I could never write a play, not if my life depended on it," Mr. Grewgious said, shaking his head.

For myself, I could not imagine anything more wonderful than writing for the stage. I rode back to Staple Inn that night in a happy daze. I hardly knew what was said in the carriage. I only wanted to get back to my room and record the thoughts churning through my mind. That night anyone looking at my window might have seen a candle burning late into the night. It was almost daylight when at last I lay aside my pen and climbed into bed. Even then my head was so full of ideas that it took me at least an hour to fall asleep.

I'm afraid we were a great trial to poor Bazzard in the weeks that followed. Mr. Grewgious never could seem to remember his lines. Mr. Tartar was so easygoing and likeable it seemed impossible anyone would challenge him to a duel. Neville, on the other hand, ought never have been allowed to brandish a revolver, not even one that was unloaded. Just seeing Rosa and Tartar talking together in the wings put him in a dangerous mood. Mr. Crisparkle was frequently absent because of his duties in Cloisterham, and when he did come, he spent more time asking me how I was doing, and what I was reading, and how I was getting on than on practicing his part.

"He likes you," Neville said one afternoon as we stood in the wings, watching Mr. Crisparkle and Tartar on stage. "I wouldn't be at all surprised if he asked you to marry him."

"If you are referring to Mr. Crisparkle, he's friendly to everybody," I retorted.

"Well, if he asked you, would you accept?"

"I'm not sure. I'd have to think about it."

"You could do worse," Neville said.

I swatted his arm with my play script.

I knew he was right, but I kept hoping Mr. Crisparkle wouldn't ask so I wouldn't be put in the position of having to say yes or no. In the beginning I had been flattered by his attentions. He was a worthy, well-intentioned man, not rich, but then that was not of great importance to me. I knew I ought to be grateful if anyone wanted to marry me. Neville and I were going to receive only a small annuity when we came of age, which was still almost a year away. After Neville completed his studies, he would be able to get a job, but what would I do? I didn't want to be a burden for him. Still, to marry for security did not seem to me a worthy motive for entering into matrimony. Was that not what my mother had done when she married my stepfather? All the same, I hoped I would not have to hurt Mr. Crisparkle's feelings by turning him down. I decided my best strategy was to keep him from asking in the first place. As a result, I tried not to let him get on the subject of marriage. If I thought he was working around to it, I promptly changed the subject or bolted. I became very good at these evasive maneuvers during rehearsals for the Thorn of Anxiety.

There were always problems during our rehearsals. Once Neville dropped his revolver. Another time Tartar charged on stage with such force that he knocked over a stone wall. Then there was the time Mrs. Billickin sat down too hard on a chair and it collapsed under her. We even had a minor fire from a gaslight on one occasion.

Bazzard kept saying he would find more actors for the minor parts, but at each rehearsal he read those parts himself. I think gradually he was becoming attached to them. In one scene, however, it became apparent that he could not be both the Surgeon and the Stranger because both had to be on stage at the same time.

"It appears we need someone to play the part of the Surgeon or the Stranger," he admitted one night after jumping back and forth between the two roles. "Does anyone know someone who might be willing to be a part of our little production?"

"I might know someone," I said.

"Who?" Neville asked, looking at me in surprise. "Who do you know in London?"

"I can't tell you that," I said. "First I have to ask if he would be interested. If he consents, I'll bring him to the next rehearsal. If he doesn't meet with your approval, you don't have to use him."

"That sounds fair enough," said Bazzard.

"You're being very mysterious," Neville said. "You

don't have some secret romance you haven't told us about, do you?"

"Of course not," I said, embarrassed by the attention I was receiving. I wished I'd kept my mouth shut.

The next morning I again donned trousers, tucked my hair under a hat, and took a cab to the East End. This time I had no trouble finding my way to the miserable little alleyway in Shadwell where Princess Puffer lived. The man with the patch over one eye who had been guarding her stair on my previous visit was nowhere to be seen. I went up unchallenged and knocked at her door. After a few minutes the door opened a crack. Princess Puffer blinked at me.

"What's your business?" she asked in a raspy voice.

I pulled off my hat so she could see me more clearly.

"Oh, it's you," she said. "Come in, dearie." She opened the door wider and I stepped in.

"So you haven't forgotten me after all."

I was relieved to see none of her customers stretched across the sagging bed as I entered the small dark room. Almost at once Princess Puffer began to cough. I waited helplessly until the spell passed. She collapsed onto her chair by the hearth.

"You ought to quit smoking opium," I said.

"Can't," she said. "Once you've got the habit, you can't ever go back."

As I watched, I saw a film pass over her eyes just as it had over Jasper's and she seemed to shiver all over.

"Can I get you something?" I asked.

She shook her head. I knelt down on the floor beside her and put my hand over hers. She was clenching the arm of the chair just as Jasper had clenched the table. When I felt her hand relax, I looked at her face. She was blinking, trying to focus on me.

"What news?" she said. "What news do you bring me?"

"News?" I said, not understanding.

"Your lawyer-man," she said. "Did you tell him about my Jenny?"

"I did."

"And will he help me?"

"He'll try," I said.

"I knew he would," she said. "Thankee. You're a good girl."

"Will you give Jack a message when you see him?" I asked.

"Jack?" she repeated. "What message for Jack?"

"Will you tell him we're putting on a play? Here, I've written down the address and time." I took a piece of paper from my pocket and pressed it into her hand.

"A play?" she said.

"It's an amateur play written by Mr. Grewgious's clerk, Mr. Bazzard," I explained.

Suddenly I felt it had been a mistake to come. The gap between Jack's world in the East End and ours in the West was enormous. Why had I thought he might want to be a part of it? In his eyes we were probably very shallow people.

"You want him to see your play?" the old woman asked. "Is that it?"

"No, I thought he might like to be in it."

"Like a sort of actor?"

"Yes."

She began to laugh, a cackle that reminded me of the witches in *Macbeth*, and then the laughing made her cough.

I found the bottle of medicine I had seen Jack give her before and helped her drink from it. When I left, I felt discouraged. My idea of inviting Jack to be in the play now seemed silly. Bazzard would have to find someone else.

But then that night when I arrived for rehearsal, Jack was waiting at the theatre door. He had changed out of his dock clothes and was wearing a jacket.

"You came," I said, feeling inexplicably pleased. "Let me introduce you to the others."

He shook hands with them one by one.

"Why you must be the Chinaman who rescued me," Neville said. "I don't remember, but I'm much obliged."

"Have you ever acted in a play, sir?" Bazzard asked skeptically, looking Jack up and down.

"No, I haven't," Jack said.

"None of us have, Mr. Bazzard," I reminded him.

Bazzard scratched his head.

"Just give him a chance," I urged.

"I agree," Mr. Grewgious said. "Let's see what the young man can do."

And so Jack was given a script. He would be the Stranger. That first night he surprised us all with his ability to fall into the character of the Stranger. He seemed to have an instinct for what would be the most effective gesture and he delivered his lines as if he had been on the stage all his life. After he skulked off the stage, everyone was silent for a minute, and then we burst into applause. He was easily the best actor of our group.

Our last rehearsal took place just one week after Jack had joined our group. On that night we donned our costumes, wigs, and makeup. Mr. Grewgious was still carrying a script and could not remember his lines. Bazzard dashed about frantically, moaning that the play ought not to go on, we needed more time to prepare, but the posters were already up, handbills had been passed out, and our lease time was about to expire.

Mr. Grewgious thought that our audience would be small, but five minutes before the curtain rose Bazzard came scrambling into the wings to announce that the street was crowded with carriages. He alternated between wild excitement and panic. He was in no condition to act in the play, but act he must.

We took turns peering from behind the curtain at the audience. I confess the sight of so many people gave me butterflies in my stomach, and I wasn't the only one feeling nervous.

"I feel ill," Mr. Grewgious said. "I don't think I can possibly go on."

"You have to," I said. "Bazzard is depending on us."

"That's true," Mr. Grewgious agreed, dabbing his sweaty forehead with a handkerchief and removing a layer of makeup in the process. "But in the future I think I will stick to the law business."

The first act went well enough, although to Bazzard's chagrin the audience laughed rather too often for a tragedy. Mr. Grewgious read in a monotone that was completely different from rehearsals and stared hard at his script, although whether this was because he had forgotten all his lines or to avoid looking at the audience, I couldn't say. It was unnerving to look out beyond the lights and know people were watching. And yet when I said my lines, they came out more confidently than I felt. But whatever the shortcomings of the play, the audience loved Rosa.

They sighed every time she stepped on stage. They laughed every time Bazzard appeared, no matter what costume or wig he wore. They began to watch for each new incarnation and whistle and clap when he stepped on stage. However, Jack got the loudest applause of all, and after he left the stage, the crowd shouted for him to come back again.

It was beginning to seem as if the play would be a great success when in the third act Rosa stopped in the middle of a line as she was looking out at the audience and turned deathly pale. I was on the stage with her and tried to cover up her lapse. But as she stood frozen and staring, the audience began to murmur.

I touched her arm, still talking, and she looked at me and blinked.

"Are you all right?" I asked in a low voice.

Her lips moved but no sound came out. I was alarmed now.

"I understand, you love the Count," I said, making up lines that weren't in the script although I knew Bazzard would not be pleased. "You are too lovesick to speak. Come. Let us talk." I put my arm around her waist and led her from the stage.

Neville, Tartar, and Crisparkle leaped into their next scene.

"What happened?" Bazzard said, strapping on his soldier's hat.

"Give her air," I said as the others crowded around. "Maybe she feels faint."

Jack rushed up with a glass of water and Rosa gratefully sipped from it.

"He's here," she whispered when she could speak again.

"Who?" I said.

"Jasper."

"Oh, my goodness!" said Miss Twinkleton and began to fan herself. "What shall we do?"

"Are you sure it was him?" Mr. Grewgious asked anxiously. "Maybe it was only someone who looked like him."

"No, I'm certain it was him," Rosa said. "I can't go back out there."

Now Bazzard looked as if *he* might faint, but he had no time to argue. It was his turn to go on stage.

Mr. Grewgious peeked from behind the curtain to see if he could spot Jasper in the audience. "I don't see him," he told Rosa. "But if you don't want to go back on stage, you don't have to."

"But no one else can play Rosa's part," I said. "Without her, we can't go on."

"You could play her part," Mr. Grewgious said.

"I'm too tall," I said. "Besides, who would play her sister?"

Mr. Grewgious looked at Miss Twinkleton and Mrs. Billickin. From the way his face fell, I knew he saw the hopelessness of it.

"It's all my fault," he said. "I oughtn't to have let her go on."

"Poor Bazzard," murmured Miss Twinkleton. "He'll be dreadfully disappointed."

"What will you tell the audience?" Jack asked.

"We'll tell them—" Mr. Grewgious paused. "We'll tell them one of our actors has taken ill."

"I suppose we'll have to return their money," Mrs. Billickin said with a sigh.

"What about the lease?" Jack asked.

We all looked at each other.

"Oh, I *will* do it," Rosa said, struggling to her feet. "I won't let him stop me. Helena wouldn't let him frighten her."

I hugged her I was so proud of her. I knew what it cost her to go back on the stage. For the rest of the play she didn't look at the audience but always at one of the rest of us. She never missed a line. And when she cried over Neville's body there could not have been many dry eyes in the audience. Backstage, Miss Twinkleton wept copiously into a handkerchief. And when Rosa kissed Tartar in the final scene, there was wild applause. The audience cheered and stamped and whistled till all of us took a second bow.

We hardly waited for the curtain to close before we started hugging each other and congratulating one another on our great success.

When it was over, half the audience wanted to crowd backstage to shake our hands. Mr. Grewgious whisked Rosa off to the dressing room and stood guard before the door, determined that Jasper would not get near her. Bazzard was surrounded by a small circle of friends who slapped him on the back and shook his hand.

Jack had his own circle of admirers, I noticed, and Tartar was surrounded by pretty ladies.

I was standing beside Miss Twinkleton and Mr. Crisparkle when red-haired Miss Ferdinand turned up.

"You were wonderful," she told Miss Twinkleton, who looked both pleased and embarrassed at this pronouncement. "I enjoyed your play very much."

"Oh, it wasn't *my* play," said Miss Twinkleton.

"I especially liked the duel," Miss Ferdinand said. "Do you suppose you could introduce me to the young man who was so cruelly shot to death?"

At that minute a portly woman glittering with jewels stepped between us to tell Mr. Crisparkle and me *her* opinion of the play. "It was," she insisted, "quite awful of course. The play was badly written and the actors, as I'm sure you all realize, were not very good. You don't mind me being honest, do you?"

"Of course not," Mr. Crisparkle said. "That's very kind of you." He shook her hand.

"I thought you were quite good," he told me when she had left.

"Well, it was fun anyhow," I said.

Turning, I saw Miss Twinkleton introducing Miss Ferdinand to Neville. They shook hands, and Miss Ferdinand immediately broke out giggling, as she was wont to do. Neville, who had been looking at Tartar's circle of feminine admirers with obvious envy, now appeared to forget all about Tartar.

When at last the theatre was empty and only the doorkeeper remained, Tartar and Neville checked out the street but saw no sign of Jasper. The fog was creeping in, so that people and carriages seemed to loom out of it, then be swallowed up again, with only the clomp of the horses' hoofs and the rattle of carriage wheels to tell us they were real and not the figments of a dream.

Jack disappeared into the fog to make his way back to the East End and Mr. Crisparkle departed for the train station. The rest of us took two carriages to escort Rosa back to Mrs. Billickin's house. I rode in the second with Neville, Bazzard, and Mrs. Billickin. Mr. Grewgious directed the carriages to take a circuitous route through the streets, to confound any watchers. At last we pulled up in front of Mrs. Billickin's house in Bloomsbury. Mr. Grewgious walked back to our carriage as Bazzard was helping Mrs. Billickin out.

"Any sign of him?" Mr. Grewgious asked Bazzard in a low voice.

"Not a hair, sir."

A carriage rattled past and we all watched it nervously until it disappeared around a corner.

"Do you think Rosa is safe here?" Tartar asked.

"I don't know," Mr. Grewgious said, frowning as he looked up and down the street.

"Maybe she was mistaken," Bazzard suggested. "Maybe it was just someone who looked like him."

"What do you think, Helena?" Mr. Grewgious asked.

"I think he was there," I said.

"If he dare show his face around here, I'll . . . ." Neville clenched both fists.

Tartar laid a steadying hand on his arm. "Don't forget, you're in danger too. Next time you might end up with worse than a bump on the head and a broken arm."

"I'm not afraid of him."

Tartar nodded. "Neither was my mate when a 30-foot wave was bearing down on us as we rounded the Cape, but he died all the same."

"Is my cousin in any danger?" Bazzard asked nervously.

"I think if no one objects I should like to spend the night in the front parlor," Tartar said.

"An excellent idea," I said before Neville could protest.

"Mrs. Billickin," said Mr. Grewgious, "would you be averse to Mr. Tartar spending the night in your front parlor? Just as a precaution."

"I don't mind," said Mrs. Billickin. "He can if he wants."

"Then it's all settled," said Mr. Grewgious. "Rosa, Miss Twinkleton, you can sleep peacefully assured that Mr. Tartar is standing guard."

"I'm here too," Neville said. "Don't forget that. And if that blackguard shows up, I'll thrash him good."

"Your arm," I reminded him. Was he going to fight Jasper with only one good arm?

"We'll fight him together," said Tartar, clapping Neville on the back.

I said goodnight to Neville and headed back to the Staple Inn with Mr. Grewgious and Bazzard.

It rained that night, and I was awakened several times by the wind howling around Staple Inn. I expect the residents at Mrs. Billickin's also had difficulty sleeping that night. And yet when dawn came, nothing had happened. They thought they had eluded Jasper. Even if he had been at the theatre the night before, he had not followed them to Mrs. Billickin's. Rosa's hiding place was still secret.

It was mid-morning when Rosa, looking out the window of her bedroom on the second-story, saw him standing opposite watching the house. But by the time she had alerted Tartar and he had run into the street, Jasper was gone. Tartar waited two hours, watching the street for

Jasper to reappear. Then he caught a cab to the Staple Inn and told us what had happened.

I had gone down to Mr. Grewgious's office to join Mr. Bazzard and Mr. Grewgious for lunch, as I frequently did these days and so heard all that Tartar had to relate.

"We must move Rosa and Neville, but where?" Mr. Grewgious said when Tartar had finished. As usual when he was faced with a problem, Mr. Grewgious paced. A worn patch on the rug showed his accustomed path between the door and the window.

"I may know of a place," Tartar said and then began to redden. "That is, if it meets Miss Rosa's approval . . . and of course yours."

Mr. Grewgious stopped pacing. "Where?"

Tartar reddened yet more. "I can't say just yet. I have to . . . look into it first, you might say." He glanced at the window, took a firm grip on himself, and then faced Mr. Grewgious again. "Would you be available for an outing this afternoon?"

"To where?" Mr. Grewgious asked.

Tartar looked at the window again. "I'd rather not say, sir. I want it to be a sort of surprise."

"And will anyone else go on this outing?" Mr. Grewgious asked, pausing by the window and rocking on his heels.

"Miss Landless, you must come," Tartar said, turning to me.

"All right," I said. "I'll come." I was curious what his surprise could be.

"And no one else?" Mr. Grewgious asked.

"Miss Bud," Tartar said. "I thought Miss Bud might like to come."

"I see. And Miss Twinkleton?"

"Yes, of course, Miss Twinkleton."

"And Neville?" I suggested.

He hesitated just a fraction of a second. "Yes, Neville should come too. You must all come."

And so later that day we all took the train to Maidstone and then hired a carriage. Tartar remained secretive about our destination, but I suspected he had told Rosa something because she seemed very excited and whenever their eyes met she blushed. Neville, on the other hand, was once again out of sorts. On the train he buried his nose in a book, and in the carriage he scowled at the passing countryside as if it offended him. It was a warm sunny day in August, a beautiful day for an outing. Rosa was delighted with everything. I had by now guessed where we were going—to see the estate Mr. Tartar had inherited from his uncle, the property for which he had agreed to sacrifice his career in the Navy. Neville looked determined not to be impressed, but as the house itself came into view, Rosa let out an "ah" of pleasure, Miss Twinkleton said, "Oh, my!" and I thought Tartar had made the right choice after all when he came ashore.

Tartar could not conceal his pride in his ancestral home as he showed us around. He watched Rosa dash from room to room, every cry of delight fetching a smile from him.

I felt sorry for Neville, who must have known he was beaten. Neville had told me Tartar had a country estate, but until I saw it, I had not realized how wealthy Tartar was. When he had simply been the resident of the adjoining building, jumping from his roof to ours, I had thought of him as being almost as limited in resources as

263

we were, although I knew he didn't have to worry about a future income, as Neville and I did.

After exploring the house, we had tea on the broad green lawn, sitting on wicker chairs carried out by servants. Tartar passed around a spyglass so we could look at his yacht moored on the river.

"So is this your idea for a hiding place for my ward?" Mr. Grewgious asked.

Tartar reddened. "If it meets your approval, sir."

"What do you think?" Mr. Grewgious asked Miss Twinkleton. "You have watched over Rosa since she was seven years old. You are the nearest thing she has to a mother. What say you to Mr. Tartar's estate?"

"It's a very fine estate," Miss Twinkleton said. "However, it won't do."

"Won't do?" said Mr. Grewgious. "And why not?"

"Unless of course a suitable companion can be found," Miss Twinkleton said.

"You mean it wouldn't be proper, a young unmarried woman staying at a gentleman's estate."

"It would not," Miss Twinkleton said emphatically.

"What say you, Mr. Tartar?"

Mr. Tartar looked at the ground, then at the sky, and then at his house before he spoke. "It might not be proper for a young unmarried woman but how about for a married woman?"

We all looked at Rosa, who was smiling and blushing as she sipped from her cup of tea.

"What say you, Miss Rosa?" Mr. Grewgious asked.

"Why, if you have no objection," Rosa said, "then neither do I. That's what I told Mr. Tartar this morning when he asked me."

"Isn't this rather sudden?" Mr. Grewgious asked. "Marriage is not something you should rush into without careful consideration. It's a contract, remember, one that should not be broken. You will be married to each other for the rest of your lives. You don't want to find out later you made a wrong decision by acting hastily."

"I *have* thought about it," Rosa said and blushed again.

"It should not be Mr. Tartar's estate that sways you, fine though it is," Mr. Grewgious said. "You must look into your heart and ask yourself if you love him."

Rosa was now so pink I did not think she could blush more. "I have," she said.

Mr. Grewgious turned to Tartar.

"I have loved her since the moment I first saw her," Tartar said, looking at Rosa in the way every young woman dreams of being looked at. "And I would be the luckiest man alive if she would consent to be my wife."

We all broke into congratulations. Everyone was happy for the couple, except Neville, but he tried to put a good face on it, realizing that he had no hope of winning Rosa now.

By the time we started back to London, the details had been worked out. It would be a short engagement and a speedy marriage, to get Rosa under Tartar's protection as soon as possible. Mr. Grewgious hoped that once Rosa was married to Tartar, Jasper would give up his pursuit of her. Considering her dread of Jasper, I was surprised when she announced that she would like to be married in the cathedral at Cloisterham.

"I thought you didn't want to go back," I told her when we had a few minutes alone on the train.

"I'm not going to let Jasper spoil this for me," she said. "Cloisterham is my home, leastways the only one I can remember very well. For years I dreamed of being married in the cathedral. I thought Eddie would be walking down the aisle with me. Now it will be someone else, but it will still be the cathedral. Besides, if I get married there after school starts, all my friends from Miss Twinkleton's can attend. They have looked forward for a very long time to seeing me married in the cathedral. I don't want to disappoint them."

17

The wedding took place on a warm and lovely afternoon in September. Rosa wore a white dress and flowers in her hair. She looked very young and pretty as she walked down the aisle of the ancient cathedral on Mr. Grewgious's arm. Tartar beamed as she took her place beside him at the altar. She was such a little thing that she did not come up to his shoulder. Minor Canon Crisparkle performed the ceremony, while overhead the rooks cawed in the cathedral tower. Many of the townspeople could be seen sitting in the pews, including Mr. and Mrs. Tope, Mayor Sapsea, the Dean and his wife and daughter, old Mrs. Crisparkle, Mrs. Tisher, and of course Miss Twinkleton, who dabbed at her eyes frequently with her handkerchief. The young ladies of the seminary were there too, decked out in their finest muslins. Mr. Datchery was seated near the back where he had a good view of everything. Stony Durdles looked as if he had given himself a good scrub, and I'm sure Deputy was somewhere about, perhaps peeking through the grillwork. Bazzard and

Mrs. Billickin had come from London for the event, and so had Jack. With Neville seated beside me, I felt I was surrounded by all the people closest in the world to me. One citizen of Cloisterham, however, was noticeably missing—John Jasper. We had all worried that he might try to attend the wedding or interfere in some way, but there was no sign of him.

When Mr. Crisparkle pronounced Tartar and Rosa husband and wife, Tartar bent down to kiss Rosa's upturned face and the young ladies from the seminary let out a deep sigh. Then we all poured out of the cathedral in a wave, and when the young newlyweds emerged we threw flowers at them as the bells rang out overhead.

I had worried about how Neville would react to Rosa's marriage, but I needn't have. Red-haired Miss Ferdinand stood beside him on the cathedral steps, all chatter, laughter, and smiles, and Neville's heart appeared to be well on its way to mending.

"Well, Miss Landless, I hardly recognized you in that dress," Mr. Datchery said as we all stood outside the church. "I suppose one of these days we'll be attending *your* wedding."

He was the second person to make that remark to me that day. The first had been Mrs. Tisher, who had said it in a consoling tone, as if to reassure me my time would come. A wedding seems to set people to thinking matrimonially. It is like dropping a rock into a pool and setting off many ripples. One of those ripples I witnessed a little later. We had moved our celebration to the Nuns' House, where I went into the garden to be alone for a few minutes with my thoughts. I was not alone long. When I heard voices approaching, I ducked behind a hedge. Through a gap, I saw Miss Twinkleton and Mr. Grewgious come into the garden. Miss Twinkleton sat down on the garden seat beside the sundial and dabbed her eyes with her handkerchief. Mr. Grewgious stood awkwardly beside her.

"Come, come," he said. "You mustn't cry. Mr. Tartar will take good care of her."

"I can't help it," said Miss Twinkleton. "She's like a daughter to me."

"And to me as well," Mr. Grewgious said.

"I always knew the day would come when I should have to give her up. You must think I'm terribly sentimental."

"I do not, madam. I have always had the highest regard for you."

"And I for you."

"I'm sure you will be invited to visit the young couple often."

"Oh, visits . . . !" she said in a trembly voice, as if visits hardly counted.

"And you have your young ladies."

She waved her handkerchief with a dismissive gesture, as if to say they counted no more than visits.

"And besides you are still young. No doubt you have 'admirers.'"

She hesitated. "I'll be truthful with you, Mr. Grewgious. There have been admirers."

"I knew it."

"But at present there are none."

"None at all?"

She shook her head. "None at all."

"I find that hard to believe," he said. "If I were not such a confirmed old bachelor . . . ."

"Old?" she said. "Mr. Grewgious, I beg to differ. You are not old."

At that moment Neville and Miss Ferdinand entered the garden and looked disappointed to find the garden seat already occupied. It seemed to be a place much in demand. Although the younger couple promptly retreated, the thread of the conversation had been broken.

"Shall we go back now?" Mr. Grewgious asked. "Are you feeling better?"

"I am, thank you," said Miss Twinkleton. She dabbed her eyes one last time, and rising, took the arm he offered, and they went back inside.

I emerged from my hiding place and sat down on the garden seat. As fate would have it, Mr. Crisparkle walked around the corner of the house at just that moment. There was no time to duck behind the hedge again.

"I've been looking everywhere for you," he said. "There's something I want to speak to you about."

My heart sank. I hoped he too was not feeling affected by the wedding atmosphere.

"May I join you?" he asked.

"Of course." I made space for him on the bench.

"I hear you are staying in Cloisterham?"

"Yes, Miss Twinkleton has offered me a position," I admitted. "Miss Weston, our French teacher, got married quite unexpectedly over the summer. It was most inconsiderate of her. I daresay I know far less about French than she did, but I'll try to do the best I can."

"You are too hard on yourself," Mr. Crisparkle said. "You have a fine mind and a lively intelligence. I have no doubt that you can do whatever you set your mind to."

"Perhaps I'm not sure this is what I want to set my mind to," I confessed.

"Would you prefer to stay in London?"

"And do what? For a while I could continue to watch over Neville. But soon he must earn his way, and I don't want to be a burden for him. No, I think this is better."

"And have you no desire for a home of your own?" he asked. "Children?"

"Perhaps someday," I said.

"But not yet?"

"No, not yet."

He looked at the sundial and sighed. I felt sorry for him. He was my friend and I didn't mean to hurt him. But I also knew that in good conscience I couldn't agree to marry him unless I could give him my heart. And I didn't think I could do that.

That night after everyone had left, I felt restless so I went for a walk. I didn't tell Miss Twinkleton I was going out because then she would have told me it wasn't proper for a young woman to go walking alone. I knew we would have to make concessions to each other's ways in the coming days, but I didn't intend to stay confined in the Nuns' House. I walked the length of High Street, following the lamplighter as he went from street lamp to street lamp. Outside the Gate House I paused and looked up at Jasper's window. It was dark. I wondered how he had spent this day, which must have been such a bitter disappointment to him. Was he lying on his bed in an opium dream? Had he gone to London to visit Princess Puffer? Would he resign himself now to the loss of Rosa?

I couldn't sleep that night after I lay down in my old bed in the room I had once shared with Rosa. Perhaps it was the events of the day, or the memories stirred up by being back in Cloisterham, or the now unfamiliar bed that made it so difficult to fall asleep. At length I arose and dressed. Throwing a shawl around myself, I slipped out of the Nuns' House. Once outside I stood for a moment breathing in the cool night air and watching clouds scud across the full moon. Then I started walking. I walked until I came to the end of High Street, and then I kept going, leaving behind the silent houses of Cloisterham. I must have walked for thirty minutes, although afterward I was as unconscious of the route I had taken as if I had been sleepwalking. Maybe I was sleepwalking, for it was like waking up when I became aware of the sound of churning water close at hand, and I realized I was near the weir. Another minute and I saw the water ahead, dark and turbulent in the moonlight. I also saw that I was not alone. A man stood at the water's edge, his back to me. With a shock I realized it was John Jasper. I hesitated, not daring to move for fear he would hear me. Something about the way he stood warned me not to interrupt his silent vigil. After a few minutes of standing there, shivering in the night air, I tried to retreat. In the dark I stepped on a branch that snapped loudly. I looked back to see if Jasper had heard, but he had vanished. I took a few steps more and then saw him standing ahead, not behind me. Somehow he had circled around me and cut off my retreat.

He wore no hat or coat, and his face was contorted with anger.

"Haven't you and your brother done enough?" he shouted.

He was clutching something in his hand—a black scarf. I realized at once the danger I was in. He had told me he knew how to strangle people. In such an isolated place, no one would hear my screams. Tomorrow my strangled corpse might be found and Jasper might be suspected, but much good that would do me if I were dead. Or I might simply disappear, as Edwin Drood had.

I turned and tried to run from him, but my path was blocked by the weir. I had to choose—plunge forward into the weir or confront Jasper. I hesitated only a second, then plunged. The chill water made me gasp. It was incredibly cold and the current was strong. I could feel myself being dragged toward the timbers of the weir, but at the same time my skirt and shoes were growing oppressively heavy and pulling me down. The water closed over my head. I struggled, my lungs ready to burst, the cold water pressing in on me. A thought flashed through my mind: I was going to die.

18

But I didn't die. When I awoke, I was in Miss Twinkleton's private sitting room, lying on her settee with a pillow tucked under my head and a coverlet pulled over me. The sun was streaming in the window. I tried to remember how I had come to be there, but all I could remember was drowning in the weir. I turned my head and saw Miss Twinkleton sitting at her little writing-table. If I had been in my own bed, I might have thought it was all a bad dream, but I knew something extraordinary had happened if Miss Twinkleton thought I needed her personal supervision.

With effort I sat up.

"Oh, you're awake at last, dear," Miss Twinkleton said, looking up. "The doctor gave you some laudanum last night to help you sleep."

"How did I get here?" I asked.

"Don't you remember? Well, I daresay you were only half-conscious. I'm surprised you don't have pneumonia. You were soaked through and shivering something awful."

"Jasper—" I said, remembering how I had been trying to escape from him.

"Yes, Mr. Jasper saved you. You're very fortunate to be alive."

"No, you don't understand. He tried to kill me." I remembered the black scarf in his hand. He had been about to strangle me.

Miss Twinkleton shook her head. "You're mistaken. You fell into the weir and Mr. Jasper dove in at great personal risk to himself and pulled you out. He got you breathing again and carried you back, which couldn't have been easy. He looked in almost as bad shape as you, soaked and white. He's not a well man, you know. Mrs. Tope says he suffers from fits, although I've never seen it myself. My dear, there's no doubt about it, Mr. Jasper saved your life."

I couldn't believe it. There had to be some kind of misunderstanding. I was his enemy. He hated me. He had threatened both Neville and me. He had murdered Edwin Drood.

"My dear, what are you doing?" Miss Twinkleton said.

"I'm getting up," I said, attempting to do just that.

"The doctor said you should rest."

"I feel fine except my throat is sore and my chest hurts a little."

"That's from the water you swallowed. Very well, if you insist on getting up, let me have Mrs. Tisher bring down something more suitable for you to wear."

I was still in Miss Twinkleton's sitting room, but I was dressed and sitting up when Mr. Crisparkle arrived to see how I was doing.

"You're looking very well," he said. He had brought along some flowers, and Miss Twinkleton, after a moment's hesitation about the propriety of leaving us alone together, went in search of a vase.

"You might have drowned!" he said as soon as she was out of earshot. "Whatever were you doing at the weir last night?"

"I couldn't sleep," I said, "so I went out walking."

"Alone? At night?"

I sighed. How could I make him understand? He didn't hesitate to walk alone at night. Why was it so different for me because I was a woman?

"So how did you end up in the weir?" he asked. "Did you fall in?"

I shook my head. "No, I didn't fall in."

"What then? Were you trying to . . . harm yourself?"

"You mean, kill myself? Of course not. Why would I do that?"

He hesitated. "For the same reason any young woman might. Because of a love gone wrong. Because of despair. Because she was . . . ." He reddened and lowered his eyes.

"What?"

"With child."

"That's ridiculous."

"Of course it is, but you must know people will talk."

"I don't care if people talk," I told him.

"So what's the truth? What were you really doing there?"

"I told you. I couldn't sleep so I went for a walk. I don't know why I ended up there. It was like I was drawn there."

He jumped up and then sat down again. "It was the

same that night I went there. It was like I knew I would find something. And the next day I found Edwin's shirt-pin and watch among the timbers."

"That's strange, isn't it?" I said.

"I think I may have been . . . mesmerized."

"By Jasper?"

"I went there directly after talking to him. I don't know how he did it, but it's the only way I can explain it to myself."

"I couldn't have been mesmerized," I said. "I wasn't anywhere near him, at least not until after I'd gotten to the weir."

"Maybe he did it from a distance," suggested Mr. Crisparkle. "I've heard such things are possible."

"I have too, but I don't believe it," I said. "I don't think he wanted me there at all. He was angry when he saw me."

"He might have lured you there to kill you."

"That's what I thought," I admitted. "He had a scarf in his hands. At least it looked like a scarf."

"A scarf?"

"I thought he was going to strangle me."

"Then why didn't he?"

"I don't know. I ran. That's how I fell into the weir, and then my skirts were so heavy that I couldn't swim."

Mr. Crisparkle shook his head. "I don't understand it. He could have let you drown. No one would have known he was there. It would have looked like an accident. Or a suicide."

"I don't understand it either," I agreed. "He swore to hurt Neville and me to get revenge against Rosa. We think he killed Edwin Drood. Princess Puffer thinks he killed her daughter. It makes no sense. Why would he save me?"

"Well, thank God you're alive," Mr. Crisparkle said. "That's all that really matters."

"Do you think he could have put the idea of going to the weir into my mind earlier?" I asked.

"What do you mean?"

I had never told anyone about dining with Jasper that night. I wondered if he could have planted the idea in my mind at that time. Nothing had been said about the weir, at least not so far as I could remember. But I could still see his dark hypnotic eyes and I remembered how I had reached unawares for my wineglass. Perhaps he had tried to use his mental powers to influence me, but when the fit had come upon him he had seemed so helpless. Then I had felt only pity.

No, I didn't think Jasper had put the idea in my mind. Yet, going to the weir had not really been a conscious decision either. It reminded me of something that had happened when I was thirteen. I had awakened in the night with the feeling that Neville was in danger. I ran barefoot to his room and found him burning up with a fever. I then woke our nurse, who was sleeping in her room, and she in turn woke the servants. By daybreak she had managed to break the fever. Afterward she always marveled about my uncanny ability to know when Neville was in danger, but I always supposed it was because of our close bond. We were like one soul that had been split apart at birth. I shared no such bond with Jasper, yet something had drawn me to the weir, something very like what drew to me to Neville that night when he was in danger.

"Why do you think Jasper was there?" I asked Mr. Crisparkle.

"I have no idea. Perhaps like you he couldn't sleep."

I saw Jasper again as he had looked at that moment I had come upon him standing at the edge of the weir with his back to me. What could he have been doing there? Had he only gone there to be alone with his own dark thoughts? Or had he some more desperate motive? Was it possible he had intended to drown himself and had I saved him from the waters of the weir?

"In any case, you must not go wandering off again to the weir in the middle of the night," Mr. Crisparkle said. "Next time there might be no one to pull you out."

I went to evening service at the cathedral that night, over Miss Twinkleton's protests. She thought I was not sufficiently recovered, but I assured her I was. She was suspicious of my sudden religious impulse, but I hinted that it was due to my recent harrowing experience. I didn't tell her I was hoping to see Jasper there and to find the opportunity afterward to thank him for saving my life. However, this I was unable to do. He was not among the white-robed members of the choir. I felt vaguely disappointed. I fancied the choir missed him too. When they sang, they seemed not quite in key without him. Still, it was consoling to hear the choir and the organ echoing in the vast space of the cathedral. I could understand how people who grew up in Cloisterham might be reluctant to leave.

When I lay down that night, I thought I would sleep peacefully, but instead I woke with a sense of foreboding as the cathedral clock chimed twelve. Again I felt compelled to arise and dress and slip out of the safe confines of the Nuns' House, careful to wake no one.

Again I found myself in the dark street with only the streetlamps to light my way. It was but a short distance to the Gate House. As I stood below the archway, above me Jasper's window glowed with the flickering light of a candle. In the distance I heard the rumble of thunder. Clutching my shawl about me, I climbed the postern stair that led to Jasper's rooms. I had no idea what I would say to him, but I felt a driving need to know if he was there and safe. I rapped on his door and waited. Nothing happened. Was he sleeping? But then why was a candle burning? Had he taken laudanum or was he in the daze of an opium dream? I pounded more loudly on his door, hoping I wouldn't wake anyone else. Explaining why I was there might prove awkward. Still no answer, so I tried the latch. To my surprise, the door was unlocked. I opened it and went in. The sitting room was empty, but a candle burned near the window. The doors to both bedrooms were open, but Jasper was not in either one. Nor was he in the little dining room. Had he gone again to the weir? I looked all around the sitting room, hoping to find some clue. Rosa gazed at me from her portrait over the chimneypiece, a hint of a smile mocking me, as if she knew where he was. From the sitting room, I went to his bedroom, where the diary was lying on the little stand beside the bed just as before. But then I noticed something I had not seen before, a folded piece of paper tucked among its pages like a bookmark. I pulled the paper out and looked at it. It was a page ripped from the diary, dated the day before.

September 14, 18--
The only reason for me to go on living was taken away from me

today. For HER I have given up everything. And all for nothing. For the eyes of the world I hereby leave my confession. I and I alone am responsible for the death of Edwin Drood.

A confession! I could hardly believe it. He admitted his guilt. He had killed his nephew. But why had he confessed? I read it again and began to shiver. Was it a suicide note? And if it was, then it confirmed my suspicion that he had intended to kill himself at the weir the night before. Had he gone back to complete the deed? Dropping the diary and the note back on the stand, I rushed back out into the night. The wind blew my hair. A silver fork of lightning rent the black sky. I had taken only a few steps when I heard the crash of thunder. I hesitated, uncertain where to go next. Then I saw the square tower of the cathedral looming above the trees and houses. What instinct told me to direct my steps to the cathedral and not the weir? I don't know. But to the cathedral I ran, certain that was where I must go.

I was out of breath when I reached the great doors of the cathedral. They were locked but I hammered on them with my fists anyway until I realized it was useless. I looked up at the dark cathedral looming above me, to its massive square tower. I knew I must find a way in if I could. There was no time to lose. I ran to the small side door where Durdles had let me in and felt a kind of terrible joy when I found it open. This was how Jasper had entered, and he hadn't bothered to lock it behind him. Without pausing, I descended into the crypt and hurried past its shadowy pillars and sleeping dead, then up the next steps, to the door that led to the cathedral, and this too was unlocked. It was as if he had left them unlocked for me. A flash of lightning illumined the room and then was gone, but the room was still lit sufficiently by moonlight for me to find my way to the iron gate—also unlocked—that led to the winding staircase of the tower. I climbed as quickly as I could, my skirts clutched in my hand. With no light, I had to feel my way, and more than once cobwebs brushed my face. Only when I reached a gallery was there light from the nave. By now I was out of breath and my side hurt, but I couldn't stop. A bird flew by my head. A bat? A rook? As I neared the top, the stair narrowed and grew steeper. And then, just as I thought I must stop for breath, I saw the open door, I felt the wind, and I stepped out into the open air.

He stood at the edge, his back to me, just as he had stood the night before at the weir. I was afraid to speak, afraid I might startle him. A single misstep could have been fatal.

A flash of lightning cut across the sky, followed almost immediately by a crash of thunder so loud that for a moment I felt deafened. He might have come to watch the storm, so peaceful he looked standing there. But then he turned. He didn't seem surprised to see me. He turned back, ignoring me. Some slight movement made me cry out. "Don't!"

"Why not?" he said, his back to me. "Would you save me for the hangman? I'm a murderer, and I deserve to die."

"Not like this."

"Better like this than a hangman's noose. This is how *he* died."

"I know that."

He turned. "How could you know?" he said angrily.

"Were you here that night? Were you watching me even then?"

"No, but I know you took the keys."

"What concern is it of yours?" he said. "Why are you meddling in things that don't concern you?"

"They do concern me," I said. "You threatened my brother. You threatened me. You murdered your nephew."

"Don't call him that!" he cried out, as if I had wounded him.

"What should I call him?" I said, my hair blowing in my eyes.

"He was my brother! I murdered my own brother! May God forgive me! My own brother!" He swayed, and I reached out, afraid that he would fall, but dared not touch him.

"He was your brother," I repeated, trying to keep him talking. I wondered if he had lost his wits.

"You loved him, didn't you?" he said.

"I hardly knew him."

"But you loved him, didn't you?" he insisted stubbornly.

"Yes," I said.

"*She* loved him too. Everyone loved him. My father loved him. From the time he was born he was loved. And I was shunted out of sight. No one knew. Not even Ned. Especially not Ned. He never knew I was his brother."

"Why did you kill him?"

"Can you ask? I loved her. They had no right to betroth her to Ned when she was just a child. It should have been me. I would have appreciated her. Ned didn't appreciate her. It drove me crazy to watch how carelessly he treated her. I wouldn't have treated her carelessly. I would have given her my very soul. I didn't want to kill him, but I knew I couldn't stand to see him married to her. It would have driven me mad. And then he would have carried her away to Egypt and I might never have seen her again. I couldn't bear it."

"So you gave him laudanum in his drink that night and then pushed him off the tower."

"I strangled him, just as the thieves do in India, just as I had done thousands of times in my dreams. I strangled him with my scarf."

"What did you do with his body?"

He threw back his head and began to laugh, and I wondered again if he had lost his mind. "You want to know what I did with his body? Don't you know what I did with it? Don't all of you know? Haven't you known all along?"

"Known what?" I said. "We know nothing."

"Don't lie to me!" he shouted. "You must know."

Lightning flashed around us and a tremendous crash of thunder made me crouch.

Jasper dropped to his knees several arm lengths from me, still dangerously close to the edge. He put his hands to his head. "I put him where he belonged. I put him with his father. With our father."

"In his tomb?"

He nodded. "A thousand times I put him there. A thousand times I unlocked and forced the top. I can't close my eyes at night without seeing him. I think I'll never be done with killing him. And that's why I must jump from here. Though Lord knows he'll probably be my fellow traveler through hell, and I will never be free of him."

"He's there now?" I said. "In his father's tomb?"

He stared at me, as if trying to understand. "No, he's not there."

"Then where?"

"I don't know. I thought you knew. You and your brother and Grewgious. All of you. I thought you found him and took him out just to confound me."

"The body's gone?"

Jasper swayed slightly. "I strangled him. It was almost too easy. I expected him to struggle more. In my dreams he always struggled. Instead he looked surprised. And then he fell." Jasper waved his hand toward the edge. "It was over in a minute. That's the last thing I remember, Edwin falling. Then I had one of my fits."

He began to tremble, and I realized he was having one of them now. He reached out with one hand, as if groping for the wall. I reached my hand out and caught his. I tried to pull him away from the edge.

"It's my curse," he said. "I might have known. Just like that night." He leaned against the wall behind us. I held his arm firmly, so he would not bolt for the edge. His body was shaking and his eyes stared blindly. I could see sweat beading his forehead. Suddenly it began to rain. It fell on our hair and ran down our faces. We slid down until we were sitting, our backs to the wall.

"I don't remember anything of that night after he fell," he said. "I woke up the next morning in my bed. I don't know how I got there."

"Don't—" I said.

"Why are you here?" he demanded. "Why have you come?"

"You saved my life."

"I might as easily have taken it."

"But you didn't."

We sat there together in the rain. I put my arms around him, waiting for his fit to pass. I could feel his body shaking. I don't know how much time had passed when Mr. Crisparkle charged out of the tower doorway, followed closely by Deputy and Durdles, then Mr. Datchery. Mr. Datchery had a revolver and Durdles was carrying a pick. They stared at us.

"Are you all right?" Mr. Crisparkle shouted through the rain.

I nodded. "How did you know where to find me?"

"I told him," Deputy said. "It was me what saw my old enemy sneaking into the cathedral in the middle of the night up to no good, and I hung 'round to see him come out again, so I could chuck a stone at him if I could, but then I saw you go in and I set off to tell Durdles, and Dick was out walking and saw us, and Durdles said we'd better get Mr. Crisparkle too, in case Jasper was too much for the rest of us."

"He's not well," I told them as they stood looking down at us. "Just give him a few more minutes."

"At least come in out of the rain," Crisparkle said. "You'll catch your death of cold—both of you."

Gradually we all retreated back into the tower. When Jasper's fit had subsided, we began to slowly descend the stair. Shivering, I followed Deputy, who led the way with a lantern. Behind us, Jasper was helped along like a blind man by Durdles and Mr. Crisparkle, while Datchery brought up the rear.

19

The one thing everyone agreed upon was that Edwin Drood was dead. Datchery admitted that the body might never be found. However, now that the authorities had Jasper's confession, knowing the whereabouts of Edwin Drood's body was no longer important. They knew who had murdered him, how the murder had been committed, where it had occurred, and even why. Jasper had hidden the body that night following his fit, but no one knew where, not even Jasper himself. The sarcophagus of Edwin Drood Senior was opened, but as Jasper had told us, it held no body but that of its rightful occupant.

Jasper was taken to the Mayfair jail to await trial. It was there I visited him in a small bare cell with a single high barred window. He was sitting on a small stool reading when Mr. Crisparkle and I entered. He looked tired and defeated. In the past he had always been a fastidious man, neatly dressed and well groomed, but now his clothes looked wrinkled, he was unshaven, and his hair was uncombed. He looked up at us and blinked as if it took him a moment to register who we were and why we were there.

"I see you are reading the book I brought you last time," Mr. Crisparkle said when the cell door had been closed and locked behind us. "I hope it has been some comfort to you."

"It has," Jasper said, looking down at the Bible in his hands.

Mr. Crisparkle and I sat on the two worn chairs the guard had thrust into the cell for us.

I held out the basket I was carrying. "We brought you some food."

"It was most kind," he said but made no motion to take it so I set it down on the narrow bed against the wall.

"Do you want for anything?" Mr. Crisparkle asked.

Jasper closed his eyes. "If you wouldn't mind, there is one small thing."

"If it's within my power, I will get it for you," Mr. Crisparkle said. "What is it?"

"My medicine. If you could get some for me, I would be very grateful."

"Laudanum," I said.

He glanced at me. "Yes, you are correct, Miss Landless. Laudanum. I'm sure you don't approve, but without it I shall die. Of course I shall die anyway, and perhaps it is of no great moment whether it be of my affliction or at the hands of the hangman, but I would prefer not to suffer the awful agonies of my illness."

Mr. Crisparkle looked uncomfortable. "They may not let us . . . ."

"We will try to bring some," I promised.

Mr. Crisparkle shot me a look which I ignored.

"I hate for others to see the fit upon me," Jasper said. "I hate them to see my weakness." He clasped his hands tightly together to stop their trembling. My heart felt moved with pity for him.

"Have you always had fits?" I asked.

He nodded. "I had my first when I was ten. I used to tell myself that was why my father didn't want me."

"Do you still believe that?" I asked.

"Well, there was that. But also he was ashamed of me."

"Why should he be ashamed of you?" Mr. Crisparkle asked.

"It's a long story."

"I'd like to hear it," I said.

"Well, I have nothing else to do," he said. "And the truth doesn't need to be hidden anymore. Why shouldn't I tell it?" He looked down at his tightly clasped hands. "The question is where to start. I suppose I should start with my father. While my father was stationed in India, he fell in love with and secretly married an Indian woman. He married her secretly because he knew his family back in England would disapprove if they found out, and he might even be disinherited. Not a noble motive, but understandable. Of course sooner or later it was bound to come out, so he was taking an enormous risk. Just think of it. He was willing to risk his future inheritance for the sake of the woman he loved. But then she died in childbirth. He was heartbroken. In his distraught state he had to decide what to do about the child to whom she had given birth. Because of his job, he saw no way that he could take care of the boy. Nor did his wife's relatives want the child of mixed blood. So he gave the little boy to an English family living in Bombay. This family had a daughter almost seventeen, but the years had passed, and the poor wife, after a series of miscarriages, had been told she would not be able to bear another child. She and her husband had hoped for years for a son. They were only too happy to give a home to the boy-child who was offered to them."

"You," I said.

"Yes, Miss Landless, me. Who could have foreseen that my father would fall in love with their daughter? He never did reveal his secret first marriage or the fact that I was really his son, although they may have suspected. No doubt it seemed best for everyone if my parentage remained a secret. After a short courtship, my father married their daughter.

"At the age of ten, I was sent to England to go to school. I didn't like England much. It was cold and I was often sick and the other boys bullied me. My only consolation was my love of music. After I completed my studies, I returned to India, intending to work as a civil servant. However, India was different than I remembered. I was appalled by the squalor. The natives looked at me with dislike because I was clearly English, but the English did not completely accept me either, because of my dark skin. Then I fell sick during a cholera epidemic that decimated the British population. I survived but was so weak I was forced to resign my position and return to England. I was a young man by then, but I didn't know the truth about my identity. It wasn't until several years later that my father on his deathbed confessed all.

"Since then I can't help but wonder, would he have confessed to me had he not wanted someone to watch over Edwin, whose mother had died many years before trying to give birth to a little girl? Had it not been his desire to provide a guardian for young Edwin, he need not have told. He could have gone to his grave with the secret. Sometimes I wish he had. Learning I was young Edwin Drood's brother as well as his uncle was an unwelcome revelation. I had been fond enough of the boy before I knew the truth, but afterward I couldn't look at him without comparing my lot with his. I began to see how Edwin had everything that I did not. Edwin had grown up loved. He had the blond good looks and sweet disposition that caused everyone to dote on him. He had a future that would take him abroad. He even had an exquisite young beauty betrothed to him. How could I help but compare my own fate to that of my younger brother? I tried hard to hide my feelings. To all the world around us, and especially to Edwin himself, I was a doting uncle. I hid my sense of injustice within my breast, but it only grew until at last I dared to imagine myself as the favored son. It seemed to me Edwin did not deserve all that he had. What had he ever done for it? In truth, he was a spoiled conceited young man who scarcely valued his birthright. Can you imagine how that galled me?

"Even then I might have lived with my terrible secret had I not started to give Rosa Bud music lessons. From that first lesson I wanted her. No amount of telling myself that I couldn't have her stopped me from wanting her. From a pretty child she was blossoming into a pretty young woman. I found myself thinking about her when I was not with her. I began to live for those lessons when we would be alone together. Sometimes I grew angry with her for little mistakes because I so desperately wanted to touch her, to crush those rose-petal lips against mine, to crush her against myself, to tell her how much I loved her. Instead I had to stifle my passion. I could say nothing. Sometimes my feeling welled up so powerfully I thought she must feel it. How could she not know? I willed her to know. I willed her to love me. It was too much for such a fragile creature. She became frightened of me. I could see it and yet I couldn't stop myself. I told myself that I deserved her. Everything else had been denied to me, but I would not let them deny me *this*. Edwin was so damnably cool about her. What did he know about love? What right had he to claim Rosa for his wife?

"After that I began to brood even more than before. Since my schooldays I had been taking laudanum for my fits. Now I recklessly sought out an opium den in London, where no one would know me. I had found that laudanum gave me dreams. In my dreams I could possess Rosa and I could revenge myself against Edwin in violent and terrible ways. The pipe proved my undoing. Having given in to it once, I must give in to it again and again. I despised myself for my weakness. I despised that old woman and her sordid den where I must share her filthy bed with the dregs of the earth. But when my dark mood came upon me, I threw all caution to the wind and there I must go and seek relief in the powerful dreams unleashed by her opium pipe.

"And so gradually I came to live a double life. In Cloisterham I continued to be the respected choirmaster, but then I would rush off to London's seedy backstreets where I could indulge my most despicable impulses. It was in those backstreets that I found Jenny singing on a street corner. Her resemblance to Rosa struck me at once—the same blue eyes and golden hair, the innocence and sweetness. I found myself drawn back repeatedly to that corner, to watch her and listen to her sing. I thought it would be a simple matter to approach her. I expected her to be flattered, but instead she seemed frightened and resisted me. I have known for a long time that I have a certain power over others if I concentrate hard on looking in their eyes. It's what fakirs do in India when they charm a cobra to rise from a basket. I tried to use these magnetic powers on Jenny. I willed her to know I was there, to sing for me, to think of me.

"I followed her through the streets, willing her to turn and look at me. Finally she allowed me to buy her a drink. I tried to tell her about Edwin, about how much I hated him, about Edwin's betrothal to the girl who ought to have been my sweetheart. But it only confused her. She didn't love me any more than Rosa did, and as she pulled away from me one night, I felt a surge of anger, and before I knew what I had done I had wound my black scarf around her throat and choked her. It happened in a minute. She didn't even have time to cry out. I looked around furtively as she slumped in my arms and saw no one. I didn't want to be caught. My first impulse was to drop her and run. But then her face, even dead, looked so much like Rosa that I couldn't bear to leave her lying in the street. So I carried her to a nearby church and laid her in an open grave, her hands crossed on her chest. That was the last I saw of her. When I went by the churchyard a week later, the grave was filled in. Whether she was in it or had been moved, I don't know."

He looked from me to Mr. Crisparkle, then back again. "So you see what I am. I don't deserve your pity. Once maybe I did, but I have forfeited all right to be pitied. If I could undo the terrible things I've done, I would. But I can't. There it is."

In the weeks that followed, I went as often as my teaching schedule permitted to visit Jasper in his cell in the Mayfair jail. Sometimes Mr. Crisparkle accompanied me; sometimes I went alone. I made sure that Jasper had laudanum and I took him whatever news I could.

"Did you go to morning service?" he often asked.

Sometimes I had to confess that I had not, but seeing his disappointment, I tried to go as often as I could. If I said, yes, I had gone, he would ask what the subject of the sermon had been and how the choir had sounded. Mr. Crisparkle could always answer both questions with more authority than I when he was with me. Without him, I did the best I could.

"And have they found a new choirmaster?" he asked me one day when I had gone alone.

"They are still searching," I told him.

He nodded. I wondered if the subject was painful for him. It surely reminded him of what he had lost, his position and the life he had led, but then no doubt everything reminded him of that. The very walls around him reminded him.

"I'm sorry I can't come more often," I said. "My classes at the seminary keep me busy."

"Ah, yes, how are you doing in your new position at Miss Twinkleton's?" he asked. He always treated me politely and asked me about myself. He never questioned why I visited but merely accepted it. I suspected that my life was of little interest to him. In his place I was sure I could think of nothing but the waiting gallows. But we could not talk of that.

"I do the best I can. I fear I'm not as good a teacher as I ought to be. I have so much to learn." I could look him directly in the eyes now. His eyes no longer made me uncomfortable. I didn't feel I'd get lost in them. They were the eyes of a man who had suffered. That was what I saw in them—suffering and regret.

"Do you like working there?" he asked. "Are the young ladies attentive?"

"I like working there very much," I said. "The young ladies sometimes don't care very much about learning French, but we progress. No doubt it seems strange to them that last term I was a fellow student and this term I'm a teacher."

"And your brother?" he said. "How is your brother doing?"

"He's doing well. He hopes to find a position soon."

"That's good," he said, nodding. "I regret all the distress I caused your brother. I hope he'll be able to forgive me someday. The strange thing is he reminded me of myself when I was younger. All that pent up anger. That desire to lash out." He shook his head, remembering. "When I looked at your brother, I saw myself. I hope he will come to a better end than I have."

"Neville will be fine," I assured him.

"And Rosa? What of Rosa?"

"She's well."

He nodded. "And is she happy?"

"Yes, she's happy."

He nodded again, his eyes closed, and sighed deeply.

Another day I told him about the ghost scream Durdles

had heard Christmas Eve the year before Edwin Drood had died.

"It was no ghost scream," he said. "It was me. I borrowed Tope's key and climbed to the top of the tower. Christmas has always been hard for me. It's supposed to be a time for family, but it has always reminded me that I was abandoned by my father and robbed of my birthright."

"So you climbed to the top of the tower and screamed?"

"I intended to jump that night," he said, "to put an end to the self I had come to loathe. I had murdered that poor girl in the streets of London in cold blood. I thought I deserved to die. But then looking down at the graveyard, I lost my nerve. I screamed because I couldn't bear my life any longer. It was followed by the howl of a dog somewhere in the night, the most mournful sound that you can imagine. *That* gave me shivers. But then there was only silence. And so I came back down again. Shortly after that I dreamed that Edwin climbed the stairs with me, and that he was the one who jumped, not I, and the scream was his. By the night it happened, I had already lived it a thousand times in my dreams."

Jasper's trial took place on an overcast day in late October. Mr. Crisparkle traveled with me and never left my side. Princess Puffer did not attend due to ill health, but Jack came and Neville was there too. Most of the people in the courtroom didn't know Jasper. They had come for other cases or were there out of curiosity. Heads turned to look at Jasper only after he was singled out by the judge as a dangerous murderer. Sitting in the iron cage with the others on trial that day, he looked thinner and older, but there was a calm about him that had not been there before. When he first came in, he glanced around the room as if he were looking for someone. I wondered if it was Rosa he was looking for. If he saw us, he did not acknowledge us. He merely bowed his head and did not look up again until his turn came. It was over in a matter of minutes. There was never any doubt about the outcome because he had confessed.

"What will happen to him now?" Neville asked.

"He'll be hanged of course," Jack said.

Knowing he was condemned to die did not change Jasper's outer demeanor when next I visited him in his prison cell. He had known from the time he was apprehended that he would die.

Now I was able to visit only if Mr. Crisparkle went with me, and we had to talk to Jasper through bars with a guard sitting near who could hear all we said.

"You're not afraid?" I asked.

"Of course I'm afraid," he said. "But at least the nightmares will come to an end."

They no longer allowed him to have laudanum. Now that he was condemned to die, they did not want him to cheat the law by killing himself with an overdose of his medicine. Deprived of it, he was suffering from vivid and terrible nightmares and frequently had the shakes. He did not look well.

"You've been very good to visit me like this," he said. "But perhaps you shouldn't come again."

"Why not?" I said.

"I'll get worse. I hate to be seen like that."

"I'll speak to the warden again," Mr. Crisparkle said. "I'll see if I can't persuade him to let you have a few drops of laudanum from time to time."

"I doubt he'll agree," Jasper said. "And it's no more than I deserve. I have committed two terrible crimes. Or rather *he* did, the monster I turned into. He's inside of me. The opium brought him out. Soon it will be time for him to die."

"Pray for forgiveness," Mr. Crisparkle said.

"I fear some things are too terrible to be forgiven," Jasper said.

Then he touched my fingers on the bars. "You've been very kind to come," he said, "but you shouldn't come again."

One day in November one of our young ladies rushed up to my room to tell me I had a visitor.

"There's a foreign gentleman downstairs who wants to talk to you," she announced breathlessly.

I couldn't imagine who my visitor might be.

Downstairs I found Miss Twinkleton also in a state of excitement when she opened the door to her sitting room. "A gentleman from India," she whispered. "He says it is very important. He wanted to speak to you alone, but I explained to him that would not be appropriate. What would the young ladies think? So I'll just sit here and sew quietly while your visitor is here if you don't mind."

I didn't mind of course. I knew Miss Twinkleton would see it as a shocking lapse of duty to abandon me to a strange man in her sitting room, and a foreign one at that.

The gentleman from India stood when I entered and bowed slightly. He was dressed all in white and wore a jewel in his turban. I recognized him as the man I had once seen standing across the street from Mrs. Billickin's house.

"You are Miss Landless?" he asked. "Helena Landless? Formerly of Colombo?"

"Yes," I said. "I am Helena Landless."

His black eyes regarded me with curiosity. "I was a friend of your father's," he said.

"Lieutenant Landless?" I said. "You knew him?" I don't know what I had expected, but not this. I had never heard anyone say they knew my father. It crossed my mind that he must have made a mistake. Surely he could not mean my father. He must be referring to my stepfather.

"His name was not Landless," the Indian gentleman said. "His name was Bhattacharya."

I glanced at Miss Twinkleton, but at that moment she seemed intent upon the needlework she had taken up. "I don't understand. My father was a British soldier."

"I realize this may come as a shock to you," he said. "Your father's name was Bhattacharya. He fell in love with your mother, and she with him. He was in the British army, but he was a sepoy, not a British soldier."

I stared at him. "If this is true, why did no one tell us?"

"He died when his company was attacked during a rebellion. Your mother had to invent a history for you to make the birth of her children look respectable. She would have been sent home in disgrace if the truth had come out."

"Have you any proof of this?" I asked.

He shook his head. "You will have to look elsewhere for proof. You will have to look in your own heart. I have only this." He handed me an envelope.

"What is it?"

"Your father asked me as he was dying to give this to you and your brother one day. I have come very far to keep my promise to him."

Inside the envelope was a thin piece of paper with writing on it in Hindi which I couldn't read. "What does it say?"

"He left all he had to his children."

"But you said he was only a sepoy."

The Indian man nodded patiently. "He was a sepoy, but he also came from a good family. He had a brother who also died. There were no other heirs. Today the money has increased and it is a respectable sum. I apologize for not being able to give it to you sooner, but it was necessary to wait until you and your brother were no longer wards. Otherwise the inheritance might have fallen into the wrong hands."

"You mean my stepfather's," I said.

"Your father would not have wanted that."

"Is it a lot of money?" I asked.

He smiled. "Quite a lot. Give this letter to a lawyer. It will be transferred between banks. There should be no problem." He stood, as if he were done.

"Must you leave?" I asked. "I have so many questions. What was my father like? Where was he from? How did he and my mother meet?"

The man smiled again. "He was a good man, a good son, a good father, a good friend. He met your mother in a public garden. That's all I know. And now that I have given you his letter, I will go. I will first, however, give you an address where I can be contacted by your lawyer if he has questions. I will be in London only a short time longer. The time approaches when I must return home."

"Thank you," I told him. "You've been very kind to bring this to us. Can I give you anything in repayment?"

He held up his hand in refusal. "It is not necessary. I have done what I had to do. Now my old friend can rest in peace. His children will not live in want." He made another small bow to me.

Miss Twinkleton stood then and insisted on seeing him to the door. It gave me a minute to be alone. I hardly knew what to think. My father a sepoy—and wealthy. It was a lot to take in.

When she returned, Miss Twinkleton looked at the letter with me. As she could not read Hindi any more than I could, we had to content ourselves with staring at the strange writing.

"Do you realize what this means?" said Miss Twinkleton. "You no longer have to worry about how to support yourself, my dear."

"And Neville can go to college," I added.

I ran my fingers gently over the letter. The paper was so thin. I regretted now that I had never learned to read Hindi. My father's language, my father's writing.

"You must let Mr. Grewgious know," Miss Twinkleton said. "We must send a letter to him immediately."

"And Neville," I said. "We must tell Neville too."

I went upstairs to my room then and took my mother's red sari from the drawer where I kept it. Once I had asked Jasper why he had taken it.

"I broke into your rooms at the Staple Inn because I

was looking for answers," he had said. "I wanted to know where Rosa was and I wanted to know what had been done with Edwin's body. That's why I watched your brother and followed him through the streets at night. I thought eventually he would lead me to them. I thought your brother was deliberately tormenting me. It began to seem like a conspiracy, with your brother at the center. I was nearly mad with rage."

"That doesn't explain why you took my mother's red sari," I pointed out.

"I didn't know it was your mother's," he said. "When I was going through the drawer, I found it. It reminded me of India, and so I took it."

"And did you know it was me who came to dinner that night?" I asked then, remembering how he had brought out the red sari.

"Of course. Did you think I would really believe you were a man?"

I wonder now if others had also seen through my disguise. Was I the only one I had deceived? I held the sari against my cheek and felt the softness of the silk. Then I stepped to the mirror and draped it over my hair. For a minute the face that looked back at me was that of a young Indian woman. I wondered that I hadn't seen her before. My eyes fell on the miniature of my mother. She had kept our true identity a secret from Neville and me, but I remembered how she had told us when we were young how much she had loved our father. When we asked to see pictures of him, she said she had none. Now, knowing she had dared to love a man in defiance of her family and society made me feel I knew her better.

. . .

Neville won a scholarship to Oxford. He came to Cloisterham in late November to tell me and afterward went for a walk with Miss Ferdinand. I watched them from my window sit on the same bench Edwin and Rosa had sat on the day they had decided to part. I felt glad that he was able to forget Rosa. I wanted him to find happiness in life, not to pine for what he couldn't have. He had been a lonely outcast for long enough. Let him find out what it was like to belong, to succeed, to be loved.

I thought hard about the money we had inherited from the father we never knew. Neville's share could help put him through school. With mine I could live independently. I wouldn't have to work at Miss Twinkleton's, but I was not sure I wanted to live idly. I asked myself what I would really like to do if I could choose. It wasn't an easy question to answer, but in the end I decided I would like to be useful. I wanted to help other people. But I was not sure how to go about that.

I brought the matter up with Mr. Crisparkle one day when we were returning by coach from Maidstone.

"Is there someone in particular you would like to help or just people in general?" he asked.

"Both," I told him.

"If the person in particular is Mr. Jasper, I'm afraid there's nothing more you can do for him."

"I know that," I said. "It isn't Mr. Jasper. It's Jack I would like to help."

He looked surprised. "What did you have in mind?"

"I wondered if I could persuade you to tutor him as you have Neville. He's very bright, but he's had no opportunity."

"Ah, your idea of helping him is for me to help him," he said, smiling.

"I would pay for his lessons," I hastened to assure him. "Only he mustn't know."

"You wish to be anonymous?"

"If he knew, I'm not sure he'd accept."

"Very well," Mr. Crisparkle said. "I'll talk to him and see if he's interested in this arrangement. And do you also have ideas for how you would like to help people in general?"

"I'm afraid I don't. The problem seems so large. I know it existed in Colombo too. The poverty, the beggars on the streets, orphans, cripples. I've seen it again in London."

"It's very good of you, Helena, to want to help," he said. "But I'm afraid you could give away all your money and these problems would still exist."

"I know that," I said. "But there must be some small way in which I can contribute."

"Have you talked to Mr. Grewgious about this? Perhaps he has some ideas."

I admitted I had not but vowed to do so at the next opportunity.

The opportunity arose soon after when I traveled to London to visit Neville, who had new lodgings now. I stopped by the Staple Inn and told Mr. Grewgious about my desire to use some part of my inheritance to help the poor of London.

"You want my advice?" he said. "Don't do it. It would be throwing your money away."

"Surely there's something I can do."

He shook his head. "I'm sorry to disappoint you, but

your fortune is too small and the problem too large. Don't you agree, Bazzard?"

Bazzard was sitting at a desk in the corner writing. "Absolutely," he said, looking up. "The problem is too large."

"Well, if you won't help me," I said, "I guess I'll have to figure out a way on my own."

"Bazzard, she seems quite determined, doesn't she?" Mr. Grewgious said.

"Indeed she does," Bazzard agreed.

"I suppose it's my duty as her lawyer to offer advice."

"You might look at it that way, sir."

"Very well, let's look at it as a problem to be solved," said Mr. Grewgious, taking his usual path from wall to window and back again. "Let's break it down into pieces. Obviously you can't help everybody. You will have to narrow it down. Who would you like to help most, the men, the women, or the children?"

I hesitated. "The children, I suppose."

"The children," he repeated. "Now we're getting somewhere. And how could they be helped?"

"I don't know," I said. "More orphanages?"

He shook his head. "Have you ever visited one of London's orphanages?"

"No," I admitted.

"Terrible places. No, I don't think more orphanages are the answer. If children survive such institutions, they are still not fit to make their way in the world. Turned out on the street, more often than not, they turn to crime or starve."

I saw what he was getting at. It was like my solution for Jack. By arranging for him to study with Mr. Crisparkle, I was trying to provide him with the means to make his way in the world. "A school, then," I suggested. "A school where poor children could get an education."

"Of course there would be no guarantee that it would solve the problem," he warned.

"But it could be a start," I said, excited now. "We could save some."

When I stepped out of Mr. Grewgious's office that afternoon, I was glad that I had turned to him for advice. I knew it would take time to find the right location and to work out a plan for how to begin, but I was determined to do it. It would be a free school, and it would be open to both boys and girls and I would teach there. In this way I would put my money to good use.

One day in December Jack sent word that Princess Puffer was dying. For a week she lay on the bed where her customers had dreamed their opium dreams. Now there were no more customers. Jack and I sat with her during her final hours, holding her hand and watching over her when she slept. Sometimes she woke and called me Jenny and thanked me with tears in her eyes for coming back again.

Jasper was hanged a few weeks later. I wasn't there to see it. I couldn't bear to watch him die. I knew he had done wrong and must be punished, but it seemed to me that he was not the man he had been when he had committed the crimes. The man I had come to know in the Mayfair jail was a gentler man. Had he been born under different circumstances, had he been blessed with loving parents, had he never taken opium, I was sure he would have been a much better man.

20

Jasper's body was brought back to Cloisterham for burial. Only a handful of people were present at the funeral. Most of Cloisterham looked the other way. I visited his grave often and when spring came laid flowers on it. The new choirmaster moved into the Gate House and like his predecessor gave music lessons to the young ladies at Miss Twinkleton's. The days passed uneventfully, except perhaps for a sudden flurry of attention from London when Durdles located a significant cache of ancient bodies in the cathedral and an eminent archaeologist from the British Museum arrived with a dozen workers to exhume them. Suddenly Durdles found himself much sought after. Reporters wanted to interview him. The Archaeological Society invited him to lecture, a proposition that initially terrified him, but in the end, after much encouragement from Mr. Crisparkle and me, he agreed to. I went to London to hear him speak. Cleaned up and wearing a new suit, he looked quite dignified, and afterward he had a cluster of people around him asking questions. Deputy was there too, almost unrecognizable with the dirt scrubbed off him and wearing new clothes. I almost didn't recognize him until he broke into a grin that revealed his missing teeth. There was no mistaking that grin.

"He ain't had a drink for three weeks," Deputy told me proudly. "I know on account of I'm the one what makes sure. I live with him now, you know. I take care of him."

"Does that mean you don't work at the Travellers' anymore?" I asked.

"I go 'round there sometimes," Deputy said. "Just to keep my hand in."

I had heard Durdles was being paid by the archaeologist, and when their work at the cathedral was done, he was going to visit several other old cathedrals using his hammer and his finely tuned ear to look for ancient remains.

"We may even go to Egypt to search for mummies and treasures in ancient tombs," Deputy said. "Wouldn't that be something?"

I agreed it would.

During this time I was content with my lot in Cloisterham. My duties at Miss Twinkleton's kept me busy. When old Mrs. Crisparkle fell ill, I helped nurse her and afterward she began to warm to me. Sometimes I wondered if I would pass the rest of my life thus. It seemed an easy, peaceful way to live. But something tugged at me too. I felt a growing restlessness. It turned out I was not the only one feeling restless.

Jack turned up late one afternoon and asked if I would go for a walk with him. Since he had never done this before, I was mystified by what it meant. I assumed he had something to tell me, but I saw that he was not to be rushed.

"Where would you like to walk?" I said. "Shall we go to the cathedral?"

He shook his head. "It reminds me of Jasper."

"Down High Street?" I suggested.

He looked one way down the street and then the other. I could tell he was not very impressed by High Street.

"Would you like to walk in the country then?" I suggested.

This seemed to interest him, so I took him along the route that Neville and I used to take which led past some ruins to a view of the river. Once we were there, we leaned against a rock and looked at the sunset.

"Do you come here often?" he asked.

"Sometimes," I said. "Not as often as I used to when Neville was here."

"Things change, don't they?" he said. He picked up a small stone and tossed it in the direction of the river. Because the river was a very long way away, the stone had no hope of hitting its mark, but that didn't seem to bother him.

"You miss Princess Puffer, don't you?" I said.

"I knew she wouldn't be around forever, but yes I miss her."

"What will you do now?"

"Leave England, I suppose."

I looked at him, surprised. "Where would you go?"

"To the States."

"What would you do there?"

"I don't know. Maybe I'll be an actor." He grinned.

"I've heard there's lots of work there. You work hard, you can be somebody."

"What about your lessons with Mr. Crisparkle?" I said.

"I've learned a lot from Mr. Crisparkle already. I'm grateful to him for that, and to my anonymous benefactor, whoever that may be." I glanced at him, wondering if he suspected that it was me, but he was busy throwing another stone. "I can't stay here for that. I want to see what's out there. There's more to the world than England."

"You've already made arrangements, haven't you?" I said, realizing that he had come to say good-bye.

He nodded. "I sail in two weeks." Another stone flew toward the river and the sunset. "What about you? Have you ever thought of leaving?"

"I miss Ceylon," I admitted, "but I wouldn't go back. There's nothing for me there. Everyone I care about is here—Neville, Rosa, Miss Twinkleton, Mr. Grewgious, Mr. Crisparkle. And soon I'll have my school to run."

"Will it be enough?"

"I don't know."

"Well, if you get an urge to travel, maybe you'll come see me in New York."

"Is that where you'll be?"

He shrugged. "Or Chicago or San Francisco. It's a big country they say. I ought to be able to find some place that suits me."

"You must write and let me know where you are."

"All right I will," he said. "And you must write to me."

One day in May I was looking out the window of my classroom at the Nuns' House when Mr. Grewgious arrived in a chaise. I was surprised to see him on a school day and wondered what had brought him to Cloisterham. The girls in my class were reading aloud from *La Princesse de Clèves*. I thought I would have to wait another thirty minutes, until class came to an end, to find out the reason for Mr. Grewgious's visit. However, ten minutes later Miss Twinkleton poked her head in the door looking excited and flustered.

"You must come right away," she said.

I left Miss Humphreys in charge of the class, knowing that no matter whom I left in charge, the class would be reduced to giggles within moments and *La Princesse de Clèves* would be forgotten.

Mr. Grewgious was sitting in an armchair near the hearth when I entered Miss Twinkleton's sitting room. "My dear, you're looking well," he said, rising, still holding a teacup.

"She is, isn't she?" Miss Twinkleton said, pouring a cup of tea for me.

"I remember when I first saw you," Mr. Grewgious said, "that day more than a year ago when I came here to talk to Rosa about her engagement to young Drood."

"How much has happened since then!" I said.

He cleared his throat and had the uncomfortable look he often got when he had an unpleasant announcement to make. "I have news," he said.

"Is it about Rosa?" I asked, suddenly fearful. I knew she was expecting.

"No, it's not about Rosa," he said. "It is about that young man to whom she was once engaged." He and Miss Twinkleton exchanged looks. His seemed to ask if he had put it right. Hers seemed to say that he had.

"Edwin Drood?" I said, surprised.

"The very same."

"Have they found his body after all this time?"

He fumbled at his pockets and produced several sheets of folded paper which he held out to me. It appeared to be a letter. "Perhaps you should sit down to read this."

"Yes, dear, sit down," Miss Twinkleton urged. "I assure you I was glad I was sitting when I read it."

I took their advice and sat before I began to read. I quickly realized the letter before me was not only about Edwin Drood, but had in fact been written by him.

March 25, 18--

Dear Mr. Grewgious:

You will no doubt be surprised to hear from me after all this time. I daresay everyone, including yourself, thinks me dead. Until quite recently I thought letting you think so was for the best. Even now I'm not completely sure that it isn't. However, someone whom I hold very dear to me has urged me to write to you.

It is hard to know where to begin. I must confess I have taken up my pen many times intending to write, but then put it down again because I was not sure you would believe the story I have to tell—so fantastic it will seem—and because even though it is so fantastic, I feel it does not excuse my actions. Nevertheless, I am hoping that when you hear what happened the night I took leave of Cloisterham, you will understand and forgive me. But before I go farther, I must confess I lost the ring you entrusted to me. I suppose you thought me little better than a common thief to disappear with so valuable an item, especially after you had impressed upon me its value. Losing it seemed to me unforgivable, and so I thought it was just as well that I should disappear along with the ring.

Having confessed the worst, here is the rest of my story.

As you no doubt know, the night I was to give the ring to Rosa, we mutually agreed to end our engagement. (I will not fall into my old lax habits of referring to her by a certain nickname which I know offended you.) Since you specified that I was to give her the ring as a seal of our intentions, and we had not sealed them, I did not give her the ring. The ring did not leave my coat pocket. I walked away from our farewell meeting fully intending to return it to you at our next meeting, as you had requested. That night I dined with my uncle Jasper and young Neville Landless. I had too much to drink, and I daresay, so did Landless. From that point on the evening in my memory is a blur. It is more like a dream than a memory, a very bad dream. Young Neville did not annoy me so much as on our previous encounters. In fact, I began to feel positively warm toward him as the evening wore on. By the time we left the Gate House, we were walking arm in arm like old friends and singing. I remember thinking he might fall down if I wasn't helping him, and then that I might fall down if he wasn't helping me. It all seemed very confused. We ended up down by the river watching the storm, and then thoroughly soaked, we stumbled back to Cloisterham. I think I remember Neville saying goodbye and I started back toward the Gate House. Before I got there, I met my uncle Jasper. I suppose he must have been waiting for me. He said he must show me something and although I wanted no more than to go back to my little room at the Gate House and fall into bed, he would not hear of it. I must go with him.

The next thing I remember is being in the crypt of the cathedral. Jack had my arm and was talking, but I couldn't concentrate on what he was saying. Then we were climbing up a narrow winding stair that seemed to go on forever. I didn't think we would ever get to the top, and when we did, the storm was quite fierce. Jack insisted we go right up to the edge of the tower. "Many times we have made this journey," he said, "but tonight is the last time." I asked him what he meant. "You will never again take from me what is mine," he said fiercely. I said I didn't understand. "You took everything in this world from me. Have you never guessed how much I hate you? Have I not warned you a thousand times? Well, there will be no more warnings, Ned. You are going to die tonight."

I told him to stop it, that he was scaring me. His face looked strange. I wondered if he had gone mad. "In India there are men adept at killing," he said. "First they befriend a fellow traveler and then they kill him. No one knows. Did I ever tell you that when I was a child I knew men like that?" As if in a dream, I saw him take off his black scarf. Before I could cry out it was around my neck. His face was close to mine. "You are my brother," he said. "I was the older, I was the first-born. All that was given you ought to have been mine." I knew then that he had indeed gone mad. As the scarf tightened, I struggled, but I was so impaired by the wine I had drunk I was at a disadvantage. And then there was a terrific flash of lightning and crash of thunder. I thought the tower had been hit. Maybe it had. The flash lit up Jack's face in a ghastly way. At the same moment I lost my footing and fell.

I would no doubt have broken my neck had I not managed to grab the hands of the cathedral clock as I went down. One broke and I clung to the other for dear life. I have no idea how long I hung there while the lightning flashed all around me and I expected every new flash to strike me. The rain poured down. I remember being cold and wet and frightened out of my mind. I knew if I fell I would die. When I thought I could hold on no longer, I started trying to climb. I dislodged stones and tore my *clothes and my hands were bleeding, but somehow I got back up on the ledge. My uncle was gone. I stumbled back down the stairs. I found my way somehow back to the door where we had entered and bolted into the night, not knowing where to go, knowing only that I could not return to the Gate House. I wanted to get as far away as possible from my uncle.*

I must have walked most of that night. Toward morning I found myself wandering on a country road and I lay down by the side, half dead with exhaustion. That's where a farmer found me and brought me home for his wife to tend. I don't remember much after that. I was sick with a fever, I suppose from the awful weather and the shock of what had happened. The farmer's wife nursed me back to health. When I had recovered, I decided not to come back to Cloisterham. I had a dread of facing my uncle Jasper. Suppose he pretended that nothing had happened? Who would believe me when I had been drunk that night? I didn't want to see my uncle ever again. I couldn't see him without remembering that look of hatred on his face. I could only conclude that he was deranged. I remembered the fits he had been subject to. Perhaps they had been the forewarning of what was to come.

The more I thought about it, I didn't see any reason I should return to Cloisterham. Rosa and I had parted. I had no need to return for her. In fact, there really was no need to return to my life in London either. I had not been looking forward to going to Egypt. Now that I would have no wife to take care of, I really didn't need to go to Egypt if I didn't want. I began to see that an unforeseen opportunity lay before me. For months—years even—I had deplored the destiny that had been laid out for me. Now I had the opportunity to change it. I would not go to Egypt. I would not take up the partnership that my father had arranged for me. I would find my own destiny.

With the farmer's help, I managed to find passage on a ship leaving for America. On the crossing I met a gentleman who promised to help me find employment. It turns out that my engineering skills are much in demand in the States. There are bridges to build and buildings and dams. Everything is new here. From the time I stepped off the ship, I have had no regrets. I feel as if I belong here. It is just the place for a young man like myself starting out. I also have a wife to think of now—the sweetest, most amiable creature—whom I'm quite sure I don't deserve. I am ever so grateful Rosa and I did not take the disastrous step of marrying. Parents ought never plan out their children's futures. I intend to remember that when mine are born. (We are expecting our first child shortly.)

I beg you not to let Jack know of my whereabouts. I really don't want to see him again, and I have no wish to place my family in any danger. You can do as you like with the information I have given to you. I have no desire to hurt Jack. However, I have lately begun to wonder if he is a danger to others, and my conscience troubles me that I have kept the events of that night a secret all this time.

But perhaps by now he has been locked away. In any case, it's best that he forget about me, as I have tried to forget about him. Someday I may return to England with my family for a visit. If I do, I will look you up. Until then I remain,
Respectfully yours,
Edwin Drood

"What do you think of that?" Miss Twinkleton said when I had finished reading the letter. "I can tell you I was astonished."

"As was I, Madam, when that letter arrived in the mail," said Mr. Grewgious. "I did not expect Edwin Drood to return from the dead after so much time."

"I wonder if he has any idea how much trouble he's caused," said Miss Twinkleton. "And think how poor Rosa suffered."

"It's just as well she didn't marry him," Mr. Grewgious said. "I always suspected he didn't love her as she deserved to be loved."

"You will write to him?" I asked Mr. Grewgious. "You'll tell him Jasper is dead?" I thought Edwin ought to know, but I did not want to be the one to write such a letter. I didn't think I would be able to hide my feelings on a subject that was still painful.

"I will," Mr. Grewgious said. "I will let him know all that has transpired in his absence."

"He might have written sooner," Miss Twinkleton said, "instead of letting everyone think he'd been murdered. It was most inconsiderate."

"He might have let us all know as soon as he recovered from his fever," Mr. Grewgious said. "Then poor Neville wouldn't have been blamed for his disappearance."

"But his desire to run away is understandable," I said, looking down again at the letter in my hand. "It was no doubt an awful shock when his uncle turned on him that night. He had no way of knowing Neville would be blamed."

"He was a young man who did not think much about the consequences of his actions," Mr. Grewgious said. "That was my opinion of him the last time I saw him, and it is my opinion now."

"Well, I must say I'm glad our Rosa is not in faraway

Egypt," Miss Twinkleton said. "And she could not ask for a kinder husband than Mr. Tartar has proved to be."

I went to visit Rosa during the summer recess. We sat out on the lawn of Tartar's estate with the bassinet close by where her baby daughter slept. Inevitably our conversation came around to the events that had changed both our lives during the past year and a half.

"There's only one thing I don't understand," Rosa said. "How did Edwin's watch and chain and his shirtpin get into the weir?"

"Jasper threw them in," I explained. "He took them from Edwin while they were climbing to the tower. It was all part of his plan. He wanted people to think Edwin had drowned in the weir. Besides, without his jewelry, no one would be able to identify his body. He intended to put Edwin's body in their father's tomb and sprinkle quicklime on it. It wasn't just revenge against Edwin; it was revenge against his father for not acknowledging him."

"Well, I'm awfully glad Eddy is alive," Rosa said. "I felt so horribly guilty every time I thought of him. I treated him so awful."

The baby cried just then, and Rosa sprang to it and picked it up. "I can't bear for her to cry, not for a minute. Nancy says I'll spoil her, but I don't care." Nancy was the nursemaid, who seemed to me to have very little to do since Rosa would not let the baby out of her sight.

"I ought to have told Eddy about his uncle," Rosa said. "It was very wrong of me not to tell."

The baby cooed softly and touched her face with a tiny hand.

"What will you do now?" Rosa asked me.

Mr. Grewgious had at last proposed to Miss Twinkleton and Miss Twinkleton was planning to close the seminary and move to London. Although I had grown fond of Cloisterham, it held sad memories for me, and once the school was gone, I thought it would be time for me to leave as well.

"I suppose I'll follow Miss Twinkleton to London," I said.

"But London's such a gritty place," Rosa objected, making a face. "Wouldn't you rather live in the country?"

"I'm going to start a school for poor children. There are far more of them in London than in the country."

"It won't be a bit like teaching at Miss Twinkleton's," she warned.

"No, I don't suppose it will," I admitted. "But it's something I want to do. Besides, Bazzard is going to help me put my play on the stage." I had been working on it in fits and starts since we had watched *Macbeth*. I didn't know if it was any good, but I was curious to find out.

"And what of Mr. Crisparkle?" she asked. "I thought you would marry him and stay in Cloisterham."

"He'll always be my dear friend," I assured her.

"You turned him down then?"

I confessed I had.

She sighed. "Do you remember that night at his house when we first met? Eddy flirted outrageously with you. I thought maybe he was falling in love with you. I revenged myself by flirting with Neville. How long ago it all seems!" She kissed her baby. "Were you in love with Eddy?" she asked.

I was about to deny it but then realized it didn't have to

be a secret anymore. I could tell her the truth. "For a long while I thought I was. He was so charming. I had never met anyone like him before. And I think I envied him. He looked as if he had never been unhappy a day in his life. He had no shadows weighing him down. He was all sunlight."

She laughed. "Eddy all sunlight! What a thought!"

We were silent a moment, each of us contemplating our own vision of the young man who had caused us such heartache.

"And what of Jasper," she said at length. "Did you love John Jasper?"

I didn't answer right away. It was a question I had asked myself many times. What had I felt for him, a man who had enslaved himself to opium, a man who had murdered? At what point had my feelings for him changed from hatred and detestation to pity, and from pity to love? Yes, he had lacked Edwin's charm, but he had something else that drew me to him—something which made me feel more akin to him than I could ever have felt to Edwin. Like him, I had suffered as a child, I had the same mixed blood in my veins, knew what it was like to belong to two worlds yet to feel that I belonged in neither. I understood the darkness in Jasper. But he had given me no reason to hope that my love would have been returned. So far as I knew, to the last he had held on to his dream of Rosa. Now he was gone and I would never know what might have been.

I looked out across the low green hills. Would England feel like home someday? Would I too have what Rosa had? I didn't know. I only knew it would be a long time before my heart felt whole again.

ABOUT THE AUTHOR

Deanna Madden has taught literature and creative writing at colleges on the U.S. mainland and in Hawaii. Her publications include short stories, essays on literature, the novella *The Haunted Garden*, and the novels *Gaslight and Fog*, *The Wall*, and *Forbidden Places*. She lives in Honolulu with her family and is at work on her next novel.